Shades

The Demise of Blake Beck

a novel by

Anders Rauff-Nielsen

A Widowgrove publication

Author: Anders Rauff-Nielsen
Cover: Anders Rauff-Nielsen

First Edition published August 2016
Published by Widowgrove IVS
www.widowgrove.com

ISBN: 978-87-998847-3-5

The poem featured in Chapter 3, II of this book is entitled "The Mistress. A Song." It can be found in the public domain book: *The Works of the Right Honourable John Earl of Rochester Consisting of Satires, Songs, Translations, and other Occasional Poems* by the author John Wilmot.

To my daughter Gaia

Thank you for the way you remind me of how the world looks
and what is important – and for your love.

CHAPTER 1

- ANOTHER ONE BITES THE DUST -

I

It was late evening and the corridors outside Blake Beck's Manhattan office were empty. Apparently, everyone else at the CAC had lives to go to after work. However, Blake – the Director of Operations – was still there. Sitting in his chair, his back to the panorama windows and a spectacular view of New York from the 61st floor, Blake looked down at his mahogany desk. It was tidy, with only a small stack of papers, a Philippe Starck lamp and a single picture frame to disrupt the level landscape of the desktop. It mirrored the rest of the office, which was appointed with a mix of old hardwood and leather furniture, spruced up with carefully chosen elements of modern design. Blake leaned back in his chair and took a deep breath, his eyes fastened on the tiny envelope in his hand. It had come with the morning mail and he had repeatedly put off opening it, but now he was going to do it. He was all alone and it was time. Definitely.

"More than twenty-five years with the agency and now this," he thought to himself as he opened the envelope and took out the small rectangular paper package. The paper felt waxy to the touch. He unfolded the paper, revealing a single razor blade. He put it down on his desk before removing a small card from the envelope. In Gothic calligraphy, a skilled penman had written only a single word. "Congratulations," it read. Blake looked at the card for a while before carefully inserting it back into the envelope, along with the razor blade, which he repacked in the waxy paper. "I guess there will be no retirement for me after all," he thought, knowing full well that that ship had sailed long ago. His wall clock told him that it was almost eleven in the evening and his "word-of-the-day" calendar sported the September 15th slip. He ripped it off and threw it in the garbage can. For some reason, he had gotten out of the habit of changing the date in the morning when he got in, and instead he ended up doing it just before he went home. The word of the day was "ces-sa-tion," meaning a temporary or final ceasing. He thought it typical, some sort of fateful irony. Of course the word of the day on this particular day would be a synonym for "end."

II

At great speed, four black Frisians pulled a beautiful black carriage down the cobbled country road. A nearly full moon rose above the horizon, preventing the darkness from conquering the mild autumn evening. The sparse lights from a small village could be spied in the distance beyond the fields. The driver sat on a bench at the front of the carriage, holding the reins with both hands to control the galloping horses, with little need for the long whip that lay next to him. He was shielded from the rushing winds by a broad-brimmed hat and a long, dark woolen coat that made him blend into one with the carriage. In the stately red velvet interior sat Dæth returning home to his mansion. He was a handsome man and, as always, he was well groomed and impeccably dressed. He wore a knee-length black frock over a masterfully tailored suit of trousers, dinner jacket, waistcoat and a cummerbund – all tailored and embroidered to match the fashion of mid-nineteenth century Victorian England, the fashion of his time. A silver chain hung from his breast pocket, hinting at the presence of what could be nothing but the epitome of chronometers. Anything less would simply be out of place in his pockets. From outside, Dæth heard the sound of the whip cracking. "Fall," he thought to himself, looking out the window at the passing landscape. "Even in life, I had an affinity for it. The trees changing their colors like a fire surging in flames of red and yellow, as if trying to fend off the coming winter's chill." He let the image linger a short while in his mind. "But inevitably, just as the fire dies out and leaves behind a pile of ash, the trees lose their battle. The leaves fall and it is time for darkness to envelop the land, at least for a time. Just like death inevitably comes to us all in the end, after a life of spring, summer and fall." He felt it and embraced it. To him there was no sadness in death – not anymore. To him, death was simply a transition into something else. Into his arms, as it were. He was Death now and had been for more than a hundred years. And for many years, he and he alone had governed Shades. But it had not always been that way. When he had died himself, there had been many different Deaths in Shades, each serving their own deity and taking care of their own peoples. One of these Deaths had taken notice of him and, on seeing his potential, had taken him in as an apprentice. But Dæth's potential had been far greater than any had dared dream, and soon Dæth had found himself his master's better. In the end, he had taken over his master's work and then moved to put all the other Deaths out of business. Over time, they fell one by one, as their deities found Dæth to be the better deal. And now there was only him. He was Death, governing the fate of all souls as they crossed into Shades from the world of the living. His angels of death welcomed all new arrivals to Shades, and his organization made sure that everyone was as comfortable as they deserved in the years, sometimes decades, it would take for their paperwork to go through with the departed soul's appropriate deity or deities. Then, once judgment had been passed on a soul, Dæth's organization would transfer the soul to its appropriate afterlife or inform the unfortunate soul that he or she would be forced to spend an eternity in Shades. "For some spring will come again. For others an eternity of winter awaits," Dæth thought as the rural landscape outside gave way to the well-groomed park that surrounded his mansion.

III

Blake picked up the picture frame that stood on his desk. "Marie. Sweet, darling Marie," he thought as he studied the photo like he had so many times before. It had been taken in front of Notre Dame on Île de la Cité in the heart of Paris. Marie was sitting on a stone ledge that framed a long bed of small green bushes on the square. She was posing. She looked absolutely stunning – her black hair flowing in the autumn wind and rays of afternoon sunlight illuminating the smile that had won Blake's heart. Her smile had a slyness to it, revealed by the way her lips curved a little higher on one side than on the other. She was utterly intriguing. Wearing a black skirt suit, she sat with her legs crossed, her long coat folded over her knees and her umbrella resting upright against her leg. The clouds on the eastern horizon were dark and promised a change of weather typical of autumn. It had been ten years since Blake had been stationed in Paris and had taken this photo. She had been working at the CAC Paris branch as one of the lead operatives and had been chosen as Blake's liaison on a cross-departmental assignment. A long assignment. He had been stationed in Paris for seven months, but it hadn't taken that long for Marie to capture his heart. It hadn't even taken seven days.

Blake had been set up in a penthouse apartment in the Latin Quarter, just south of Île de la Cité, with a view of the Pantheon on one side and Notre Dame on the other. The apartment had soon become their little oasis where they could escape the world and, for a short period, forget the fact that they had both chosen to go through life alone. If only for a little while, they could have each other and once again know what it was like to be close to another person. "Goddammit! I loved her," Blake thought as he looked at the picture, feeling his body urge his eyes to begin watering – an urge that he soon subdued. They had walked around Paris pretending to be a normal couple by day. They had seen the sights, dined in small cozy cafés and returned to Blake's apartment to make love in the afternoon before getting a few hours sleep in each other's arms while the pigeons cooed on the ledge outside the open window. They did it all so that their nights would make sense.

The clouds had closed in on the city and the wind picked up. Marie shook her coat before putting it on in one clean, swinging motion. She opened her umbrella and took Blake's arm. As they walked off the square in front of Notre Dame and over the Petit Pont towards the Latin Quarter, the rain began to fall. Marie put her arm around Blake and pulled herself even closer to him, shielding both of them from the rain with her umbrella. They walked through the streets of the Latin Quarter saying nothing, savoring the sounds, sights and smells of Paris in the autumn rain. Outside the building that housed Blake's apartment, they stopped.

"I just have to stop by the offices before we go out tonight," she said. "Is it OK with you that we just meet at the club?"

"Sure," Blake said. "I'll see you there." She gave him a kiss goodbye. It was a long and wet kiss, partly from the dampness of the air. Then she turned and walked away towards the metro, looking back only once to give him a wave.

They had been hunting Vincenzo in Paris for months and he had continued to elude them. They had followed his tracks through the abandoned metro tunnels. They had followed their leads through museums, churches and bars, and they had walked the city streets endlessly. On several occasions their hunt had even led them to back-alley abattoirs where Vincenzo had disposed of those who stood in his way. This was something uncommon for his kin, as they usually left their victims in a quiet place, out of the way, where no one would find them for at least a few hours but preferably longer. This allowed one of their kinsmen to take over the body rather than having it go to waste by decaying, being buried or cremated, or – in the case of Vincenzo's victims – being dismembered and destroyed. The dead, soulless body was a valuable vessel for them, as this was what allowed them to travel into the world of the living once again. Of course, many retained their own body from life, but those who had been so unfortunate as to lose their own body were forced to take a new one. And it was much easier and a lot safer to take a soulless body than a living one. But for some reason, Vincenzo had taken to destroying his prey, perhaps to obscure the fact that he killed so many. Once Blake and Marie almost caught up with Vincenzo in an abattoir that he had recklessly used twice in a row. The girl's body was still in one piece and several degrees above room temperature when they arrived. She was young, maybe sixteen or seventeen, but it was hard for Blake to tell because her half Asian heritage somewhat concealed her true age from him. On her back, she bore a large tattoo of a white tiger guarding a lotus blossom. In life she had been very beautiful and gracious – it was obvious. But as she lay there naked, all grey and cold on the table amidst the saws and butcher's knives, she was a horrible sight. Blake felt a memory struggling to surface and finally he realized that he had seen the girl before.

"I've seen this tattoo before," Blake said. "I saw her in a Montmartre nightclub, so at least now we know how he likes to feed. This wasn't business – this was pleasure!"

"Mmmhh," Marie murmured in agreement as she took her cellphone from her jacket pocket.

"Are you calling the gatherers?"

"Yes."

"Good. Then let's get out of here."

This had been the night before the photograph was taken.

It was already dark when they met up outside the nightclub Le Chat Blanc. Blake had been waiting in a small café across the street for about an hour, enjoying several cups of espresso and the fact that he had time to read the paper. Marie saw him through the large café window and tapped the window with one of her rings. Blake looked up from the newspaper and out the window at Marie. She had her hair in a long, single braid

13

and was wearing a short black leather jacket, black leggings and a pair of Dr. Martens boots. Blake walked out of the café to Marie, leaving the waiter with a "merci beaucoup" and a generous tip. They walked together across the street and into Le Chat Blanc. Once inside, Marie made her way to the bar while Blake walked over to one of the dancers who stood chatting with a patron. Blake tapped the girl softly on her shoulder, provoking an annoyed and slightly hostile glare from the man she had been talking to.

"Excuse me, miss," Blake said.

"Yes," she replied, her pronunciation revealing that English was not her strongest suit.

"I'm looking for one of the girls who works here. She's got a big tattoo of a tiger and a flower on her back. Is she here tonight?"

"Fabienne?"

"Yeah, Fabienne. That's right," Blake replied.

"No. She is not here. Maybe she is sick – she should have been dancing at seven o'clock."

"Do you know where she lives?"

"No. I'm sorry. But her friend is sitting right over there, maybe he knows about her. They left together yesterday." She pointed across the room to a man sitting in one of the VIP booths that offered a perfect view of the flesh on stage. He was a stately looking man with a presence that couldn't be denied. His long, dark hair was combed back, and he had a slightly greying and perfectly groomed mustache and goatee, which made Blake think of Vincent Price in his portrayal of Cardinal Richelieu in *The Three Musketeers*. Even the man's clothes had a slight air of olden days to them. The cut and style of his tailor-made outfit looked like a quaint mix of contemporary fashion and Italian Renaissance. Blake couldn't believe that he hadn't noticed the man the second he walked in, but he hadn't. They were somehow able to do that – the vampires, that is. They could stand out like a sore thumb, but still remain unnoticed until attention was called to them.

"Thanks, miss," Blake said. "I think I'll just go have a drink with my date, otherwise she might get upset. I'll catch up with him later." Blake gave her a smile.

"You're welcome," she said. "I guess you won't want a dance since you brought a date?" Blake noticed that her companion flinched ever so slightly at her question.

"No, thank you. Not tonight."

Blake walked over to Marie, who had easily gotten the attention of the barman and was already sipping a cosmopolitan.

"I'm quite sure he's here."

"Where?" she asked, keeping her cool and focusing her gaze on the bar.

"He's sitting in the VIP booth closest to the stage," Blake said. "Once you take a look, you'll wonder how on earth you missed him."

"I think I'll just go and powder my nose," Marie said as she hopped off the barstool. She gave him a kiss. Then she walked off to the ladies' room in order to get a good look at the man in the booth along the way. They were right. It was Vincenzo.

They left the nightclub and walked just around the corner to where Marie's yellow Citröen 2CV was parked. Marie picked up a slim aluminum suitcase that held the pieces of a high-powered rifle, designed for easy transport and quick assembly. Blake picked up his katana, which had been his favorite close combat weapon since the late eighties. He hid it in the folds of his grey trench coat and tipped his fedora hat slightly to one side. They were ready. This was the night they had been waiting for.

They waited in the small café where Blake had enjoyed his paper and espresso earlier in the evening. At a quarter to two in the morning, Vincenzo left the nightclub across the street. He wore a long scarlet coat that draped him like a blanket of blood flowing in the autumn winds. Blake and Marie tailed him at a distance, following him through the night streets of Montmartre, biding their time until they would finally be alone with him. Vincenzo turned up the stairs of Rue Foyatier towards the Sacré-Coeur Basilica high atop the hill overlooking Montmartre and the rest of Paris. Halfway up the stairs, Marie took Blake's hand. She pulled him in and gave him a peck on the cheek. Then, with a wave, she beckoned him to head up the stairs. He took off his hat and placed it on her head with a grin, and then continued up the stairway. He unbuttoned his coat as he walked, letting the hilt of the katana out into the moonlight. Marie knelt down and opened the aluminum rifle case. She took out the stock of the rifle, and less than a minute later she had the weapon assembled. She closed the rifle case, and with Blake's hat resting on top, set it next to the fence that separated the stairway from the dual tram tracks that ran up the hill. Then she jumped the fence with the rifle slung on her back, and she ran into the park that stretched down the hill from Sacré-Coeur beyond the tracks. By the time Marie made it across the tracks, Blake had reached the top of Rue Foyatier with a clear view of Vincenzo who was leisurely strolling along the white stone column railing of the viewpoint square just a little way down from the church itself. Vincenzo was looking out over the park at the evening lights of Paris, which were rivaled only by the light of the nearly full moon. No one else was there, save for sleeping pigeons.

Vincenzo stopped and turned around, and Blake stepped out of the shadows, flinging his trench coat to one side, readying to draw his sword. They stood there in the dead of night among hints of shadow drawn by the cold moonlight and the lights of distant street lamps.

"Vincenzo . . . It's time to go!" Blake said with the confidence of a male lion challenging another to a fight for domination with a roar and baring of teeth.

"Signore Beck," Vincenzo replied with a smile on his lips, "such a nice night for this." He shifted the side of his scarlet coat slightly to reveal an old longsword. Vincenzo had been given the sword by his father when he was a young man coming of age in Siena, but in the end the sword had failed its charge during the Battle of Marciano in 1554 when Vincenzo was killed – sword in hand – at the tip of a Spanish soldier's blade. Both men drew their swords in silence. With nothing but the sounds of their feet to disturb the pigeons, they started towards each other. Vincenzo moved to strike, raising his sword high above his head. He struck hard, aiming for the sword to cut through Blake's ribcage and straight into his heart. Dodging the blow, Blake jumped, and with one foot on the stone column railing, he somersaulted past Vincenzo, landing right behind him. Before Vincenzo could steady his sword and turn around to face his opponent, Blake moved to strike. Blake knew that he was fighting a being whose long death offered a degree of skill, knowledge and experience which was poorly matched by that offered by Blake's short lifespan. He knew that he would not get many chances, if any, and that there was no glory or honor to be found in fighting fair. He would defeat Vincenzo by any means possible, and any chivalrous ideals would only bring about his own downfall in a battle like this. In one swift, flowing motion, Blake raised his katana before turning around and guiding the blade downwards. He drew the blade from left to right, seeking to cut Vincenzo in two from behind. In response, Vincenzo dropped to his knees and raised his sword over his head and down his back, letting the blade run along the length of his own spine. Then he shifted his balance and turned his torso to parry Blake's attack, the sound of the two swords meeting piercing the chilly November night. In the hope of finishing the fight right then and there, Vincenzo made his move. Still on one knee, but with his other leg stretched out, he turned and swept Blake's feet out from under him, sending Blake crashing down on his back. He landed with a muffled "Umpfh!" as Vincenzo sprang to his feet with a feline grace. In a series of movements flowing seamlessly into one, Vincenzo brought his sword back around. Then Vincenzo let his defenses give way for the strike, his sword looming in the night air above his head, about to be thrust down into Blake's chest.

"Arrivederci," Vincenzo whispered, as much to the shadows as to Blake. He leaned into the strike, letting his full weight drive the sword downwards. Lying on his back, Blake saw death's reflection in an instant as the blade gleamed in the silvery moonlight.

Marie had gotten into position. High up one of the park trees, she sat straddling a thick branch. Her aim had been on Vincenzo since the fighting started, but she found no reason to reveal herself or to draw attention to the fight by firing her rifle, which, although silenced, was not silent. That was until she saw the moonlight gleam in the polished blade with Vincenzo about to strike. As she pulled the trigger, she felt the force of the recoil, and she saw through the scope how the blade shattered and split as the bullet hit Vincenzo's sword just above the cross-guard.

"You fucking coward!" Vincenzo bellowed, displaying the strange sense of betrayal he felt. He stumbled forwards, trying to regain his balance and recover from the attack. "You dare not even face me alone!?!" A small stream of smoke rose from the muzzle of the rifle as Blake quickly took advantage of Vincenzo's disarming. The distant ring of a bullet casing hitting the ground scarcely registered with Blake. Still lying on the ground, he kicked Vincenzo straight in the gut, sending him stumbling back. This left Blake just enough time to get to his knees and ready his sword. Vincenzo pulled a dagger from the folds of his coat and launched himself at Blake, knowing that he would have to end it before the rifle could be reloaded and re-aimed. As Blake saw Vincenzo coming at him, he heard the distant sound of a rifle bolt sliding and he knew that the fight had come to its end. With his dagger raised to strike, Vincenzo was just about to jump Blake when another bullet split the air. Flesh and bone were sent flying everywhere as the bullet ripped through Vincenzo's knee. What should have been a powerful pounce suddenly became an uncontrolled topple, and as Vincenzo fell to the ground, Blake struck. He drew his katana upwards, the blade cutting into Vincenzo underneath his left arm and running all the way through to his right shoulder. As his soul retreated from his dismembered body, Vincenzo looked up at Blake.

"You'll never get me Beck . . ."

"Vincenzo, let me enlighten you," Blake replied. "We just did. Now have fun with the Hunters."

Vincenzo's body fell limp as Blake wiped his blade in the

sleeve of Vincenzo's scarlet coat. Then Blake rose to his feet and sheathed his katana.

It took a couple of minutes before Marie reached Blake.

"So, I saved your life," she started. "Now you owe me one, but I will settle for a cup of coffee and a kiss," she continued with a smile.

"Well, that's all you're gonna get, sweetie. 'Cause I still had to do all the hard work – what the hell was that all about?"

"What?" asked Marie with a shrug.

"I mean . . . his sword?" Blake paused. "Why not just shoot him in the head and be done with it?"

"Honey, what fun would that be? And also, I wouldn't get to see you fight, all . . ." she searched for the word for a second or two. "What do you say? Macho?"

Blake didn't reply. He just smiled at her and gave her the kiss she was due.

They got into Marie's yellow Citröen and drove through the Paris night towards the Latin Quarter. In the silence that followed, they each battled the invading feeling that this night not only saw the end of Vincenzo, but also the end of them. Marie parked the car outside Blake's apartment, but they didn't go up. Instead they went just around the corner to their favorite late night café. Neither of them wanted to go to bed and end the night because chances were that Blake would already have to travel back to New York the next day. It was the day they had both been dreading.

21

They sat in the café, each sipping their coffee and praying that they would never reach the bottom of their cups. However, despite their prayers, the café eventually closed and they had to go back to Blake's apartment. They didn't really sleep. They didn't even make love. They just lay there until morning broke, neither of them saying what they were both thinking. When the sun had made it above the rooftops, Blake got up and walked to the windows and drew away the curtains. Marie was still in bed, sitting halfway up, resting her back on a huge pillow. She had the sheets pulled up to her chin. She looked changed. She looked neither sly, nor dangerous – and she didn't smile, which she almost always did. Rather, she looked like a young girl stricken down by the profound sadness of death, guarded only by a shield of cotton.

"So, I guess this is it?" Blake asked, staring out the window with his back to the bed. He knew that he couldn't say the words and look into her eyes at the same time. He simply didn't have the strength. "I'll be leaving now and who knows when I'll be back."

"Blake, you could put in for a transfer," Marie parried his words in a vain attempt to save what they had together.

"Sweetie, we both know that won't work. The agency doesn't exactly encourage this, you know."

"But . . ." She tried, but it was no use. There were no words that would serve her. No words that could shield her from the truth, and deep inside she knew he was right.

"I know. I want to keep seeing you too, you know. I love

you," he said, his voice trembling slightly. "But we'll have to keep a low profile and see where time takes us." He paused as he turned around. "If we make this official, they'll probably just have one of us hunting in Outer Mongolia," he said, hoping for a hint of a smile. There was no reward. "And I guess we both knew that it would come to this." He tried to believe it himself. He didn't though, so he shrugged his shoulder in an attempt to excuse himself. He stood there looking at Marie in silence, and she eventually took mercy upon him by finally rejoining the conversation.

"Well," she started, "at least give me another kiss and come back to bed."

IV

As Blake put down the picture frame, he thought about the first couple of years after Paris. They had seen each other as often as possible, but it was hard. Neither Marie nor Blake had much free time, let alone vacations – both of them climbing the career ladder, advancing within the ranks of the agency. In the end, Blake had been the one to break it off when he had finally convinced himself that the pain of saying goodbye again and again, and not knowing when or where – if ever – they would meet again was greater than the joy of being together. But he still loved her, even to this day. He took out the picture of Marie and stuffed it into the breast pocket of his jacket that was hung over his chair.

It was almost midnight now. Blake picked up the small envelope containing the card and razor blade and put it in his jacket pocket. He got up, put his jacket on and left his office, not bothering to lock the door behind him. The hallway outside was empty and the lights flickered as they switched on from the hallway motion sensor. As he reached his secretary's desk, he stopped and bent over it, picking up a yellow pad of Post-it notes and a ballpoint pen. "Dear Marcia, thank you for these last five years. You've been an ace. Have them pick me up at home in the morning. Take care," he wrote. Then he walked away, not looking back once. He took the elevator down to the parking level where his white Jaguar E-type was parked in his reserved stall.

Blake drove across the Brooklyn Bridge to his home on the waterfront of Brooklyn Heights. He parked the car at the curb and went up the stairs, holding his bundle of keys in his hand. He unlocked the front door and entered the stately hall of the old but newly renovated building. It was three floors of beautiful, perfectly styled home. Most people would have given their right arm to live in it, but Blake seldom had time to use it for anything other than sleeping. He hung his jacket on the coatrack by the door and unbuckled his belt. He took the picture of Marie and the small envelope from his jacket pocket and went upstairs to his study. Tall bookcases lined the walls from top to bottom. He picked up a bottle of whisky from the table in the corner and poured himself a glass before lowering himself into his favorite chair. He felt the leather embracing his body as he sat down. He sat there in silence, drinking his whisky, staring out into nothing.

"I guess it's time," he thought, having finished his drink. Then he got up and picked up the envelope, the picture of Marie and the bottle of whisky, leaving the empty glass behind. He went into the white-tiled bathroom adjacent to the master bedroom. He looked around in the same manner as when deciding whether or not to use the toilet before or after showering. He decided on the toilet and lifted the lid. Then he placed the whisky bottle and the envelope on the edge of the bathtub and the picture of Marie on the sink opposite it. He opened his pants and let them drop to the ground. As he sat down, he thought about the fact that people always seemed to do this kind of thing in the bathtub. Something quite undesirable, he concluded, having seen enough dead people to know what happens when all the muscles of one's body relax as you enter death. "No one is going to find me floating like a great big raisin, marinated in my own filth," he thought to himself as he took his belt from his pants and used it to fasten himself to the toilet to keep from toppling over. Then he took a great big swig of the bottle before grabbing the envelope. He took out the razor blade and looked at it. He shifted his gaze between the razor and the picture of Marie every other minute or two, interrupting the process only to take another drink. He repeated this for about half an hour, until the bottle was empty and he could feel the alcohol flowing through his veins, numbing his body more and more. Then he took the razor blade in his hand and slashed deep into his wrist. It didn't hurt as much as he had feared, at least not physically. Then he rested his arm on the edge of the bathtub, allowing the blood to run into the tub and down the drain. He sat there alone, the color fading from his skin and his mind gradually losing its grip on reality. He sat there and he died.

CHAPTER 2

- AIN'T NO GRAVE -

I

Dæth's mansion was built in the Jacobethan style typical of the early Victorian era, and the magnificent building held more than 150 rooms all together and sat on a well-kept estate that stretched far beyond the horizon. Dæth's carriage halted by the stairs that led to the front door and two servants immediately lay a stepping-stone in place in front of the carriage door. Another servant opened the door and Dæth stepped out, donning a black top hat and holding a silver-tipped ebony cane in one hand. He took no notice of the servants as he stepped onto the stone that kept his boots from the mud of the driveway. By the stairs, his butler – aptly named Elijah Butler – stood waiting patiently.

"Good evening, sir," he said as his master approached. "I trust you have had a pleasant journey. Mr. McCoy is waiting for you in the drawing room."

"Yes, thank you, Elijah. The journey itself was quite pleasant, though its object was not. However the battle was won and that is what matters – not whether it was pleasant or not," Dæth said as he made his way up the stairs.

"Indeed, sir," Butler replied, following his master up the stairs at a fitting distance. Two guards opened the large double door that led into the hall, allowing Dæth to enter unhindered.

"Has my wife returned?"

"Yes, sir. She arrived early this morning and she bade me to tell you that all is taken care of." Elijah paused for a second before continuing. "That is all she said, sir."

"That is fine, Elijah. I will talk to her in the morning." Much to Dæth's dismay, the servant responsible for taking his coat had failed to do so immediately. Having finished his conversation with Elijah, Dæth shifted his voice to a more authoritative pitch.

"Will you ever take my frock, you imbecile? Or will you have me stand here forever?" he yelled at the idle servant who gave a jolt as he was instantly pulled back from wherever his mind had wandered off to.

"Yes, sir! I mean no, sir! I . . . I am sorry, sir!" the servant blabbered, desperately trying to remove Dæth's frock in a speedy, yet controlled and worthy manner, but failing miserably.

"My apologies, sir. I will set him straight," Butler said when the young man had finished removing the frock and had stepped away.

"Yes, do that. I simply cannot comprehend the incompetence of some people. But in the end that is why he will spend eternity holding my coat and not the other way around."

"Will there be anything else, sir?" was Elijah's only reply, as he knew full well that his master's intention was not to start a discussion about the competence of the people in the employ of the household.

"Yes, go inform Mr. McCoy that I will be with him shortly, and have the maid lay out my white walking suit for the morning."

As Dæth walked up the stairs to his private chambers, Elijah bowed and turned to walk away. He headed into the drawing room, picking up a tray holding two porcelain cups and a matching pot of black tea from the kitchen on his way. When Elijah entered the drawing room, Mr. McCoy was sitting in one of the Rococo chairs that made up the lounge arrangement in the middle of the room. He knew not to sit in the chair next to the carved ivory chess set where a game was underway, as this was where Dæth usually sat. McCoy was impeccably dressed, wearing a suit of clothing also fitting the late nineteenth century, but which – contrary to Dæth's Victorian attire – was clearly of American heritage. His Stetson hat lay on a table nearby, and his dark hair was freshly combed to make sure that his hairdo bore no signs of him wearing a hat. When Elijah entered the room, McCoy got up.

"Elijah," he said, giving a friendly nod to the butler, who walked over and put down the tray on the lounge table.

"Sir," Elijah replied in a friendly tone, giving the man a slight bow. There was a short pause before McCoy took the conversation further.

"Did he say anything when he arrived?"

"Not much, sir, no. But he did say that the battle was won, and then he inquired to the presence of his wife, sir."

"Thank you, Elijah. I guess I'll just have to wait and hear the news straight from the horse's mouth."

"Sir," Elijah replied, unsure of how to react to the way this American idiom resulted in his master being called a horse. But he decided to think nothing more of it, putting it aside as a cultural difference. The double doors to the hallway swung open and Dæth entered. He mimicked the movement of the doors with his arms, welcoming McCoy into his home. Dæth had left his jacket behind upstairs and the bare white shirt, vest and sash made him look much more relaxed and a lot less intimidating to Elijah's eyes.

"Harlan, my friend!" Dæth said, his arms open wide. "Welcome! I trust you to bring pleasant news, for such is much too scarce these days."

"I am pleased to say that I do, sir," McCoy replied. As they sat down, he continued, "And I hope that you do not bear ill news yourself?" Elijah immediately began pouring two cups of tea and then turned to take two glasses and a decanter of what looked to be cognac from a nearby cabinet.

"So, Mr. Beck has chosen to join us?" Dæth asked after a few seconds of contemplative silence.

"Yes, sir. He should be in the Entrance as we speak." Harlan paused briefly, before deciding to elaborate. "I have sent Virgil to greet him to make sure he gets a proper welcome."

"Fine. When the opportunity presents itself, please let Mr. Beck know that I would like to meet him here in person."

Harlan gave a smile and a nod as Elijah put the two glasses down next to either cup of tea.

"Will there be anything else, sir?" the butler asked.

"No, Elijah. That will be all and I shan't be calling upon you further this evening. So, I bid you a good night."

"Thank you, sir. And the same to you both," Elijah said, giving a small bow to excuse himself.

"May I ask how the meeting went?" Harlan tried again once Elijah was out of the room.

"Of course – It went well, I think," Dæth said with a smile. "I am glad to say that it seems that we were one step ahead of Mr. Ferre this time around and our Hunters have managed to make quite a killing, so to speak."

"I'm relieved to hear that, sir. And I gathered from Butler that your wife has returned sound and well."

"Yes, but sadly she shan't be joining us tonight, as she has retired to her room – tired from the long journey." Dæth picked up the crystal glass, holding it in his palm for a while before raising it and taking a deep breath through his nose, savoring the nuances of the olfactory experience. Harlan took up his glass, as well. Dæth raised his glass in a toast, catching Harlan's eyes. "Let us toast to victory and a happy death."

"To victory and a happy death," Harlan replied.

II

At first, Blake couldn't make out what the bloody hell had happened. Had he fallen asleep? In that case, he had been having a very disturbing dream in which he had killed himself on the toilet. He thought about it. It could have been a dream – it made sense. But in that case, how had he ended up in the back room of what, judging from the view through the open door, appeared to be a New York City diner closed down for the night? As he came to, he tried desperately to get the pieces of the puzzle to fit. However, no matter how hard he tried, the pieces didn't fit because it wasn't a dream and he wasn't in New York. Blake got up from the floor of the back room where he had found himself lying between industrial sized jars of mayonnaise and various crates of foodstuff that didn't require cold storage. He slowly made his way into the diner, half expecting to run into a waitress who had stayed behind to close up and who would throw a hysterical fit and go for some kind of blunt instrument under the counter, intent on knocking the burglar over the head. To his great relief, nothing of the sort happened. He walked through the diner, undid the lock on the front door and walked into the street. That was when he began to realize that something was definitely off and that this was not New York. At least not any New York he came from. While the many black London taxis driving by could reasonably be explained as being some kind of image renewal scam decided upon by Europhilic politicians, the presence of a half-finished Eiffel Tower, illuminated by thousands of small light bulbs and located about half a mile down the road from him, could not as easily be accounted for. This was all too much, and despite having a dreamy recollection of having drunk a whole bottle of whisky not that long ago, he decided that he needed a drink. He noticed a bar across the street claiming to have live music every night. "They'd better not serve me a full night of some bikini-wearing teen pretending to sing and trying to draw attention away from the fact that she can't by way of anatomy," he thought to himself amidst the many questions of "how, where and why?" that filled his mind. Walking across the street, bewildered and uneasy, he eyed a big blue neon sign above the entrance to the bar that said "Kingsland."

The club was filled with groups of people sitting at small round tables, drinking, talking and enjoying themselves. An elderly gentleman wearing a black suit and shirt was setting up on the stage and he hooked up his black western guitar to an old amp just as Blake entered. "That's more like it," Blake thought as he made his way over to a vacant table in the corner, bent on keeping as much to himself as possible. He had only just sat down when a waitress came over.

"And what can I get you, sir?" she asked.

"Just a beer – whatever you fancy, as long as it ain't light," Blake replied. She nodded, turned and headed for the bar. Though it didn't take more than a few minutes before she returned with a pint of pale ale, it felt like hours in Blake's mind. His mind desperately fought a losing battle to make sense of it all, but there seemed to be no way he could win. Blake took a drink, almost emptying the glass in one, leaving only a mouthful of beer at the bottom. A man wearing a tight-fitting black robe and leather belt stepped up to Blake's table as he drank. None of the other patrons seemed to notice the man. He appeared a fit and rather anonymous middle-aged man at first glance, but as Blake let his eyes linger on him for a couple of seconds, the man seemed somehow slightly blurred. Blake decided that it had to be because of the alcohol.

"Excuse me, sir. May I join you?" the man asked.

"Sure. Sit down," Blake said. As the man sat down, the elderly gentleman on stage struck a chord to make sure that his guitar was in tune. The other guests started clapping. Then he began to play, filling the room with the heavy presence of a D minor tune. Blake shifted his gaze from the man on stage to the man in front of him. Then Blake raised himself off his seat and put out his hand to greet the man properly.

"I'm Blake Beck. Nice to meet you," Blake said, struggling slightly with the last sentence.

"My name is Virgil and I know very well who you are, Mr. Beck," Virgil replied.

"How on earth – or wherever this is – do you know who I am?" Blake asked.

"As I said, I am Virgil. I am one of the angels of death and I have been sent here to welcome you into Shades and help you find your place." He paused, giving Blake enough time for his words to sink in, but not enough to reply. "Something which should be easy, as I understand you are a valued associate of Mr. McCoy and of Dæth himself."

"Then would you please start by telling me where the hell I am?" Blake said with mixed feelings of impatience and profound relief.

"Certainly. You are in Shades, the world beyond the veil of life. Where every soul comes when it is time to leave life behind," Virgil started. "Each and every soul steps into Shades where they bide their time until it is clear to the appropriate authorities whether or not they move on from here. Until they have been judged, you might say."

"So, this is purgatory?" Blake asked after a few seconds contemplation.

"You might say that. Others have called it Limbo or Barzakh, but the truth is that they are all just different names for the same thing."

"I have to say that it is not like I imagined it."

"No," Virgil paused. "It never is. But there is much more to Shades than this place we are in now. Right now we are in the Entrance, the place your soul was drawn to when you died, and it is filled with new arrivals like yourself," Virgil said, trying to offer Blake the comfort of knowing that he was not alone in being newly dead. "To lighten the transition, the Entrance always resembles life. It has different areas matching the different lands and cultures of the world of the living. And like life, the Entrance is forever changing," Virgil noted. "Now, most souls try to make do and just continue on as before until they go on from here – which is why this place is a lot like the world you came from."

"But you said that everyone is judged after coming here. I'm guessing that this means that some of us will be sentenced to remain here? Otherwise, it wouldn't be much of a judging," Blake said.

"True," Virgil replied. "And that brings us to the rest of Shades which is divided into numerous areas, each of which has, at some time in the past, served as the Entrance. As time goes by and the world changes, the Entrance moves around. When this happens, the old area is left behind, filled with those unfortunate souls from the many cultures of that age who have been doomed to an eternity in Shades."

Blake drained the last mouthful of beer from the bottom of his glass.

"For instance, you could travel to the Norman Dark and find the destitute souls from Europe around the year 1000. Or – as you will soon experience for yourself, as Dæth has requested a visit from you – you could go to the Empires of Industry, which is home to Dæth himself and millions of souls from the late 19th century."

Virgil took his time before continuing, observing Blake who sat still and listened with the expression of a man who was desperately trying to make sense of it all. "In this way, Shades is divided into areas where souls of a certain age and culture have congregated and created societies as best they can – trying to hold on to what little they have: namely, the memory of life. A life they have been doomed to contemplate for eternity."

"So what? All these souls . . . they just get left behind and go on as before?" Blake asked, struggling to understand.

"Well, not exactly. Most souls try to go on, but they can't. As time goes by, they begin to realize that all they are doing is merely postponing the inevitable and that this pantomime of life is all just an act. There is no meaning anymore." Blake looked puzzled and Virgil continued. "Let me give you an example. You are sitting here drinking your beer, but unlike in life it serves no purpose. It won't get you drunk and you don't need liquids. You can't really die of thirst now, can you?"

"Then what?" Blake asked, beginning to follow what Virgil said.

"At some point, most souls break and begin to neglect the act. Instead they start looking inside themselves, pondering the only thing that really mattered to them: their life." Virgil paused. "As time goes by, these lost souls begin to look more and more inside themselves. As they retract, they start to neglect the daily act and the area they inhabit starts to decay, becoming more and more grotesque as their memories of life become more distant and distorted. In the end, sometimes after thousands of years, all that is left of these souls are merely inanimate shades of their own former selves left in a catatonic state of contemplation, forever burning in the fires of their own conscience."

"You said *most* souls?"

"Well, yes. Obviously there are exceptions. There are those who do not just lie down beaten. Those who will not stay in their grave, so to speak."

"The vampires."

"Yes, the undead. The undead and then the few of us who serve Dæth."

III

In the far corner of Shades lies the Gothic, homeland of the undead and the largest area in Shades outside of Dæth's control. At the heart of the Gothic lies the medieval city of Aquraa. Concentric city walls divide the city into quarters surrounding Aquraa Castle, Mr. Ferre's castle, high atop the castle hill. The castle stands as a Gothic monument looming above the city like the cathedrals of old reminding the inhabitants of the supreme, omnipresent authority governing their deaths. Reminding them of *Him*, the first undead.

The pale moon rose above the horizon, nearly full. It cast its light down on Aquraa to accompany the flaming lights of the many braziers, torches and lamps burning throughout the city. The moonlight shone through the tall stained glass windows of the castle's grand dining hall. It was as if the moon wanted to help illustrate the story told in the glass mosaics - the story of Mr. Ferre's fall and rise. The light fell on Bahij Khaleel, Mr. Ferre's most trusted adviser, as he walked across the hall towards Teresa Ammon, the designated lady of the house. In life, Bahij had been born just in time to see the end of the Islamic golden age and he had only been a small child when the Mongols laid siege to the city of Baghdad in 1258. This made Bahij a few hundred years older than Mistress Ammon, and one of the oldest remaining vampires in Mr. Ferre's service.

Musicians were getting ready to accompany the great feast of the nobles by way of lute, viol, flute, drum and song. When Bahij reached her, Teresa Ammon had just finished correcting the table-setting skills of one of the servants, wanting everything to be ready and perfect before more guests arrived.

"Mistress Ammon," he said, giving a deep, courteous bow.

"Master Khaleel – a great pleasure to see you." She curtsied, bowing her head slightly.

"I know this may come as an inconvenience to you, but I must be allowed to see *Him*," Bahij said with a grave voice.

"And on what business may I say that you approach *Him* as he readies himself for the ball, wishing not to be disturbed?"

"You may tell *Him* that I believe I have finally found the way back. That is all you need to say, and I will wager you what is left of my soul that *He* will thank you for the disturbance. Now please go, Mistress Ammon, and I shall remain here until you return."

Heeding Bahij's request, Teresa walked out of the hall towards the castle wing where *He* – Mr. Ferre – had his private chambers; it was a part of the castle no one but his most trusted servants and advisers were permitted to enter. What Teresa didn't notice in her hurry was the figure that followed her in silence, keeping at a safe distance. The figure belonged to the Earl, one of the noblemen of Mr. Ferre's court. Having overheard the exchange of words between Bahij and Teresa, the Earl had taken an interest in the subject of their conversation and he had decided to follow Teresa. For he, if anyone, knew that knowledge is what allows you to be the author of your own story, while a lack thereof would resign you to the mercy of others, leaving you as a mere actor or even a spectator – something the Earl found to be most undesirable. He followed Teresa through the castle along the thick, cold stone walls that made the corridors feel like tunnels running through a mountain. On the walls hung paintings and tapestries, competing with beautiful marble statues for the attention of those who walked these hallways. The greatest artists of the world had created all these splendid pieces of art, some of which dated back thousands of years. While some works had been recreated in the image of artwork made during their lifetimes, the masters had created many of the pieces in death – offering a beautiful and profound finale to each artist's life's work.

Teresa stopped at a heavy oak door and drew a deep breath. Then she knocked.

"My Lord," she said, uttering the words as loudly as she dared, secretly hoping that he might not hear her. "I'm sorry, but Master Khaleel has requested to speak to you urgently," she addressed the still-closed door.

"Come in, Mistress Ammon." His reply came in a deep, calm voice that filled the halls. The door opened to Teresa and she walked in. The antechamber was dominated by beautiful stained glass windows set in the far wall, and majestic Gothic arches held the ceiling high above. A long massive table made to seat twelve on either side filled the room.

Mr. Ferre stood before her wearing only a pair of black leather pants and a belt with a silver buckle. *He* was lean and muscular, with the powerful build of an Olympic swimmer. Judging only by his physique, one might have thought *Him* to be in his late thirties, but his grey eyes and weathered face, framed by a powerful jaw covered in dark stubble, told a different story. Despite having been part of the household for centuries, Teresa was always taken aback by his presence and gravity of being. His cold, calm gaze, his voice and his gestures clearly belonged to a being who had seen millennia pass and yet still remained unbroken. *He* carried himself like someone who had been around for aeons and had witnessed and embraced all the facets of mankind. *He* was like a mountain and she stood at his base. Mr. Ferre turned towards the heavy wooden cabinet that stood against the wall and picked up a crystal decanter by its polished silver handle. As *He* poured two glasses of the decanter's crystal-clear contents, Teresa couldn't help staring at the bulging scars on his back, one on either side of his spine where his wings had once been. Filling her with sorrow and despair, the scars told her of the fall, the birth of her race and of the wounds that would never heal. Only when *He* turned to face her, did she manage to revert her eyes.

"A glass?" *He* asked, handing her one of the glasses, aware that what is but a moment and a slight gesture to the master is an eternal memory to the servant.

"I . . . ," she started, her faculties of speech failing her. "Yes, my Lord. Thank you."

"You are aware that I asked to not be disturbed," *He* said before taking a sip from his glass, showing no discernible hint of emotion.

"Yes, my Lord. And I *am* sorry . . . I would not have disturbed you had Master Khaleel not insisted upon it."

"And what, pray tell, would Bahij want from me that could not wait but half an hours time?"

"Well, my Lord, he simply bid me tell you that he believes that he may have finally found 'the way back.'"

"Were those the very words he used?" *He* asked.

"The very same, my Lord." For the shortest of moments, his eyes betrayed *Him* and revealed to Teresa a longing for reunion, retribution and revenge that was so clear and determined that she could barely fathom it.

"Teresa, my dear. Before you go and bid Master Khaleel to join me in my study, let us make a toast and drink together," *He* said, raising his glass. "To what would you propose a toast?"

"I . . . I would propose a toast . . ." She thought about it for a second, which seemed to her like ages. "To both the father and his children. To the understanding with which the father does what is best for his children, and to the love with which the child remains true and faithful."

"A fine toast indeed. To father and child!"

"To father and child." As they emptied their glasses, the Earl walked away from the door, making sure that he was neither seen nor heard.

Bahij caught the eyes of the Earl, who entered at the other end of the grand hall. The two bowed to each other despite the distance between them – Bahij because he felt that he ought to, and the Earl because he was sure that Bahij expected him not to. As Bahij rose from his bow, he saw Teresa approaching.

"*He* will see you now, Master Khaleel."

"Thank you, Mistress Ammon. Now, before I take my leave, I trust that I will see you tonight and I would ask to be allowed the pleasure of your company on the dance floor."

"We shall see," she replied, her smile clearly stating that he would.

Bahij entered the antechamber of Mr. Ferre's private quarters and, as *He* was not there to greet Bahij, he called out.

"My Lord?"

"Bahij. Come join me in my study." Bahij walked through the antechamber, trailing his right hand across the long table until he reached the door to his master's study. The room had a view of the surrounding city and landscape through the leaded windows. The walls were lined with heavy bookcases holding thousands of books and tomes – the most ancient of which dated back to the dawn of man. Various artifacts, relics and objects pertaining to the practice of the dark arts lay on tables, cabinets and pedestals around the room. In the middle of the room stood a huge desk. Numerous tomes, scrolls and drawings claimed the entire desktop, save for a small corner that held a goose quill pen, an inkwell, a stack of blank paper and an ancient Arabian chessboard on which a game was underway. *He* was standing with his back to the door, looking over the books and papers that lay on the desk. As Bahij entered, *He* spoke.

"Do you know why I have not only kept you in my employ for the better part of a thousand years, but have also come to count you as a . . ." *He* thought about it, letting his words float on top of the silence like oil on water. "As a friend?"

"No, my Lord."

"It is because you are utterly dependable. For more than five hundred years you have served me as a scholar and adviser, and not once have you failed me. It almost makes me feel." *He* turned around to face Bahij, offering him a hint of a smile. "And now, here you come bearing the best of news once more, I hear."

"Thank you for the kind words, my Lord," Bahij said, lowering his gaze. "I merely do my best and I am happy and honored if that not only suffices, but may even merit your friendship, my Lord." *He* gestured for Bahij to come closer.

"Well, friend. Pray tell me of your discovery while I listen and pour you a glass." *He* took up a decanter from the side table that stood near the wall between two old leather armchairs, pouring two glasses of the same crystal-clear liquid that *He* had offered Teresa.

"As you know, I have long believed the Voynich manuscript to hold, among its many undisclosed secrets, the dark way to summon a soul between the worlds – even back into life," Bahij started. "However, for hundreds of years the manuscript has managed to keep its secrets hidden within, despite the fact that the brightest minds in both life and death have sought to wring the secrets from it." Bahij paused, taking the glass of soul as *He* offered it to him. "Yesterday, one of my most promising initiates discovered that another vellum manuscript dating back to medieval Europe has been put up for auction in London next week. It's a manuscript that has previously remained hidden in a private collection, and which was reportedly written at the hand of Flamel, whom we know to have possessed knowledge of at least part of the summoning ritual." Bahij leaned over the desk, trailing his fingers across the documents until he found what he was looking for. "Here. According to these documents, the Voynich manuscript was written by the Sol Niger alchemists of the Baltic region. And we know that they carried on the works of Flamel after his death," Bahij said, giving the documents a tap to underline his point.

"So this," *He* started, but was interrupted by Bahij who, in a great display of eagerness, got a bit ahead of himself.

"Yes, this and several other pieces of the puzzle have led me to believe that the newly discovered Flamel manuscript will contain the information required to decipher the Voynich manuscript," Bahij said before realizing that he had just interrupted his master. *He* let the silence linger for a few seconds before *He* began to speak.

"Well, we will see when you bring me the Flamel

manuscript. And when you do, make sure not to draw unnecessary attention. Not from the living, nor from the whelp who thinks he can rival me."

"Yes, my Lord. With your permission, I would suggest that we merely wait for the auction and buy the Flamel manuscript," Bahij replied.

"That will be fine – as long as I get the manuscript," *He* said before raising his glass. "Let us drink to our endeavors, and then you should go and enjoy the banquet. I shall join you shortly."

"Yes, my Lord," Bahij said, silently raising his glass to his master's toast.

Blake and Virgil sat through the whole concert, talking only when Blake reengaged in the conversation as new questions surfaced. Virgil didn't mind. He knew that new arrivals had to adjust and get used to the idea of being dead and to the whole concept of Shades, which – as Blake had noted – was far from what people expected.

There was a chill in the air when the two men walked into the street. A large clock hanging on the wall of the building on the opposite side of the street told Blake that it was just past eleven in the evening. They walked down the street until Virgil suddenly stopped by the metaphysical equivalent of a 1964 silver Aston Martin DB5 and began rummaging in the pockets of his robe for the keys.

"I have arranged for you to have a house and a car, and, of course, if there is anything else you need, just let me know," Virgil said as he threw the keys to Blake, who stood admiring the car, unaware that it was actually his. Blake caught the keys, turning to Virgil with a surprised look on his face.

"Thank you."

"No need. You're in the employ of Dæth and thus will be taken care of – a task with which I have been charged." Virgil opened the passenger-side door, which was already unlocked to him. "I tried to get you something that matched your life, but which was slightly different than what you were used to."

He got into the car and waved his hand, letting Blake know that he should get into the driver's seat. "In my experience, those who arrive here thrive best with a bit of change. In the end, at least," Virgil said once Blake had gotten into the car. "It doesn't really help to deny the fact that there has been a change from life. I hope this is OK?" he continued. Blake turned the key in the ignition, giving the car just a little gas. The engine roared to life.

"Sure it is. I'll be alright with this one once we get to know each other," Blake said, blatantly understating his own excitement. With the engine running, Blake turned to Virgil.

"So tell me, Virgil. What happens now?"

"We drive. I'll let you know when to turn." Blake rolled away from the curb and briefly looked with wonder at the half-finished Eiffel Tower that grew ever smaller in his rearview mirror. "Well, as I said," Virgil started, "you have been invited to Dæth's mansion, and I'm sure I don't need to tell you that this is an invitation you do not turn down."

"Of course not. And what on earth, or . . ." He let it slide. "What would I do instead, anyways? It's not like I have a life, you know."

"No, I know. But in time you will settle down and develop your own routines. Turn left here. You will make acquaintances, maybe even friends, and, for a time at least, Shades will seem a lot like life." Blake turned at the intersection, barely making the green light. "That is until you realize that everything around you changes and deteriorates.

When all of those whom you have befriended begin to decay and become more and more distant." From the faraway look in Virgil's eyes, it was clear to Blake that Virgil's mind had begun to wander. "That is when you realize that the only ones you really have left are the few of us who work for Dæth and thus remain ourselves – at least to some degree."

"You don't sugarcoat it, huh?" Blake asked, halting Virgil's flow of words and forcing Virgil's mind back in the car.

"Well, my job is to welcome you here and guide you. I am just trying to offer you a few hard-learned lessons of my own for free." As they drove through the city night, they sat in silence, neither of them feeling the need to speak. Leaving the skyscrapers behind, they drove onto an old bridge that bore a strange resemblance to the Brooklyn Bridge, which Blake had been accustomed to crossing at least twice a day. Blake rolled down his window to feel the chilly autumn air and when he rolled it back up after a couple of minutes, he decided to break the silence.

"So, seeing as I am invited to visit Dæth, how the hell do I get there?"

"Well, first I am going to show you where you live and then I will leave you to get yourself sorted," Virgil said, pausing for a second. "Then tomorrow morning you should leave and head for Dæth's mansion in the Empires of Industry. There's a map at your house, but please don't show it around. The other souls will not understand. They need the illusion that they try to uphold."

"So I shouldn't draw attention to myself?"

"Exactly. And for that reason I have made sure that you have a number of appropriate outfits to change between on your journey. You always need to fit in as a Hunter when you travel around Shades. Normal souls never travel outside their own land. They simply cannot, and therefore it is not prudent to draw attention to the existence of the other lands, by – say – looking like *that* as you travel through the past lands," Virgil said, gesturing at Blake's suit.

"I'm guessing that this also means leaving my new car behind?"

"Yes. Well, you can drive this car all the way through to the border of the Empires. From there you will have to travel by coach, but I will make sure one is there to pick you up. I've left a note explaining the essentials by the map on your desk, and I've taken the liberty of packing a bag so that you have everything you should need for the trip. Now, take a right the first chance you get after the bridge – that should take us down by the promenade to your house." The promenade was a lot like the area of Brooklyn Heights where Blake had lived the last years of his life. However, there was something fundamentally different that Blake couldn't immediately put his finger on. As they drove along the waterfront, Blake struggled to figure out what it was until it finally dawned on him. There was something distinctly Parisian about it. It was as if he found himself driving along the south bank of the Seine bordering the Latin Quarter in Paris. However, where Notre Dame and Île de la Cité would have been, Blake found

51

only a barge floating by on a dark river much wider than the Seine. On the far side of the river lay a bustling city, which to Blake looked much more like Manhattan than Paris.

"Hell, I have to say it again. This is not at all what I imagined it to be," Blake said, breaking both the silence and his own chain of thoughts.

"No, my friend. It never is. But you will get used to it. Now, just park the car by the curb up ahead," Virgil said and pointed to a house further down the street. "It's the one over there." Blake stepped on the clutch and allowed the car to roll along while easing the breaks. The car stopped just outside his new house and they both got out. Virgil walked around the car and shot out his hand to Blake, who was looking up the stairs at the house and admiring the fact that Virgil had taken time to arrange two flowerpots with some kind of white flowers, which were actually gardenias.

"I have left the house keys under the flowerpot. Take care," Virgil said as they shook hands.

"You too. And thank you for all of this."

"As I said, don't mention it. I am just doing my job," Virgil replied with a smile. Then he turned and headed down the street. As Blake walked up the stairs to his new home, he paused and looked back down the street. As Virgil walked away, Blake saw him slowly shift and blend into the shadows that filled the night, and then Virgil was gone.

Blake bent down by the door and lifted the nearest flowerpot in search of the key. "Fucking typical," he muttered, finding nothing under the flowerpot but small insects and a little dirt that had fallen through the hole at the bottom of the pot. He found the keys under the other flowerpot and let himself into his new apartment, which was decorated very much like he would have done himself in life – a decor dominated by old, heavy wooden furniture in stylish white rooms, spiced up with elements of modern design. In his study, he found a large map of Shades laid out on his desk, and on top of it was a letter from Virgil.

Dear Mr. Beck,

I will be brief, as I will have explained most of what you need to know about Shades by the time you read this. Tomorrow you should leave early and drive west towards the Parted, which you should reach tomorrow evening. This area is inhabited by the souls of the Cold War era and you shouldn't have much trouble blending in. I have booked you a room at the Hotel Marina for your first night. It should be quite a treat for you to revisit the seventies for just a night.

The next day you should be able to clear the rest of the Parted and reach the borderlands to the Empires of Industry in the early evening. From there you will have to travel by foot for a few miles until you reach the Broken Pail Inn inside the Empires of

Industry. Here I have made sure that you will have a room for your second night – and remember to change your clothes in the borderlands. They are in your bag, together with fitting currency and all else you should need.

From the Broken Pail, I will make sure to have a coach pick you up and take you directly to Dæth's Mansion so you will have no trouble traveling through the Empires of Industry. It should all be marked out on the map, and all your things are packed in the leather bag in your bedroom closet. I believe that is all.

Have a pleasant journey!

– Virgil

V

In Aquraa Castle the minstrels started playing, filling the grand hall with the songs and tunes of five centuries past – the tunes from their own time. They played with the skill of musicians who had had centuries to master their instruments. The castle was bustling, as all of the most prominent undead were gathered there for this night. The long table where all the guests had been seated for the banquet, with Mr. Ferre at the head of the table, ran half the length of the hall and was covered with the remnants of a magnificent feast. The souls served had been prepared and distilled into drinks and exquisite dishes before serving, for just as no king in the world would ever serve his guests with raw flesh, *He* would never dream of serving unprepared souls for his guests to devour as if they had just hunted them down themselves. It would be savage, and if there was one thing *He* was not, it was uncivilized. As the feast ended, the dance floor filled and only a few noblemen remained seated at the table. Among them sat the Earl only a few chairs down from *Him*, who also remained at the table. The two sat in silence observing the gathering of nobles dancing the minuet, both noticing the beauty of Teresa Ammon dancing gracefully with Bahij Khaleel.

The corners of Mr. Ferre's mouth curved slightly in what could have been the indication of a smile as the Earl stood up and excused himself. The Earl's audacious way was one of the reasons why *He* kept the Earl at court, despite his obvious deficiencies. The Earl offered a slight relief to the staleness of eternity – something to be valued, *He* thought, as the minuet ended and *He* watched the Earl walk towards Bahij and Teresa.

"Thank you for saving me this dance, Mistress Ammon. It is indeed a pleasure and a privilege to have the first dance of the night with the lady of the house," said Bahij as he bowed to her following the last steps of the minuet.

"Teresa, please. I insist. And you are most welcome," she replied with a smile before continuing. "You are such a fine dancer, Bahij, if I may say so."

"Thank you, Teresa. As are you, if you will allow me to repay the compliment," Bahij said, so lost in her presence that he did not notice the Earl approaching.

"I see that your dance has ended and I endeavor to ask for the mistress's hand so that we may show master Khaleel how a proper European would lead the minuet," the Earl continued before Bahij found words to retort. "Not that I did not find your performance a splendid attempt for a soul three hundred years too old to have danced the minuet in its time and place."

"Sir, I think I would kindly reject your offer just . . ." said Teresa, trying to diffuse the situation.

"Oh, but Teresa, what a waste of amusement," Bahij interrupted. "I would surely like to see the boy dance, yet I would be surprised to see that he had time in life to learn to dance, between all his drinking and whoring," Bahij said before taking another stab at the Earl. "But perhaps in the time of your lordship, mastering the arts of whoring and drinking were considered virtues fit to pursue, just as those of knowledge, common courtesy and good manners."

"Indeed," replied the Earl, allowing a sly smile to creep across his face. "Perhaps not by all in my time, but certainly by myself. And none were, nor ever have been since, a more virtuous man than I!" Annoyed that Bahij's temper and vanity had bested his natural flair for gallantry, Teresa turned to the Earl.

"Very well," she said. At her reply, the Earl turned on his feet and bellowed to the minstrels on stage.

"Play us the tune once again, so that I may show how one confidently and truly leads in the minuet!" Disarmed by Teresa's response, Bahij was forced to step back. Fuming with anger, there was nothing he could do but watch the two dance. "Wonderful! As I expected, milady's beauty perfectly matches the grace of her movements," the Earl noted with great conviction.

"You flatter me, sir. But still, I have to say that your grace, at least on the dance floor, greatly exceeds my expectations," Teresa replied with a smile.

"I always strive to surprise, so I will take that as a compliment, if I may."

"You may, indeed," she said, trying to figure him out as the steps of the minuet drove them apart for a moment. Once the minuet led the two to rejoin hands, the Earl turned his head towards her and spoke in a low voice.

"I understand that our well-mannered friend has made quite a discovery."

"But how?" Teresa replied.

"Let us, for a second, not pretend that secrets are meant to be kept, and instead set out to mirror the world as it is, rather than how we think it should be," the Earl said. "I simply desire knowledge, therefore, I seek it where it lies; knowledge is always accessible to those who know where to look."

The minuet again tore the two apart, leaving Teresa just a few moments to wonder before the Earl once again took her hand and moved to speak.

"A slight glimmer of uneasiness in your gaze gave you away, and I must say that as I found myself captivated by it, I could not help but notice." Teresa's sense of wonder shifted as she began to feel both uncomfortable and intrigued. "You had to disturb *Him*, something I know you would do only if utterly necessary and that – of course – sparked my curiosity," said the Earl as the minuet called for him to give a bow and allowed Teresa time to respond.

"Let us hope that it will not be that very same curiosity that becomes the end of you," Teresa replied, hoping that her wit might put off the Earl's questions, yet knowing full well that it wouldn't.

"I am sure it will not," he said, "and that is also why I wish to inquire more of you. Knowing you to be a true lady, I know that I can expect nothing but discretion of you."

"But what is it that you think I would have to tell you?" Teresa asked, curious to see where this would take her.

"From the way our courteous friend found me to be a competitor, I am guessing that he has a fondness for you, milady – something which is understandable," the Earl said. "Now, I myself am fond of many things about you – especially your loins, with which I hope to get further acquainted later on." Taken aback by the Earl's rude flattery, Teresa chose to ignore his last remark and tried to put the conversation back on track.

"And thus you think he confides in me?"

"Indeed – just as you will confide in me. If not now, then later when we are in bed. Just because we are dead does not mean that we should forsake lust or pleasure." A short silence fell between them, softened by the tune of the minuet.

"You are very confident, are you not?" Teresa ended the silence.

"Yes. Confident that you will come to dislike me, yet feel a strange longing and desire towards me. For I am my own man and follow only as long as it pleases me and my endeavors – something all men envy and all women desire in a man," he replied to her before finishing their dance with a bow and a last remark. "And then I will make you shiver and I will show you the dark corners of your soul that you have never dared enter before ... even in death."

Blake had been underway for almost two days and had driven more than 1,500 miles. However, Blake felt like years, not miles, were the right way to measure distance in Shades. Trying to keep to himself as much as possible, he had made it through the Entrance and most of the Parted, each mile taking him further back in time.

As the sun set below the horizon, Blake turned off the highway at a junction and headed into the downtown area of the large city he had reached. According to the map Virgil had given him, this was about as far has he could go by car. As he drove onto the city streets, Blake rolled down the window and slowed down the car. Looking around, he felt like the sole spectator at a play set in the seventies, played out by flawless actors with all the props built to immaculate perfection. But Blake knew that none of these people, with their bell-bottom jeans and Volkswagens, saw this as the performance it essentially was. Blake scouted for a place to park his car and found a vacant spot by the edge of a large park, the trees of which had just about shed the last of their leaves. He parked his car and got out, picking up his bag before heading across the street and into the park. Blake put on his fedora and buttoned up his coat as he walked, trying to make as little contact as possible with the inhabitants of the city. He walked along a park path until he reached the massive concrete wall that cut through the city and which was covered in graffiti protesting its existence. As he turned right along the wall, the last rays of sunlight hit the treetops and the street lamps lining the path came on. Blake kept walking as he pulled a thin paper binder from his bag. A small note on the front read: "For your crossing out of the Parted." Blake opened the binder and found a number of official documents filled out and stamped to ensure his unhindered passage through any checkpoint in the city. After a quick look through the forms, Blake closed the binder and found that he had reached the edge of the park and the street that lay beyond it. "Gartenstraße" read a sign above the bakery that lay on the corner across the street. Blake looked to his left, and some thirty yards down the street he could see the wall that cut through the city, scarring the skyline. By the wall, he saw a small white building in the middle of the street, with a red and white painted toll bar ensuring that no unauthorized traffic came through. A tall sign next to the toll bar informed Blake that "You are leaving the American sector" in several languages. The baker was closing down his shop for the evening as Blake crossed the street and walked past. Heading towards the checkpoint, Blake couldn't help but notice the people he passed. Some were clearly on their way home from work, while others seemed on their way out to enjoy the city by night – but it was common to all of them that this was clearly just another night. But in his mind, Blake could hear Virgil's words: "Most souls try to go on, but they can't. As time goes by, they begin to realize that all they are doing is merely postponing the inevitable and that this pantomime of life is all just an act. There is no meaning anymore."

As Blake neared the checkpoint, he saw a young man in uniform standing guard by the toll bar, beyond which lay the no-man's-land between the walls. From the checkpoint ran an asphalt road lined by barbed-wire fences, leading to another checkpoint at the foot of a tall concrete guard tower on the other side of the wall, about a hundred yards away. Behind Blake lay a city that, at a glance, seemed like most western cities in the seventies. In front of him lay the memory of the iron curtain.

The young MP standing guard turned as he heard Blake approach.

"Good evening, sir," he said, letting his M16 hang down by the shoulder strap.

"Good evening," Blake replied, "Is this the right checkpoint to cross by foot?"

"Yes, sir. Provided that you have all your documents in order."

"I believe I have," Blake said, removing the binder from his bag and handing it to the MP.

"So, where are you from, sir?"

"I'm from New York. Well, at least that's where I've lived for most of my life," Blake said.

"You're kidding. Me too," the young man said as he started reviewing Blake's papers.

"Really?" Blake replied, feeling that he had to.

"Yeah. From the Bronx – and I can't wait to get back there

when I go on leave next month. Get some real home cooking and then go to see the Knicks at the new Madison Square Garden. Can't wait to see it – they say it's huge." He flipped over another page.

"It's pretty big," Blake said, trying to keep the conversation as smooth as possible.

"You've been there?"

"Yes. I went to a ballgame there a while back."

"It can't be that long ago. They'd just opened when I came over here for my first tour." The MP looked up at Blake with a slightly puzzled look on his face.

"No . . . I mean a couple of months ago. Just before I came over here myself," Blake tried to save it.

"Mmhhh," the young man returned his eyes to the documents and left the conversation at that. "Well, it all seems to be in order," he said after looking over the last couple of pages. Then he closed the binder and handed it to Blake.

"Thank you," Blake said as he placed the documents back in his bag.

"You're welcome. Have a nice evening, sir," the young MP said as Blake walked past him and around the toll bar. From there, Blake walked into no-man's-land.

He traversed the walkway, which was enclosed by tall wire mesh fencing and bathed in floodlight. All around him, Blake could see the two cities that should have been one divided by concrete and barbed wire. He looked ahead to the tall guard tower at the end of the walkway. A searchlight pointed to the ground a short way ahead of him, the cone of light standing still as if it had forgotten what it was looking for. Blake walked through the light and through the checkpoint at the foot of the tower. He looked around to find a guard to clear his papers, but found no one. Then he looked back over his shoulder and saw the young soldier from New York standing guard by the checkpoint some hundred yards behind him. Blake walked around the white concrete tower.

"Hello?" Blake called out, scarcely expecting any reply. Beyond the tower lay a small square lit up by the same tall light posts that kept the stretch of no-man's-land illuminated. A couple of small one-story buildings lay around the square, dwarfed by the tall apartment buildings beyond it. As Blake looked around, he did not find a single soul, so he started walking across the square towards a street that headed west. On the corner he could see a small grocery shop occupying the ground floor of the six-story apartment building. It seemed to be closed down for the night. The streets were dead empty, and as Blake made his way across the square away from the wall, the sounds of the city slowly died out. As Blake walked past the grocery shop, he saw empty rooms through the street windows. There was nothing inside, yet he found that he had accepted the place as a grocery store simply because of the sign above it. That was enough. He walked through the empty streets, feeling how he had always imagined that it would be to visit the city of Chernobyl. As he walked deeper into the city, he found the buildings had even fewer details. After about half a mile, he walked around the corner of what was merely the relief of a building. There were no windows, only ledges. There were no doors, only frames lining where the doors should have been, with doorknobs and keyholes placed into the brick wall behind the facade. As Blake walked around the corner, he found the building was only a wall about a foot deep, like a theater stage set. Wild, uncultivated fields lay beyond it as far as he could see. Blake walked well into the fields before turning to have a last look at the city. From where he stood, it looked like a theater stage built for a play with no audience, only performers. It existed only to let those beyond the wall believe that there was an enemy to guard against, and so they would believe that there was a world beyond the iron curtain. "Perhaps," Blake thought, "there is a different city elsewhere in the Parted where the souls of the Eastern Bloc have built their own memory, guarding against their own fears." He started to feel the weight of Shades, realizing then how these souls would try to keep up the act for as long as they could, each decade forgetting and ignoring more and more details until one day they would stop and forever contemplate their wasted lives.

VII

The light of the low moon flowed through the open window, losing the battle to illuminate Teresa's bedroom where all remained mere silhouettes. The cold autumn winds pulled at the curtains of the canopy bed, as if seeking to draw them aside. Teresa and the Earl lay naked on the bed in silence among the shadows, both fully awake. He turned his head and looked at her. She was beautiful lying there with the moonlight caressing her black hair and white skin, the light blazing like a fire in the whites of her eyes. He breathed in, savoring the smell of her.

"Now, my dear. Pray tell."

VIII

Elijah Butler stood ready to greet Blake as he stepped out of the carriage.

"Welcome to Dæth's mansion, Mr. Beck," he said with a bow. Blake nodded, preoccupied by the breathtaking spectacle of the mansion, which was unlike anything he had ever seen in his life. The places Blake had visited in life that could be said to come close in their grandeur had all been museums and tourist attractions, with their air of past and pretense. Here there was no pretending, no staging of the past for the sake of the visitor. This was the home of Dæth, as real as anything Blake had seen in life. As he started up the stairs, he found Harlan McCoy standing halfway up.

"Welcome, Mr. Beck. Your arrival has been much anticipated. I trust you had a pleasant journey?" McCoy said, his presence demanding Blake's full attention. Harlan McCoy was impeccably dressed, wearing a black suit, white shirt and a black tie, with a vest that was barely revealed by his unbuttoned jacket.

"Sure," Blake said, deciding not to go into details.

"Good. Virgil usually does a damn fine job getting the new arrivals settled," McCoy replied.

"I'm sorry – may I inquire who you are?" Blake asked, trying his best to not be indelicate.

"Oh, it is I who am sorry. Where are my manners?" McCoy replied. "I'm Harlan McCoy, one of Dæth's closest associates.

You might call me his right hand in many affairs, but you will come to know me mainly as the one who deploys and instructs the Hunters."

"Oh, nice to meet you then, *sir*," said Blake with added emphasis.

"Likewise," McCoy said with a smile, gesturing for Elijah to approach. "And this here is Elijah, but he prefers to be called Mr. Butler by the houseguests. He is Dæth's valet and butler, and he is chief of the household."

"Mr. Butler," Blake said with a nod of acknowledgment.

"Sir," was all Elijah replied, as always bent on keeping up much more than appearances. Elijah guided Blake and Harlan up the stairs and into the hall.

"Mr. Butler?" Blake asked with a puzzled look on his face.

"Yes, sir. By both name and occupation."

"Oh, I see," Blake replied, a great deal less confused about the butler's name and title.

"Will that be all for now, sir?" Elijah inquired, addressing both men at the same time.

"Yes, thank you, Elijah," McCoy replied.

"Then I will take my leave to see to the preparations, sir." As Elijah left, McCoy showed Blake up the stairs towards the first floor landing.

"This way, Mr. Beck."

"Thank you," Blake replied, his mind preoccupied with the eerie feeling of being back in time.

They reached Dæth's study and McCoy knocked on the door.

"Sir. Mr. Beck is here to see you."

"Harlan, come on in," said a calm voice beyond the door. As Blake and McCoy entered the spacious Victorian study, they found Dæth sitting behind his desk. He raised himself off his chair slightly to give the men a courteous welcome. As he sat down again, rays of light from the setting sun shone through the garden windows behind him, giving him an angelic aura of golden light. "I bid you give me but a minute, and then you shall have my full attention. Pour yourselves a drink, if you please," Dæth said. McCoy poured three cognacs and then they stood there in silence, waiting for Dæth to finish his work. Finally, he pushed the chair out and got up. Walking over to Blake, Dæth picked up a glass. "So, you are Blake Beck," Dæth said, his gaze scrutinizing. "It is nice to finally meet you in person. Harlan has told me promising things about you."

"It's a great pleasure to meet you too, sir," Blake replied.

"I am sure it is," Dæth said without a hint of arrogance – to him it was undoubtedly a pleasure to finally meet death. "Did Virgil get you settled alright?" Dæth inquired.

"Yes. Perfectly, sir. House, car and all. I think he made sure that I would have all I could want in life – well, in death, obviously."

"Not all you could want in death, but you will come to see that. For now, I merely wanted to greet you personally before

69

your initiation."

"Initiation, sir?"

"Yes. Tonight you will have your initiation into the ranks of the Hunters, and when the deed is done we will celebrate." Dæth took a drink from his glass, closing his eyes for a moment as if trying to recall how a sip of cognac had tasted in life. "Tonight we will hold a veritable danse macabre, you might say," Dæth said before McCoy rejoined the conversation.

"Sir, I also bring word from one of our sources in the Gothic. Something I think would interest you." Harlan unfolded a letter and handed it to Dæth.

"Thank you, Harlan. Now let us see," he said as he ran his eyes down the page, rapidly extracting the better part of the letter's information. "Harlan, my friend. Once again, you have bested yourself. Now let us see if we can keep one step ahead of Mr. Ferre, thanks to his lordship," Dæth said with a smile as he folded up the letter and placed it on his desk. His smile reminded Blake of the smirk of a conman who had just been handed a free con. "Harlan, please look into the specific circumstances in the morning. And Mr. Beck," Dæth said, pausing for a moment to give Harlan time to step behind Blake. "It is time for you to become one of us – and I must ask you – are you ready for this?"

"Of course," Blake said, reassuring not only Dæth, but also himself.

"Good man! Harlan, will you do the honors and escort Mr.

Beck downstairs?"

"Certainly, sir," Harlan replied as he pulled a linen bag over Blake's head.

Blake was guided through the halls and down a long, winding stairway into what Blake thought had to be the basement of the mansion. When the bag was removed and his eyes adjusted to the light of hundreds of candles, the blurry shadows that lined the circular room developed into robe-clad figures. A rosewood veneer completely covered the walls, creating a warm, unbroken surface. On the floor, Blake noticed an intricate system of strange symbols and elaborate drawings. He looked around at the people standing by the walls, wearing dark robes and what Blake saw as grotesquely twisted, white porcelain Guy Fawkes masks. Four of the figures carried large brass trumpets similar to the ancient Norse lur but more delicate and adorned with elaborate patterns hammered into the brass. The door across from Blake opened, and Dæth walked into the room wearing a dark robe embroidered with countless small symbols and sigils in thin threads of silver. Dæth let a solemn silence linger a moment before he spoke.

"Kneel before your death and master!" he said with a voice that could only have been rivaled in authority by the voice of Moses as he commanded the Red Sea to part. Even if Blake would have wanted to defy Dæth, he couldn't have. "You have walked through life and into death to be here in this congregation," Dæth continued. "On this night you will leave behind all ambitions and vow to serve death in eternity – a

deed that will be repaid with an eternity of life in death."
Blake was struck by the fact that he could almost feel his heart
pounding wildly in his chest, although he knew that it
couldn't. "Your soul will belong to death, and as you will
wholly be a servant, you will be nothing without your master."
Dæth paused, letting the silence that followed underline his
point. "As eternity will be granted to you by your master, so
may your master take it away upon his pleasing." Blake
lowered his head. "You will serve as one of the Hunters: the
eternal legends that hunt the scourge of the dark one until the
final day of judgment when all will be resolved by powers
beyond any of us." Dæth rested his eyes on Blake, who sat
kneeling before him. "You will bring final death and judgment
to those who seek to avoid the death and judgment already
passed onto them. In the dark war against the undead, you will
be the spear point of justice and light. You will be an angel of
judgment, and as you hear the trumpets sound, calling you to
battle, you will rise from the ground to serve death." In the
distant corners of his mind, Blake could hear the elderly
gentleman from the Kingsland bar in the Entrance still
singing his song.

*"When I hear that trumpet sound, I'm gonna rise right outta
the ground. Ain't no grave can hold my body down."*

"Are you ready to take this upon your soul, Mr. Beck?"
Dæth asked in a low, friendly voice as if he was inviting Blake
into his arms.

"Yes," Blake replied, his eyes still on the floor.

"Then rise as a champion of death and receive my blessing

so that you may wield my powers in my stead." Blake got up, feeling the weight of death lifted from his shoulders – feeling as if he had made his way home by uttering that single syllable. "Let the trumpets sound to tell the world that a new champion has risen from the grave!" Dæth bellowed. In response, the four trumpeters sounded their trumpets and the robe-clad figures began to chant melodious sounds and words that made no sense to Blake. As the sound of the trumpets died out, the chanting figures lowered their voices to a near whisper, allowing Dæth to continue. "Receive Death's blessing at the hands of those who are now your equals. Receive the blessing so that you may carry out my bidding." Dæth stepped back, allowing four of the robed figures to step forward, each carrying their own symbol. One held up a sickle, one bore a handful of earth, one carried a heavy, leather-bound tome, and the last one had an ox heart in his hands. "First, we present you with the cold earth. From now on you shall be the master of the earth that is your grave until the final day of judgment. You shall have life in death," Dæth said as the robed figure knelt down before Blake, placing a small mound of earth in front of him before stepping back to the wall. "This tome represents the knowledge that you now possess and that which you will come to have. Knowledge that will guide you and let you stay true to your calling, even when darkness tries to corrupt you." The tome was laid down next to the earth before the figure stepped back. "Into this heart you shall pour all your dreams and ambitions – all that which serves only to distract the Hunter from his true course." The third robe-clad man knelt down as Dæth spoke, placing the ox heart at Blake's feet before stepping back with a ghostly glide. "And lastly, you shall take up the sickle. A symbol of the weapon you will wield in death – a weapon blessed to strike both living and dead so that you may reap the souls you hunt." The sickle was laid down next to the heart and there was a short silence while the last figure walked back to the wall without a sound. "Now take up the sickle," Dæth commanded. Blake knelt down and picked up the sickle as Dæth continued. "The first soul is now yours to reap and destroy. Take up the heart and slice it through to let your master and peers know that the Blake Beck that once was will be no more – that before them stands naught but a Hunter." As Blake rose from the floor, the chanting stopped. He held the sickle in his right hand and the ox heart in his left. He drew a deep breath, slowly raising the sickle before slashing downwards and severing the heart with remarkable ease. As he did, he felt death once more. It seemed like an eternity to Blake as he watched the severed heart fall to the floor. All his dreams and aspirations came tumbling down with it, and the silence of the room was unbearable to him. Just before the heart hit the floor, his master took mercy upon him and began to speak again. "Then I give you the blessing of death. You shall serve me and be allowed to share my powers. You shall be absolved from judgment for as long as you serve death. You shall be a Hunter!"

CHAPTER 3

- BACK IN BLACK -

I

Astrid Sigurdsdottir was an attractive and bright young woman about to turn the dreaded 30-year corner. She was a woman of many gifts and talents, but unfortunately for her, she seldom put them to much use. Instead of using her gifts to make an extraordinary life for herself, she had – unconsciously – chosen to use them to make an easy life instead. She had skated through a life's worth of schooling, enjoying the free education of the Danish state, always getting above average grades by making a below average effort. Her free time she spent with friends or nurturing one of several hobbies. She was the lead singer in a small symphonic heavy rock band that was – she had recently admitted to herself – not going anywhere, and she played role-playing games twice a week. She was also a volunteer guide at the cathedral in Aarhus, which earned her a lot of goodwill with the parish administration and the church servant. Goodwill she relied upon in her research for her master's thesis, which she was writing at Aarhus University. She had been studying history for six years and was writing her thesis on the religious art of medieval northern Europe, with a particular focus on the

Lübeckian painter and sculptor Bernt Notke – the Michelangelo of the north – and the altar he had created for the cathedral in Aarhus in the late 15th century.

Astrid was on her way to the cathedral to study the altar for the hundredth time – a sort of acceptable procrastination, as she could reasonably argue that it was relevant to her thesis. She had permission to study the altar up close where she could better see the details of its many sculptures and painted wings that were opened and closed according to the liturgical calendar – an undertaking which took some effort, as the altar stood more than thirty feet tall. On this particular day, she was on her way to study the left wing of the predella where Bernt Notke had depicted the mass of Saint Gregory.

Astrid took the bus downtown and got off at Cloister Square, which was aptly named after the adjacent cloister. From there she walked to the nearby Small Square, which was right next to Large Square. To Astrid, it was as if these uninventive names were a manifestation of the lack of vision and imagination she found to be missing not only in her own life, but in the entire nation around her. Over the years, her views on these kinds of matters had become more and more jaded, and with her thirtieth birthday on the horizon, they were threatening to cause a total eclipse in her view of the world. However, while Astrid believed that she was just about the only person in the world to clearly see what was wrong with everything, all of her girlfriends seemed to agree that

Astrid's negative outlook would be wholly cured if she found herself a man. To Astrid's great annoyance, these very same girlfriends constantly insisted on aiding her in the search for this cure through well-meaning advice and forwarded links to profiles on various dating sites.

However, as Astrid walked across Large Square, the dark thoughts fighting to ruin her day received a forceful knockout. It happened every time she walked across Large Square to the cathedral. She snickered as the two large side buildings, with the massive church tower standing between them, obscured the rest of the cathedral from her view. It left a vision, which – even in the mind of the holiest of nuns – could be seen only as a giant phallus reaching toward heaven. The fact that the contrail of a long gone airplane drew a thick white line from the top of the tower into the vast blue emptiness of the morning sky didn't help at all. She snickered to herself all the way to the church door where she took a deep breath. Then, with a somewhat somber look on her face, Astrid entered into what was, in her mind, a gargantuan penis rather than a grand Gothic cathedral dating back to the late 12th century.

II

The Earl had asked Teresa to join him for a morning stroll through the streets of Aquraa, and she couldn't wait to see him. She found that the night she had spent with him had awakened all sorts of feelings inside her – feelings she had forgotten existed. She had gotten so used to being part predator and part servant that she had not felt such affection and longing for hundreds of years. It was as if he had touched a part of her soul she had thought long gone, and he had thrilled her with both his words and affectionate gestures. She yearned for him.

He had asked her to meet him at the gates of the innermost city wall so that they could take a walk in the misty morning sunrise. Even though she savored the sunrises in Shades, she recalled the colors in life being, in a strange way, more real and colorful. Ever since her death this had filled her with a touch of melancholy, but on this day it did not – she simply had other things on her mind. She was meeting the Earl and she felt joyous. She walked across the courtyard of Aquraa castle, and from there she followed the street that sloped down the hill towards the gate of the innermost city wall. From a distance, she could see the Earl standing by the gates, looking as gallant and confident as ever. He wore a beautiful lace and embroidered Baroque walking suit and held a silver-tipped ebony cane in his hand. As she approached, he turned to her, lifted his feathered hat and gave a deep bow before offering her his arm to walk.

"You are extraordinarily pleasant to behold, even to the eyes of a nobleman, I would say should you permit me to," he greeted her.

"You may," Teresa tittered.

They walked side by side out through the gate and into the city of Aquraa, savoring the beautiful autumn morning. While the inner city and castle had been kept in the Gothic style of medieval Europe, the city has much more to reveal as one walks through its streets. Aquraa is home to thousands of undead, all from different times, places and cultures, and like Shades, the city is a patchwork of quarters where different times and cultures prevail. On this particular day, the Earl sought to lead Teresa down the hill to his native Baroque quarter and back up to the castle through the exotic medieval Arabian quarter. They walked through the streets for several minutes before Teresa broke the lingering silence that the Earl had left for him to savor and her to break.

"John, please speak to me of love. They say you are a great poet and I long to witness your talents myself," Teresa pleaded.

"I thought you experienced my talents just the other night, my dear," the Earl replied, raising his cane slightly, making no uncertain insinuations.

"John," she said, shaking her head in disdain, though her smile gave away her true thoughts on the Earl's manner and ways.

"Very well. I shall conquer you with my words, rather than by my scepter. But do not retort and revenge should my words leave you weeping for eternity or hungry for more, like the drunk hungers for the barrel and the lecher longs for his whores." As they turned down a small alley enclosed by half-timbered houses standing several stories tall, the Earl began to speak to the world, with Teresa as his sole audience.

"An Age in her Embraces past,
Would seem a Winter's Day;
Where Life and Light with envious haste,
Are torn and snatch'd away.

But, oh! how slowly Minutes roul,
When absent from her Eyes;
That fed my Love, which is my Soul,
It languishes and dies."

As he spoke, Teresa held his arm tightly and drew herself in closer to him, as if it would somehow help her grasp his words.

"For then no more a Soul but Shade,
It mournfully does move;
And haunts my Breast, by Absence made
The living Tomb of Love.

You wiser Men despise me not;
Whose Love-sick Fancy raves,
On Shades of Souls, and Heav'n knows what;
Short Ages live in Graves."

She looked at him with eyes that told him that she wanted him to never be absent from them, and that she wanted him to never have to rave on about the despairs of love.

"Whene'er those wounding Eyes, so full
Of Sweetness, you did see;
Had you not been profoundly dull,
You had gone mad like me.

Nor censure us, you who perceive
My best belov'd and me,
Sigh and lament, complain and grieve,
You think we disagree."

For a short instant, the Earl's words conjured up the image of Bahij in her mind. She knew that he would disapprove of her actions and feelings for John, but who was he to judge?

"Alas! 'tis sacred Jealousie,
Love rais'd to an Extream;
The only Proof 'twixt them and me,
We love, and do not dream.

Fantastick Fancies fondly move;
And in frail Joys believe:
Taking false Pleasure for true Love;
But Pain can ne'er deceive.

Kind jealous Doubts, tormenting Fears,
And anxious Cares, when past;
Prove our Hearts Treasure fix'd and dear,
And make us blest at last."

He let his words ring out and linger in the morning air before he turned to face her as they walked along.

"It was beautiful, John! You truly are a man of many and surprising talents, I have to say. Not at all what I had wrongly judged you to be," Teresa said.

"My dear Teresa, you should not be so hard on yourself, for I am sure that your judgment is not wholly unjust and that my character is indeed one to judge," the Earl replied before Teresa stopped the stream of his words with her lips. She felt alive as she kissed him, alive and free. Sadly for Teresa, she had missed a subtle point in the Earl's poetic praise of her. He had spoken to his mistress, not his true love.

They walked on with the taste of each other still on their lips, saying nothing until they reached the Earl's majestic home in the Baroque quarter. With a gallant gesture and unmistakable ulterior motive, the Earl invited Teresa inside and led her through his house, upstairs to the master bedroom.

III

At the banquet that followed his initiation, Blake got the opportunity to meet his fellow Hunters who had come from all corners of Shades, and he found himself enjoying the company. He was one of them now. As Dæth's guest, Blake had been given the use of one of the mansion's many guest rooms, and he only made it to bed just before the break of dawn. The following day he slept until almost noon, and after lying in bed for a few minutes, he figured that he had better get up and get on with things – whatever those things might be. He got out of bed and found that his clothes had been washed and dried since his arrival the day before. They were laid out for him on one of the beautiful Rococo chairs that formed the small sitting arrangement in a corner of the room. As he put on his pants, he felt the fading warmth of the autumn sun on his back through the window, and he looked down at himself. He was pleased with the way he looked. Fit and rather muscular, especially for a man around fifty years of age, and he found himself wondering if he would now look this way forever. If that was the case, he was glad that he had kept himself in such good shape and had not just let himself go as his workload had shifted from field to office. He finished putting on his suit and walked out of the room in search of someone he knew or had at least met the day before. He made it all the way down to the hall before he found Elijah Butler. Blake was just about to hail Elijah with a "good morning," but then Blake realized what time it was and decided to draw his attention with a "Mr. Butler?"

"Good day, sir," Elijah replied, immediately turning to face Blake coming down the stairs from the guest quarters. "I trust you have slept well following last night's festivities, sir?"

"Very well, thank you." Blake decided not to inquire into whether or not the butler had slept well, as he thought – correctly – that this would not be a pleasantry pleasant for any of them, least of all for Mr. Butler.

"I took the liberty of having one of your suits cleaned after your journey here, and I had it laid out for you to wear. I hope it was not a liberty taken too far, sir."

"Not at all, Mr. Butler. It was very considerate of you."

"Thank you, sir. Mr. McCoy and my master have kindly requested that you join them in the lounge. I would have offered you a spot of breakfast prior to this, sir, but unfortunately Mr. McCoy was adamant in his request that you would join them as soon as you got up. And besides, lunch will be served in just forty minutes. Is that alright with you, sir?"

"It's perfectly alright, Mr. Butler. It's not like I become hungry anymore, is it? These days it seems to be more the ritual of it."

"Indeed, sir."

"But thank you for the thought. I'll find my own way to the lounge so that you can get back to business."

"Thank you, sir!" Elijah said before going about just that.

Blake walked down the east wing hallway, still finding himself enthralled by the beauty and reality of Dæth's Mansion and Shades in its entirety. He walked in silence, soaking up all the impressions as best he could, but he was far from able to hold them all. Blake reached the lounge doors and knocked. From behind the door he heard Dæth's calm voice asking him to come in. As Blake walked in, Dæth and McCoy got up from their seats as a simple courtesy to welcome Blake into their midst.

"Good day, Mr. Beck," Dæth said.

"Good day, gentlemen," Blake replied, trying his best to not look like someone who had slept until noon on his first day of work.

"Please join us," McCoy said, gesturing to the chair next to him. Blake walked over and sat down, eyeing an unfinished game of chess on the side table next to the sofa where Dæth was sitting. A letter with the words "Bishop B7 to C8" lay open on top of the chessboard. Blake could see that the black player had just taken out the white rook that had previously held the black king in check. "Thanks for joining us, Blake," McCoy started.

"You're welcome, Mr. McCoy," Blake replied.

"Harlan, please. If we are going to work together forever, we might as well dispense with the titles sooner than later."

"Harlan it is then," Blake said and paused before taking a bold move. "And what about you, sir. What should I call you?" Blake asked Dæth. As soon as the words were out of his mouth, Harlan's face creased and it was clear to Blake that it was not the right question to ask.

"*Sir* will do just fine, Mr. Beck," Dæth replied before Harlan took hold of the conversation again to save Blake from making another faux pas.

"As you probably gathered from yesterday's conversation in Dæth's study, we have received interesting information from an informant among the undead nobility in Aquraa." It didn't really ring any bells with Blake, but he kept his mouth shut, allowing McCoy to continue. "It seems that Mr. Ferre has finally found the key to deciphering the famous Voynich manuscript. The manuscript is a medieval text written in an unknown language, which no one – despite the fact that every effort has been made – has been able to decipher over the centuries. So far the text has kept its secrets from the world, but perhaps it will not keep them for long now. We know that Mr. Ferre has sought to decipher the manuscript for several centuries as he believes it to contain the description of a powerful dark arts ritual that would let him summon souls from one world into another."

"Sir?" Blake remarked to let Harlan know that there was a considerable risk of losing him.

"Well, there are several worlds in existence, as you know?" McCoy paused, waiting for Blake to give some kind of acknowledgment that he understood this.

"Yes. The real world and Shades."

"Yes, that is sort of true, except the real world, as you call it, is no more real than any of the other worlds."

"I know, but . . ." Blake was unable to finish his sentence before Harlan continued.

"Now there is Shades, where we are now, as you mention, but there are also other worlds. There are several afterlives where some souls are sent after judgment, but in this case there is one world that is of particular interest: the world we call the Grey."

"The Grey, sir? I mean . . . Harlan."

"Yes, the Grey is a virtually empty world of infinite size, said to be like an infinity of thick grey fog. This is where we – the Hunters – exile the undead we capture as a punishment for their crimes. A world where they will be completely alone with their own thoughts until the end of eternity. This is generally considered the harshest punishment that we are able to measure out. Especially since there is no known way to return from the Grey, so those there are lost with the full knowledge that there is no hope for them."

"OK," Blake replied.

"Now the Voynich manuscript is known to have been written by the Sol Niger alchemists. They were a congregation of alchemists, most of whom lived in the area of Schleswig-Holstein in the lower part of the Jutland peninsula during the 15th and 16th century." Harlan paused for a second or two just to let Blake catch up. "We know that the Sol Niger carried on the works of Nicolas Flamel, who is one of the most accomplished alchemists of all time and who is thought to have found the way to immortality. Some call it the 'elixir of life,' some 'the fountain of youth' and yet others equate this with the legendary 'philosopher's stone.'"

"Immortality?" Blake asked.

"Yes – immortality. However, contrary to the common belief of alchemist lore, we are convinced that Flamel discovered a way to immortality that was, in fact, a ritual that allowed the summoning of souls between worlds. This would effectively allow for the resurrection of the dead and thus potentially an eternity for them in life."

"And this is the ritual you believe is described in the Voynich manuscript?"

"Exactly. Which brings us back to where I started. While the alchemists sought everlasting life, the ritual presents a much more grim prospect. It is thought to offer the power to summon back willing souls from any afterlife, which means that it will offer Mr. Ferre the power to summon back his old allies whom we have exiled into the Grey."

"So he will be able to bring back those undead destroyed by the Hunters?"

"Not those destroyed, no. They are gone forever, like those who have been consumed by the vampires. But Mr. Ferre will be able to bring back those whom we have sentenced to an eternity of punishment – which is most of the undead we have been able to hunt down. We destroy them only if we do not have the option to exile them into the Grey – for destruction offers them a peace that we do not see fit to grant them," McCoy said.

"So this means that the most powerful and vile undead ever caught by the Hunters will return if Mr. Ferre gets his hands on the ritual?" Blake asked.

"That is the concern, yes," McCoy replied. Blake sat there in silence pondering what Harlan had just told him.

"So? What do you want me to do about it?" Blake finally asked.

"Our source has informed us of another manuscript reportedly written by Flamel himself. This manuscript has been unearthed in a private collection in Bath, England, and it is now being put up for auction by the newly deceased collector's son." Harlan halted his speech and took a sip of water from a glass on the table in front of him. "This Flamel manuscript is thought to be a 'Rosetta Stone' for deciphering the Voynich manuscript. That is why we need to get our hands on it without anyone – living or dead – getting wind of our actions."

"OK," Blake said in a tone of voice that clearly implied his next question. "How?"

"We have discussed it and our solution is actually simple," McCoy answered, looking rather pleased with himself. "We know that the manuscript will remain at the deceased collector's home for the next few days until the auction house collects it for safekeeping prior to the auction," McCoy started. "Now, a CAC unit from the London branch already has the house under guard, but that is of little issue as our source has led us to believe that the undead will buy the manuscript at the auction. Thinking that we do not know of the existence of the manuscript, the vampires will be intent on drawing as little attention as possible." Blake nodded, urging McCoy to continue. "Tonight a CAC operative will gain access to the manuscript and photograph it in such detail that we may fabricate a slightly altered copy." McCoy looked over at Dæth, who sat silently on the sofa across from them like a king letting his general lay out the plans to the officers. "We will then sell this copy at the auction house at a decoy auction that will take place at the same time and date as the real auction. We will make sure that the vampire buyer will be guided to this fake auction, which is possible because neither Mr. Ferre nor his buyer knows exactly what the real manuscript looks like." Dæth smiled as he diverted his attention to the chessboard and moved the white queen from B3 to C4. "Now while the undead buys the fake manuscript from our decoy auction, our buyer will buy the real manuscript from the real auction and no one will ever know. The auction house gets a sale, the undead get a manuscript that won't help them decipher the Voynich manuscript as they had hoped, and we win by taking not only the real Flamel manuscript, but also Mr. Ferre's money. And no one expects any foul play because everyone gets what they came for," McCoy said with a con man's smile.

"Sounds like a plan," Blake said in full agreement with McCoy that this seemed to be a good plan, if not even a great one. "There is just one thing," Blake said after a short pause.

"Yes?"

"Why don't we just switch the fake and the real manuscript before the auction, taking the real one for ourselves and letting the auction house sell the fake? No one would know," Blake asked McCoy.

"That is true, but while we can gain access to the manuscript in Bath tonight, by the time we have fabricated the fake, the manuscript will no longer be accessible. At that point it will be kept in the high security vault used by the auction house to store their most prized items – and I don't have to tell you that gaining access to that vault is difficult, to say the least," McCoy said.

"Fair enough. So what? You want me to set up the fake auction on the big night?" Blake asked with a smile, anxious to get to work as a Hunter.

"Yes. Think of it as easing into your new position," McCoy replied, looking to Dæth to see if he had anything to add.

"Well gentlemen, now you will both have to excuse me for I have business to attend to. I trust that you can see yourselves out," Dæth said as he rose from his seat, forcing Blake and McCoy to mind their manners and do the same.

"Of course, sir," Harlan said as Blake gave a nod to let Dæth know that he too could find his own way out. Dæth straightened his lapel before he turned and walked out of the lounge, leaving Blake and McCoy alone.

"So, how do I get to London?" Blake asked, feeling that this was a very relevant question.

"Because this is your first time, I'll send Virgil to your

home in the Entrance to see you off. But in the future you will be free to travel into life from anywhere in Shades." Harlan started out of the lounge and walked down the corridor towards the hall with Blake following his lead, walking beside him. As they walked, McCoy continued to explain. "As you know, you can only travel into the world of the living during the night half of the day, just like the undead. We simply have no power strong enough to bind your dead soul in life during the daytime. Like the undead, if your soul remains in the world of the living beyond the night, its connection with Shades is severed and your soul will float off into the Grey."

"OK," Blake said. They reached the hall and Harlan stopped.

"Seeing as there are a few days to the auction, I will let you take time to get settled here in Shades. Now, I also have some business to attend to. I have to go riding with Dæth's wife, so you will have to excuse me." Harlan picked up his coat and put it on. "Have a great journey back, and if you need anything before you leave, I'm sure that Elijah will oblige you."

"Thanks," Blake replied. Then McCoy put on his Stetson and snapped the brim before he stepped out into the cold autumn rain.

IV

For ten long years since that fateful night at Sacré-Coeur, Vincenzo had been stuck in Shades. Blake Beck had won that night, but in Vincenzo's mind it was only because Blake had fought like a coward. Although Blake had destroyed his physical body that night – a body that Vincenzo had managed to preserve for almost five hundred years – forcing his soul into Shades, Vincenzo had managed to elude the Hunters long enough to seek refuge in Aquraa. There he had stayed for the last ten years, knowing full well that a vampire restricted to Shades is a much easier target for the Hunters than one who has the possibility to shift into the world of the living. But staying in Aquraa, he knew he would be safe. It had been a long wait, and at one point he had even contemplated attempting to shift into the body of a living person. However, Vincenzo knew it was too dangerous and that there was a reason why almost solely those undead that had gone mad from the strains of the afterlife or from too little feeding did this. He knew that entering a living body meant two souls contesting the same body, and if he lost the battle for control he would be imprisoned in the body until its death. Then, when the host eventually died, he would pass into the Grey rather than into Shades, as that ticket would be taken by the body's genuine soul. Finally, relief had come in the unexpected form of Mr. Ferre's right hand Bahij Khaleel, who had approached Vincenzo and made him a proposition. Vincenzo knew that Bahij disliked him and the feeling was mutual.

Bahij belonged to the group of conservatives who still upheld certain ideals of the living, which Vincenzo found both naive and inopportune: ideals such as honor. They restrained themselves from feeding on living souls unless it was necessary, limiting themselves to feeding on souls in Shades – presumably to draw less attention to the existence of their race. Vincenzo, like many others, thought differently. Their ideals had died with them, freeing them of the shackles of life and morality. To them, the restrained ways of the conservatives were a sign of weakness and lack of will to take the appropriate place of the alpha predator atop the food chain. However, no matter their differences, Bahij Khaleel had made Vincenzo an offer. Vincenzo would be granted a new body in the world of the living in return for serving Bahij in a venture, the details of which remained undisclosed to Vincenzo so far. He had accepted despite the lack of information because Bahij had given him one overshadowing reason to accept. Vincenzo would get the chance to face Blake Beck again. Finally, he would get a chance for revenge.

Vincenzo stood looking out over the eastern city through the window of the room he had been given at the castle. He felt at home and more powerful than ever as he slept here at the proverbial bosom of *Him*, the first undead; he was in the house of the light bearer – the one who sheds light and brings hope to those doomed to an eternity in Shades. Vincenzo walked into the bedroom of his guest quarters and lay down on the bed, gazing into the canopy overhead. It was painted with a series of murals that depicted the myth of the fall of *Him* and the origin of the undead race. Vincenzo closed his eyes and felt the evening breeze extend its airy claws into the room through the open window. Khaleel had sorted out Vincenzo's new host body and it was only a few minutes ago that a servant had knocked on the door and told him it was time. Vincenzo closed his eyes. Finally, after almost ten years, he would go back. He would go to London and aid Bahij Khaleel in his venture, and then he would once again be free to help himself from the buffet of life. Vincenzo had traveled into his own body thousands of times before Blake had destroyed it, but this was the first time he had ever taken a new body. With his eyes closed, he envisioned the two worlds flowing together. In silence he called upon the powers of *Him* that had been offered to Vincenzo in his second birth. The curtains of the bed gave way and he felt his soul dissipate as it shifted into the world of the living and into the waiting vessel.

Vincenzo waited for his soul to settle into the new body, and as the thumping bass of the club's electronic dance music manifested to his new senses, he slowly opened his eyes. He knew he had to take it slow at first, waiting until a full symbiosis was established between his soul and the new body. This process usually took a few days, during which he was likely to reminisce as the host body revolted. During reminiscence, experiences and memories stored in the host body's physiology surface, causing the invading soul to experience intense flashbacks to the body's lifetime. Some vampires would embrace these memories and the skills stored in the new vessel in order to become even stronger. Others would see the new vessel as merely a tool, insisting on subduing the body and fully remaining themselves – a battle that would sometimes prove hard to win. Vincenzo found himself sitting very uncomfortably, slumped back over the cistern of a white porcelain toilet in a small stall. His new body was aching from the onset of rigor mortis, but the body still had warmth to it, revealing that the kill had been very recent. The body was fresh. He felt light-headed – as if slightly drunk – and overwhelmed by the sensory impressions that flooded the reanimated body. As Vincenzo looked down, he felt the anger well up inside him. While looking down the impressive, pushed-up C-cup cleavage of the young female body he was in, he noticed that he was wearing a strategically torn, tight-fitting black dress, matching black stockings and pointed-toe pumps. The natural inclinations of his soul took precedence over the body's natural response to rage. As he sat up, he rammed his small, white fist into the stall wall, which gave way slightly and cracked. A few scratches appeared on his knuckles and a little uncoagulated blood oozed out.

"Are you OK in there?" a drunken female voice called from outside the stall, forcing Vincenzo to get a grip of himself.

"Yes, I just slipped and banged into the wall," he replied, surprised by the lightness and grace of his new voice. "I'll be alright!"

"OK, party on, girlfriend!" the woman called out over the muffled thumping bass electronica. Seconds later, Vincenzo heard her opening a door nearby, briefly causing a distinct increase in the volume of the music. "A woman! Khaleel must be amused with himself," Vincenzo thought as he got up from the toilet, trying to get a feel for his new body as he looked around to see if there was anything he had missed. Apart from the inane scribblings of previous patrons on the stall walls offering important information like "Jeanie is a cunt" and which number to call for a good time, the only thing he found was a black leather bag caught halfway down behind the cistern. He bent over to pick it up, and as he did, he cursed the nature of high heels and wondered why on earth women willingly went to so much trouble to attract a male specimen. He opened the bag and found a pair of shoes, presumably in there for the owner to wear on her way home. He kicked off the high heels and put on the flat shoes. Better. Then he closed the toilet lid and sat down to check the remaining contents of the bag: a couple of condoms, a set of keys, make-up and a small wallet. The wallet held nearly a hundred pounds, credit cards, a membership card for a Beckton martial arts dojo and a driver's license. Vincenzo got up and undid the lock on the stall door. He opened the door and peered out into the restroom to check if anyone else was there and found no one. He walked to the sinks, and as he stood in front of the mirror, he held up the driver's license to check the resemblance. The young, fit brunette with the sharp A-line bob haircut in the mirror in front of him definitely matched the driver's license, although the girl's hair had been blond and considerably longer at the time when the photo had been taken. Vincenzo stood still, gazing at the mirror. Although he resented Bahij for serving him with a female body, he couldn't help feeling that it might be an interesting change that would bring about whole new possibilities. The girl was definitely in prime condition, and at the age of twenty – according to the driver's license – she was in the early prime of her physical development. And she was beautiful, there was no denying that, he thought as he gazed into his own deep brown, almond-shaped eyes. He picked up the bag and turned his head to check out his new body in the mirror as he left the ladies' room.

As Vincenzo opened the door into the heart of the club, the intense electronica and the noise of hundreds of partygoers drowned out all other sounds and the shifting faces around him filled his mind. Suddenly, it all began to flow together in a liquid haze of checkered vinyl floor and laughing, shouting faces. In a blur of sight and sound, Vincenzo felt his new body revolt. He struggled to keep his mind in the same place as his body, staggering drunkenly towards the exit, but his thoughts were swooped away into the young woman's past memories. Vincenzo learned then that reminiscence is not at all like recollection, and he found himself a passenger in a body he couldn't control. It was as if he was actually present, as if he *was* the girl, and yet he had no control at all because what he was experiencing had all occurred in the past. He heard the music, tasted the lingering flavor of beer on his lips, and felt a drunken young man bump into him without even a slight mumble of an apology. It was still the same club that he had reanimated in, but it was only 8:35 p.m. according to an old 1950's wall clock. If this was his body's memories from the same night, he gathered that it was about four hours prior to her death. Straightening his dress – a gesture that felt very strange to him – Vincenzo walked over to the bar. As he placed his half empty bottle of Heineken down on the bar, Vincenzo got the distinct impression of being on the prowl for a nice time – a quick cuddle, a snog or perhaps even a bit of bonking in a parking lot or some other sordid place. Next to him, a man with a strong, trim build was standing with his back turned, talking to another guest at the bar. The man was clearly of Arabian heritage and he was old enough to be the girl's father. Yet the girl had been checking out this man all night, and despite feeling very uneasy inside this memory, there was nothing Vincenzo could do. The man turned to face him, and to Vincenzo's great surprise, it was Bahij he suddenly found standing in front of him, wearing a stylish grey suit and a friendly smile. The smile that had conquered the girl in the fatal final hours of her life.

"I can see that you are in need of a new drink. Something colorful, sharp and tasty to fit the rest of you instead of that out-of-place beer, I would imagine," Bahij started. "Now if you offer me your name, I will offer you that drink in return."

"Carrie," Vincenzo heard himself say in an endearing female voice. "And what's yours?"

"Bahij. Bahij Khaleel. It means cheerful friend," he said with a smile.

"Will you be my friend tonight then?" Vincenzo heard himself say and felt the batting of his mascara-coated eyelashes.

"Absolutely, my dear! What do you fancy?"

"Well, another drink, some dancing and then perhaps a bite before we might go somewhere else later on."

"Right you are, my dear. What are you having?" Alongside the conversation with Bahij, Vincenzo could hear the faint calling of a man's voice. It seemed like it was coming from another world, calling in a deep, slow voice like a 78 LP record played at 33½ rpm.

"Aaarree yyoouu aallrriigghhtt, mmiiss?" As the distant voice spoke, the memories shifted and Vincenzo felt himself rushing through hundreds of thousands of emotional and sensory shifts in a split second as the memories fast-forwarded through the night. Suddenly, he found himself with his eyes shut, kissing Bahij wildly, hardly aware of his surroundings. He felt his back being slammed against the stall door, which opened with a bang, echoing as the door hit the stall wall. They were kissing madly and he could feel his body getting aroused. He felt himself lift up his dress to the waist, and as Bahij moved his kisses from his mouth and down to his neck, Vincenzo opened his eyes again. Then he felt a sharp pain as Bahij sank his teeth in. As the blood began to flow, Vincenzo felt the rush of adrenalin as panic set in. He felt himself kicking and letting out a scream that was muffled into a low sob by Bahij's hand covering his mouth.

"Mmiissss!?! Ccoommee oonn, lleett'sss ggeett yyoouu ssoooommmeee ffrreesshh aaiirr." Vincenzo felt life slipping away as Bahij placed him gently on the porcelain toilet. He didn't struggle anymore. Death had taken its hold, and as he closed his eyes, Bahij began to wipe the stray blood from his dress with a piece of toilet paper. As Vincenzo closed his eyes to the memory, he opened his eyes in reality. He was outside the club, half hanging by one arm around the neck of a young man helping him to the curb. The youth was clearly under the impression that this young woman had had too much to drink and needed a bit of air, and perhaps she needed to bake a pavement pizza, as well. He sat Vincenzo down on the curb of the small paved area that separates Old Street from Hoxton Street in northeast London. Vincenzo looked up towards the club, which was located in a series of old Hackney apartments on Old Street. At street level, the wall was painted bright blue, with 12-foot tall black and white lettering reading "Exciting!" all the way around the end of the building to Hoxton Street.

"Are you OK, miss?" the young man asked again.

"Sure, I just need a minute," Vincenzo replied with a smile before continuing. "Will you stay with me?" he asked.

"Of course!" the youth replied as he sat down next to Vincenzo. He sat there silently for a minute or two to let the girl catch her breath and get her bearings. As always, Vincenzo played his part brilliantly.

"I don't think I need anymore to drink," he said, breaking the silence between the two.

"No. I don't think so either," the young man replied.

"Would you walk me home? I'm sleeping at my friend's flat. It's just a couple of minutes up Hoxton Street," Vincenzo said, scooting in closer to his companion, who – like most young men – was helpless against the endearing gestures of a beautiful woman in need of assistance and male protection.

"Sure," he said and got up. "You need a hand?"

"Yes, please," Vincenzo said, letting his new friend take his hand and help him off the curb. Vincenzo straightened his dress and took the boy's arm as they started up Hoxton Street. Vincenzo cuddled up to the young man as they walked, wanting to keep the small talk to a minimum. After a few minutes, they reached a small communal garden that lay quiet on this Tuesday night. Vincenzo stopped and moved to kiss the young man. He didn't feel any stranger doing this than a fisherman feels reeling in his catch. To Vincenzo, the kiss was merely a means to an end. "Come on. Let's go in there," he said, pointing to the garden with an unambiguous glimmer in his eyes.

"OK," the young man said with a slightly goofy grin, thinking he knew what was about to happen. Vincenzo took his hand and walked into the garden where he looked around to see if there was anyone nearby, and finding no one, Vincenzo leaned in and kissed the boy. Even by his lips, Vincenzo could feel how the blood started rushing as the young man's pulse rose. Then he felt the young man caressing his back and looking for a way to unzip Vincenzo's dress.

"What's your name?" Vincenzo whispered, running his fingers down the boy's throat.

"Why?"

"I'd just like to know."

"Martin," the young man replied. Vincenzo kissed him and saw how he closed his eyes to the kiss.

"Well, Martin, thank you for this," Vincenzo said, kissing him on the cheek before moving his kisses downwards.

"Mmmhh . . ." was the last thing the boy said as he stretched his neck to let the girl kiss him. Vincenzo sank in his fangs and immediately tasted and felt how arousal turned into panic. Vincenzo covered the young man's mouth with one hand, silencing his screams while pulling back his head by his hair with the other. The young man fought to break free, but to no luck. Vincenzo swept away his legs and let the young man fall on his back as Vincenzo got on top. Then Vincenzo drank, feeling his own powers grow and his soul bolster and renew as the young man's dwindled away. He closed his eyes, reveling in the taste of fear. As he felt the boy's body relax, Vincenzo sat up on his chest and looked into his eyes. Even though Vincenzo had removed his hand, the boy didn't scream. There was no strength left in him, and in his eyes was the despairing look of an untroubled youth who had met the devil for the first time. Vincenzo smiled.

"Why . . ." the young man stuttered, finding no strength to go on.

"Because I hunger." Vincenzo leaned down. "But if it offers

you any comfort in your last moments, know that I am likely to have saved you from an eternity of punishment. For I am sure that you – like all the others – would have eventually squandered your life away in sin." As Vincenzo spoke, he saw blood filling the boy's mouth and knew that he would soon be gone. Vincenzo sank his teeth into the boy and consumed the last of his soul, feeling life leave his body as he did. Then Vincenzo sat up and ripped a clean piece off of the young man's shirt, using it to clean as much of the blood off his dress as he could. Then he got up and hid the body among the bushes with a makeshift cover of leaves and branches. This would keep at least until morning when Vincenzo would be long gone.

Vincenzo walked out of the garden and back down Hoxton Street to Old Street where he managed to flag down one of the characteristic black London taxis. He got in and told the driver to take him to the address Bahij had given him in Wandsworth. They drove in silence through the streets of London towards the suburb in the southwestern part of the city. Vincenzo's body language made it clear that he was in no mood for idle chatter. After about half an hour, the taxi halted outside one of a great number of identical, two-story, yellow brick houses with bay windows framed by white painted wood. The houses were built together and formed what appeared to be a great wall that enclosed the street, as if they were meant to keep people from escaping from suburbia. Vincenzo paid the taxi driver and got out without replying to the taxi driver's "sleep well, miss," which had a distinct ring of disapproval to let Vincenzo know that young girls shouldn't be out that late drinking on a Tuesday night. Vincenzo walked up to the house bearing a sign stating that it was a bed & breakfast run and owned by a Mrs. Miller, which was aptly named Mrs. Miller's B&B. Below the sign, dangling by two hooks, another sign revealed that there were, in fact, "no vacancies." This sign – to the marvel of all the neighbors – was never taken down. This had resulted in the general agreement that Mrs. Miller and her husband Clive had to be very well off given all their business, even though they certainly did not flaunt their riches. To the neighbors it was this presumed restraint that ensured that Mrs. Miller and her husband were still a welcome and valued part of the community. They were certainly much more welcome than the family who had moved in next door to Mrs. Miller's a few years back with their uncontrollable teenage son Aidan who would play that awful rock and roll music until late at night – and even on weekdays at that. However, the truth about Mrs. Miller's B&B was light-years away from what any neighbor could have dreamed of.

Vincenzo knocked on the door of the house where Mrs. Miller had run a vampire safe house for more than thirty years. She offered cheap rates at the price of life in death – a death that would no doubt be confined to Shades when her life's work was added up. Seeing as Mrs. Miller was a stalwart woman, she would have none of that and had taken charge of her own destiny and afterlife. As for Clive, he seemed to do mainly what his wife told him. It was a couple of minutes before the door was answered by a little, elderly lady wearing what secondhand stores would peddle as a vintage nightgown.

"Yes, dear?" she said.

"I believe that a room has been reserved for me for the next few days by Bahij Khaleel."

"Oh, you must be Mister Vincenzo. Pardon me, dear. I had expected you to look a bit different. Come on in," Mrs. Miller said, stepping aside to let Vincenzo enter before she closed the door. "I have reserved our best room for you; it's a single. We can't have anyone associated with *Him* sleeping with the crowd of box-heads, if you don't mind me saying." Vincenzo simply ignored her – a hint she clearly understood. "It's up the stairs and to the right, dear." He started up the stairs, finding that the house appeared to have been unchanged in its furnishings for the better part of the thirty years it had been in the care of Mrs. Miller. The carpeted boards creaked as he walked up the stairs with Mrs. Miller following behind him. "That's the one," she said, pointing to the street-side door down the hallway to the right. As Vincenzo opened the door, a rush of cold air met him. The house lay silent, save for the humming of the air conditioning running on full blast and the muffled sound of Aidan's stereo playing in the neighboring house on the other side of the wall. Vincenzo's en-suite room had rather sparse furnishings, but the room offered the choice of a bed or a box, as some undead had gotten used to inanimating in boxes or coffins. Wherever it was done, the most important concern was to keep the body cool and out of direct sunlight while it lay inanimate without the undead's soul to keep it from decaying.

"This will be fine," Vincenzo said.

"That's nice to hear, dear. Now, is there anything else I can do for you? Otherwise, I will be getting back to bed."

"No. I will be fine. Just make sure that the room remains undisturbed."

"Of course, dear. Discretion is our creed."

"Good. Now I bid you goodnight."

"Good night, sir," Mrs. Miller said and left the room, closing the door behind her. Vincenzo walked over to the door and locked it. He looked at himself in the mirror that hung on the wall and examined the well-trained body of the young girl. Then he removed the black dress and stockings as he went into the bathroom. He gave the clothes a quick rinse in the sink to remove the bloodstains and then hung them to dry in the shower. He walked back into the bedroom and pulled the blinds of the bay window that faced the street. The music coming through from next door disappeared for a second while the track changed before returning with the sound of tight drums, bass and an electric guitar blasting. The vocals joined in at the same time as Vincenzo reached the bed. As he lay down, he savored the feeling of being back in the world of the living. He could still taste the young man on his lips. "It is good to be back among the prey," he thought, feeling like a wolf returning to a field of sheep. It didn't matter now that he had been forced to remain in Shades for all those years. All that mattered was that he was back. He closed his eyes. It was time to return and he began dislodging his soul from the vessel. As he felt the pull of Shades, the world dissolved around him and he felt as if he rose up out of his body and floated into the sky like a wisp of smoke.

V

The Earl got out of bed and put on the trousers of his walking suit. His white, embroidered shirt was unbuttoned and draped around his upper body, revealing the Earl's physique as slender and lean, albeit muscular. Teresa lay across the bed, spanning its entire width – uncovered and unashamed. She let her love soak up the sight of her. The Earl turned his back to her in order to pour them both a glass of that most precious drink – that of distilled soul.

"So, my dear. Have you been so fortunate as to have been further blessed by the company of our honorable and courteous, yet love-stricken friend?" the Earl said with customary arrogance, offering Teresa a glimpse of jealousy to assure her of his love for her. Although he felt no such thing, he played it out as the finest actor, knowing that it would suit the play.

"John!" she said with slight disdain, feeling both assured and assaulted by his jealous demeanor. "You speak of Bahij as if he is a lovesick puppy intent on following me around – and one that I allow to follow me, if I do not mistake your words. But that could not be further from the truth," she said as he turned and walked over to the bed. Teresa sat up and he handed her one of the two glasses, along with an endearing smile. "I know Bahij has pursued me for a while now, and I must admit that I have been flattered in the past and have laid my thoughts upon accepting his advances. But that is in the past. A past where I did not know you, John, but was resigned to knowing *of* you." She took a sip from the glass before continuing. "I trust you do know that you have showed me things and feelings that I could never hope for Bahij – or anyone else for that matter – to show me again. You make me feel life again, and for that and because you are you, I love you. This I trust you do know?"

"Yes. And I apologize sincerely, my dear, if I have offended you. It was not my venture to speak ill of you nor to show you mistrust." As he spoke, he ran his hand over her hair and down her cheek before bending over to kiss her on the forehead. "Now let us speak no more of my ill manners and the misplaced words of unbefitting feelings. Rather, having touched upon the name of Bahij Khaleel, I have a matter that I would much like your advice upon." He lay down in the bed next to Teresa, resting his head on his arm to allow him an optimal view of the topography of the bed. She smiled at him.

"And what may this matter be, my love?" Teresa asked with a slight titter and a smile, giving away the fact that she – as the Earl had expected – had placed him on a pedestal adequately high for it to be slightly strange and amusing for him to ask her for advice.

"Like all who serve *Him*, I too strive to make sure that Dæth is unlikely to be dealt a better hand than *Him*, and should it happen, it would be without my knowing or consent."

"Mhhh," she murmured as she took another sip, urging him to go on.

"I have come to know that Dæth is aware of the existence of the manuscript which Bahij has discovered – the one which we so inappropriately discussed in bed the other night. As Dæth knows of the manuscript, he will inevitably take precautions to make sure that *He* does not obtain it." Teresa sat up, looking just as strikingly beautiful to him in death as she ever could have in life. The sparse light flowing through the window caressed her features as the gravity of his words sank in.

"John. This is not a matter between you and me. If the advice you are looking for is about what you must do, then there is only one advice I can give. You must tell *Him* or Bahij!"

"Yes. That I know very well. However, it is not as strikingly clear from my perspective, as there are different ways to go about this. You are right that I could go to *Him* and reveal the fact that Dæth has caught on to his plans and will inevitably try to foil them." She looked at him, nodding her head in agreement. "But seeing as I am not entitled to know of Bahij's discovery of the manuscript and how *He* intends to acquire it, it would be hard for me to justify making inquires with my sources into how much Dæth knows on the matter. That is, without revealing the fact that someone has spoken out of turn." Looking at Teresa, the Earl could see a glimmer of panic in her eyes, as she knew very well who this someone was. "Now you know that I have no love for Bahij, but still I am a gentleman and I do not wish to bring harm to a friend of yours. And as for you, my feelings would not allow me to put

111

you – unnecessarily, I might add – in the awkward position of having to explain why you disclosed this information to me."

"But what do you propose then, John?"

"I would ask you to go to Bahij and tell him of my discoveries as if they were your own. He trusts you and knows full well that he disclosed the fact that he has discovered Flamel's manuscript to you himself. Then Bahij will enlighten *Him*, probably without reference to you, and the end is the same. The means, on the other hand, are not, and this way no one is embarrassed or that which is worse."

"Thank you, John! I know that I was in no position to disclose to you that which Bahij had secretly entrusted to me and put you in this awkward position. But even though I did, you are still a gentleman and seek to protect me, even though I am the one who stepped out of place." She gave him the long kiss of a woman who had just been delivered from despair.

"Do not be so hard on yourself, my dear. Had you not told me, I would not have known. Had I not known, *He* would not have been warned and that could have been a far less appealing scenario. The means might not be fully desirable, however the end seems to be."

VI

Vincenzo had spent the last couple of nights in London preparing for the evening's auction. His soul had taken full control of the young girl's body, which had proven to be in better shape than he had dared hope for. Bahij had done a great job picking her out, Vincenzo concluded after he checked up on Carrie's background. She had been in her first semester of studying economics at a London business school while still living with her parents in their Beckton town house. She was an only child and her recently retired parents were away for two months in the Caribbean. It was unlikely that anyone would really miss Carrie for a least a couple of weeks, which would be plenty of time for Vincenzo to build the story of Carrie's voluntary disappearance from her old life. But first, there was a more important task at hand.

Vincenzo roared down Battersea Park Road in his newly acquired 1965 Cadillac convertible, enjoying the feel and sheer power of the car. He grabbed one of the mixtapes left in the glove compartment by the previous owner and shoved it into the tape deck. Rock n' roll rhythms immediately shot from the speakers of the heavy metal monster that was piloted by a young brunette through the streets of London. Vincenzo smiled finding that he favored the electric guitar much more than the lute of his own time. One thing he had enjoyed over the last five hundred years was keeping up with the world – something most undead struggled with. Many of them struggled to such an extent that they would completely refrain from traveling into the world of the living as time passed. But not Vincenzo. If change was a liquid, it would be his favorite cocktail. He had witnessed the Renaissance, the Enlightenment, industrialization, two world wars and a cold one, and still he wanted more. He swerved and hit the gas to overtake an old Vauxhall with elderly lady behind the wheel.

Although Vincenzo had only served Bahij for a few days, it had become clear to him why Bahij Khaleel served as right hand to *Him*. Bahij had shown just how well connected he was when he had provided Vincenzo with an identity and high clearance ID badge for Christie's Fine Art Storage Services, the location where the Flamel manuscript was housed until the auction. As Vincenzo roared through the streets high on three nights of feeding and the prospect of revenge, he felt as if nothing could stop him. Bahij had meticulously planned the con, and Vincenzo's orders were clear. According to Bahij, Dæth had managed to create a fake of the Flamel manuscript that he planned to sell to Vincenzo at a decoy auction while buying the real manuscript from the real auction for himself. Vincenzo thought switching the auctions rather than the manuscript was a great idea, but there was just one flaw. Someone somewhere knew about the plan and hadn't kept quiet, and it seemed that if Bahij began to dig, there was no limit to what he could uncover. Bahij's plan was simple. While Blake switched the auctions, Vincenzo was going to switch the manuscripts. "And he'll never see me coming," Vincenzo thought to himself, looking down at his sleek female figure dressed in a stylish black pinstriped suit and white blouse. He slowed the car down as he turned down Ponton Road, which ran past office domiciles and warehouses, until the road made a sharp right turn. He drove slowly around the bend and along the railroad tracks that ran atop a red brick embankment as far as the eye could see. To his right, he saw the words "Christie's: Fine Art Auctioneers since 1766" written in thick foot-high letters adorning the massive building that stretched far down the street. It looked like a yellow brick cross between Fort Knox and a medieval castle to Vincenzo.

Vincenzo pulled over and stopped the Cadillac, and as he pulled the keys from the ignition, the music stopped. He picked up his briefcase, which contained a number of old books and manuscripts in different bindings. Then he clipped the ID badge he had gotten from Bahij onto his lapel and strode across the street and back around the bend to the entrance. He took a few seconds in the parking lot to straighten his suit and go over his story in his mind. Then he opened the door and went into reception where he found a young woman sitting behind the reception counter.

"Hello and welcome to Christie's Fine Art Storage Services. How may I help you?" she asked.

"Hi. My name is Carrie Charlton and I am here to check a reference in one of the manuscripts being put up for auction tonight in King Street."

"Oh, OK. Could I see your ID badge, please?"

"Of course," Vincenzo said as he unclipped the ID badge and handed it to the woman with a smile. The receptionist wriggled her mouse and tapped the keyboard in front of her.

"It seems to be cleared all the way up."

"It'd better be," Vincenzo replied jestingly, sending Bahij a stray thought.

"I can see that you're new to the firm. Is this your first time at the storage?" the receptionist asked.

"Yes."

"Well then, let me show you the way down to the holding facilities. That's where the lots for tonight's auction are being kept." She looked over her shoulder to a nearby office where an elderly gentleman sat staring at his computer screen. "Excuse me," she said before getting up and walking over to the office. "Ralf, I'm just going to pop down to the keep with Carrie out here. Be a darling and mind the desk for me." Ralf replied with a nod and a grunt. "Come on, Carrie. Let's go." The receptionist guided Vincenzo down the hallway, deeper into the windowless, high-security part of the complex. "Nice suit. I bet it cost a few bob?" she inquired as they walked down the hall.

"Sorry?" Vincenzo said.

"The suit. It looks like a million on you, so I just said that I'd bet that it had cost quite a bit."

"Thank you," Vincenzo replied, seeking to avoid any further conversation by neglecting to return the compliment.

This put a damper on the receptionist's endeavors, and they walked in relative silence down the hallways into the heart of the complex. After a few minutes, the receptionist halted in front of a heavy fireproof door and entered a code on the security touch pad next to the door.

"Here you go. The guards in there will clear you through the rest of the way 'cause this is as high as my clearance goes," the receptionist said with a smile.

"Thank you, miss," Vincenzo replied, repaying the courtesy. "I'll be back later on to oversee the loading of some of the items that will be going to the auction – in an hour or so, I guess. Do you have an exact time for the scheduled loading?"

"Oh, I'll just check that for you and then give you a shout when you're on your way out."

"Thanks." Vincenzo stepped through the doorway into the security gateway and shot a smile to the two uniformed guards who were courteous or well-trained enough to get off their seats when a lady entered the room.

"Miss," the older of the two men greeted Vincenzo.

"Hi. I'm Carrie Charlton from King Street and I'm just here to go over a few of the lots for tonight's auction. I'll be back again later on to oversee the loading."

"Sure thing, miss. Just let me have your badge and I'll give it a quick scan 'n see if we can let you in. Just have to make sure you're not a robber," the younger guard said with a slight chuckle. Vincenzo handed him his ID badge, which was scanned before keypads were punched, screens were scrutinized and facial resemblance was checked. Then he handed the badge back to Vincenzo. "Looks fine. The lots for tonight's auction are kept in vault 3b. It's just down the hall, and then the second hallway to the right." He pointed to the only other way out of the security entrance, where a heavy steel door slid open revealing a maze of windowless hallways.

"Thank you, sir," Vincenzo said and left the two men with a warm smile as he walked into the inner sanctum of Christie's Fine Art Storage Services. He walked down the hall to vault 3b and punched in the code Bahij had given him. The door slid open, withdrawing into the adjacent wall. Inside the vault, he looked around for any security cameras and found one overlooking the room from high in the corner. He walked over to the stand that held the Flamel manuscript and took a good long look at it. Then he opened his briefcase and found the manuscript that was closest to the Flamel manuscript in size and looks – at least at a glance. With his back to the camera momentarily obscuring its view, he switched the Flamel manuscript for a near worthless binding of late 18th century music sheets and placed the Flamel manuscript in his briefcase. This would do to make sure that no one noticed any change on the security camera. By the time anyone would pick up the manuscript by hand, Vincenzo should have returned and replaced it once again with the immaculate fake produced by the CAC. Playing his part, Vincenzo looked over the manuscript as he had said he had come to do, and then he exited the vault, closing the door behind him. On his way out, he shot the guards a smile before he headed down to reception. As he walked past the young receptionist, Vincenzo caught her eye.

"It's going to be at 8:45 p.m., Miss Charlton," the receptionist called out as Vincenzo walked by.

"Perfect. That will give me just enough time to pick up a few things on my way home. You're a dear." As Vincenzo walked across the parking lot and around the bend to his car, he shuddered – as if to shake off the role of Carrie Charlton for a while. He cared very little for the niceties and small talk of the living and found it unnatural for the wolf to chat with the sheep. However, his talent for playing the part, which he had developed over hundreds of years, served him well and he knew this. Not only did it serve a higher cause, but it also provided him a way back to feeding fresh – and a way to get Blake Beck.

VII

Blake had returned to his new home in the Entrance while the creation of the forged Flamel manuscript was underway. He tried to get settled in, but found that he still struggled to wrap his head around the concept of being dead, yet still being asked to walk through life as Dæth's vicar. On the eve of the auction, Virgil arrived to guide Blake through his first reanimation. Blake had half expected a grand ritual with humming, chanting, verses and candlelight like on the night of his initiation. However, this time the ritual was more like an instruction and cordial send-off. The initiation ritual had, in fact, imbued Blake with the powers of Dæth that allowed him to travel into life by sheer force of will. As Blake lay down on his bed, Virgil explained to him how to dissipate his soul and focus on the receiving vessel – his own body – in the world of the living. Then he closed his eyes and did as Virgil had instructed, feeling his soul dissolve and float out of Shades.

As his soul settled into his body, Blake heard the sound of muffled voices and he slowly opened his eyes. His body lay on its side with the knees pulled halfway to the chest. It remained in the position in which he had left it for the rigor mortis to set in – perched on the toilet in his New York City apartment. Blake stretched out his legs, feeling stiff and a little sore. He was wearing a white hospital gown and he found himself lying inside a man-sized metal tube on a thin mattress – which reminded him of the stasis capsules he had seen in sci-fi movies. A thin sheet of condensation covered the window that made up most of the capsule door, obscuring Blake's view of the world outside.

"He's up!" said a man's muffled voice. Seconds later, the capsule began to move, raising itself into a semi-upright position that forced Blake to stand on his feet. He felt his legs twitch, and as the capsule door opened, the blurred white shape outside was replaced by the figure of an elderly gentleman wearing a white lab coat, blue rubber gloves and a pair of thick spectacles. "Welcome back, Mr. Beck," the man said in a distinct British accent, nearly causing Blake to expect an offer of tea and biscuits. Blake shook his head, trying to remove the dizziness of reanimation. "So this is your first time up. Well, welcome to CAC London's mobile lab. Or as we call it, the Hunt-mobile." In case Blake had missed it, the man smiled to indicate that he had said something amusing, but Blake didn't bother to raise his cheeks. The man took Blake's hand, partly as a gesture of welcome and partly to help him out of the capsule.

"My name is George Thompson and I will be overseeing both your reanimation and inanimation tonight."

"Nice to meet you, George." Blake paused for a moment, straightening his gown. "Is it alright if I call you George?"

"Certainly, sir."

"Well then, let's get down to business," Blake said just before tripping over his own feet like a small child who has recently learned to walk. He would have fallen over if Mr.

Thompson had not been there to support him.

"Sir, might I suggest, since this is your first time in reanimation, that we just sit you down for a moment until you've settled in fully."

"That might be a good idea, George," Blake said as he regained his balance and looked around. What seemed to be a small, tightly packed room now revealed itself to Blake as the inside of a truck trailer, which appeared to be staffed only by Mr. Thompson and a young blond woman in a lab coat. Mr. Thompson helped Blake to a seat at a table in the corner before sitting down himself.

"Everything should be in order, sir. Our agents are setting up the surveillance as we speak, and the decoy auction has been staged. Every eventuality has been covered and every detail, from fake posters and fliers to CAC agents posing as prospective buyers, has been taken care of," Mr. Thompson said with a self-satisfied smile before emptying a lukewarm cup of tea that had been given a helping of milk and sugar some time before Blake reanimated. "Judith! Be a dear and bring me another cup," Mr. Thompson called out. Judith, the young CAC lab tech, turned her head. After sending Blake a warm smile, a frigid look crept over her face.

"Yes, sir."

"It is so nice to have these young people around. In this high tech day and age, it is almost impossible to run even a small CAC lab without assistants," Mr. Thompson said, clearly unaware of the fact that he had, with a great lack of respect, just reduced a presumably brilliant young PhD to a mere gofer. Blake let it slide, but sent Judith an empathetic smile. "So all you need is to get dressed and have a quick look around, sir. Then I'm sure that you will find everything to be in order and on track."

"Thanks, George," Blake replied. "One thing is missing though."

"I'm sorry, sir?" Mr. Thompson said in a slightly indignant tone of voice.

"Where are my clothes?" Blake said with a smile.

"Oh. . . I'm sure Judith will fetch them for you, sir." Mr. Thompson looked to Judith and she nodded. "I hope you will excuse me while you get dressed. I just have to make sure that they are on schedule with the surveillance setup."

"Sure," Blake said and got up, following Mr. Thompson's lead.

"Right this way, sir," Judith said to Blake and showed him to a small stall that provided him with a little privacy for him to put on his clothes. "Your clothes are set out for you. I thought a dark suit and black leather shoes would look good on you and fit the occasion."

"Thanks, Judith," Blake said before he stepped into the stall to change. Judith returned to check the feed from the heat scans that were set up in the auction house foyer, which had just come online.

"Please let me know if there is anything else you need, sir," Judith called out.

"There is one thing. The manuscript – do you have it here?" Blake asked as he buttoned his shirt.

"Yes, it's right over here on Mr. Thompson's desk."

"Perfect. I'll just do a quick check of the auction house and then I'll be back to pick it up. I want to make sure that it gets to the right auction room myself."

"OK. I'll let Mr. Thompson know that then," she said as Blake walked out of the dressing room wearing a sharp, stylish black suit.

"How do I look?"

"Very nice, sir."

"Thanks. I'll just head over to the auction house. What's the easiest way to get there? I mean, where are we parked?"

"We're just across the street. Apparently, there was a leak in one of the sewage pipes that run beneath King Street, so we're here to do the repairs tonight to make sure that we disturb the traffic as little as possible."

"Ah, OK. I'll let you get on with that then," Blake said with a smile before letting himself out of the back of the trailer. Once outside, he navigated the maze of traffic cones, roadwork signs and plastic tape that were closing off the area around the trailer, and after making his way around two other vans, he walked across the street to Christie's.

Vincenzo was on his way to King Street to make the second part of the switch, his speakers filling the streets with rock n' roll. He drove along the south bank of the Thames knowing full well that the timing would be more than tight. He had to reach King Street, locate the fake Flamel manuscript, make the switch, and bring the fake back to vault 3b before 8:45 p.m. at the latest. He looked at his wristwatch. He had just about an hour, and if traffic was reasonable and there were no traffic jams he would spend half that time in the car. "It shouldn't be a problem because there is no way Blake will see this coming," Vincenzo thought to himself. Then he let his mind drift into the music and left his body to pilot the Cadillac through the early evening traffic of central London. As the song faded out, Vincenzo saw the great London Eye, wreathed in hundreds of lights, looking down upon him from the edge the Thames until it disappeared out of sight behind the Shell Center.

Inside Christie's, Blake began his tour to check that all was ready and in place for the auction, starting with the foyer setup that included a team of five CAC agents. Two of them were set up as Christie's security guards, and the remaining three were posing as part of a TV crew doing a documentary on Christie's. However, the innards of their cameras, sound desk and other gear were unlike those found in real TV production equipment. As Blake walked through the front entrance and made his way over to the CAC team, he eyed the team's lead operative, Clarence Jacobs, an overweight, but muscular Englishman of African heritage. He was setting up and testing an infrared heat signature camera and several pieces of high tech abomination detection equipment that had been developed by the CAC over the years.

"So?" Blake said as he reached the agents.

"Sir!" Clarence replied, turning his attention to Blake and standing at attention. "We're just setting up the heat scans and are running the final tests, so we're on schedule. Also, the basic detection is already in place and running, so we should pick up any suspect entrants even now, sir!"

"Good! And just so we are clear about it, there are no excuses for not being on your posts tonight – for either of you. No sneaking away for just a minute for a quick phonetic romance with your girlfriend, and no unscheduled bathroom breaks! If you need to take an unauthorized piss, you do so in a cup with your eyes on your target and not your johnson," Blake barked, beating the agents to their reply. "Are we clear?"

"Yes, sir!" all three men said in unison. This time around, Blake was not just the Director of Operations. He was the Hunter brought in to make sure that everything was done with immaculate precision. The CAC agents knew this only happened on the most important assignments and that the authority of the Hunters was literally out of this world. Blake took a quick look around before giving Clarence a nod, and then he turned on his heels and headed up to the auction room where the real auction was being held. On his way up, he ran into Judith who had left the truck in order to assist with some tech difficulties in the auction room. Her phone rang as she passed Blake, but she refrained from answering it. Instead, she looked at the number and sighed, rolling her eyes as she hung up.

A few minutes earlier, Mr. Thompson had returned to the truck trailer. Upon his arrival, he moved to take the faked manuscript to the auction room, but Judith stopped him. She explained that Mr. Beck had given specific orders that the manuscript should remain in the trailer until he returned. Angry that he had not been included in the decision-making process, Mr. Thompson accused Judith of using her feminine wiles to bend Mr. Beck to her will to disrupt Mr. Thompson's own well-laid plans. While Judith had been just about ready to – at least, verbally – rip his head off, her focus was broken by her cellphone. The CAC agents in the upstairs auction room had problems with the abomination detection setup and needed her ASAP. Judith gave Mr. Thompson a quick passive-aggressive verbal lashing, which, to her great annoyance, escaped him completely. Then she headed into Christie's to aid the agents, leaving Mr. Thompson behind in the truck accompanied only by his slightly enlarged prostate. He realized that he had been so focused on getting back to the truck and taking the manuscript to the auction room that he had completely forgotten to urinate. The urge to relieve himself grew stronger as the minutes passed, and what was worse, he had spare time in the back of the truck to think about it. "Dammit," he thought to himself, "just as that damned girl has stepped out . . . Why is she never around when she's needed and able to do something useful for once?" He gave Judith a call on her cellphone, but she didn't answer. He couldn't hold it much longer. "Damn, Damn, Damn," he thought to himself as he looked around the trailer hoping to find a suddenly materialized loo to save him from the horrors of incontinence. He would have to step out. "Or use a cup?" he thought in a moment of weakness before deciding that he – Mr. Thompson – could not pee in a cup. It was simply beneath him. That was the sort of thing young people did. But he couldn't risk leaving the truck and walking into Christie's to use the loo because someone would undoubtedly notice him. Then an idea popped into his mind as he realized that he had noticed a pub just a few yards down the road. He thought they must have a toilet and he quickly decided to go for it. He was certain that he would make it back before Judith could return to have her ill misconceptions of him validated by seeing him sneaking out. It was something he would never do – except this was an emergency, although she would obviously never understand.

Vincenzo drove past the massive roadwork roped off outside Christie's and parked his Cadillac in a vacant parking space just outside the Golden Lion pub. He sat in the car for a minute to get the lay of the land, scoping out possible locations for the CAC agents who might be set up outside, as well as inside Christie's. His theory was validated by an elderly gentleman in a lab coat stepping out of a large Volvo truck that was supposed to belong to the roadwork crew fixing a sewer leak beneath King Street. The man seemed to be in a hurry and looked worried that someone might see him. Half running and looking over his shoulders, he passed Vincenzo. Vincenzo knew that this could very well be his moment and –

briefcase in hand – he got out of the Cadillac and hurried down the street to the truck. He tried his best to listen for anyone inside the truck before he slowly opened the trailer's back door and peered inside. Finding the truck abandoned, he jumped in and closed the door behind him. Without delay, he searched for the faked manuscript, disturbing the order of the truck as little as possible. He soon found the manuscript, which was carelessly left on Mr. Thompson's desk, barely covered by miscellaneous paperwork in an attempt to keep the manuscript out of plain sight. Vincenzo took the fake manuscript and put it in his briefcase. Then he placed the real Flamel manuscript on Mr. Thompson's desk, already savoring the fact that this would be on the head of Blake Beck. He quickly let himself out of the truck and walked back to the Cadillac. As he opened the car door and got in, the elderly gentleman exited the Golden Lion looking relieved but slightly guilty. As Mr. Thompson noticed the attractive young woman getting into the Cadillac, he sent her an awkward smile and a courteous "hello" before hurrying back to the truck. Once inside the trailer, Mr. Thompson checked on the single most valuable item in the truck – the manuscript fake. He realized it was still there and breathed a sigh of relief.

Vincenzo had already turned off King Street by then. While Blake examined the auction rooms and made sure that the decoys, guards, flyers and greeters were in place, Vincenzo drove back to Christie's Fine Art Storage Services, making good time. About the same time as Blake returned to the

CAC truck to take the manuscript up to the decoy auction, Vincenzo walked into vault 3b and placed the fake Flamel manuscript on the stand, returning the old sheet music binding to his briefcase. Now he just had to wait for the transport to take the fake manuscript to the real auction before he could drive back to Christie's to buy the real manuscript from the fake auction set up by Blake Beck. And that was just what he did.

VIII

For the second time that evening, Vincenzo parked his Cadillac on King Street, but this time he strode into Christie's boldly. "It's perfect," he thought. For once he didn't have to hide from the CAC. He wanted them to know that he was there. And sure enough, as soon as he walked through the front door he saw minute telltale signs that several people in the crowded hall were with the CAC. As he approached the stairs that led to the auction room, a young blond woman wearing a long, black dress approached him.

"Excuse me, miss. Can I offer you a catalog of the lots of rare books and manuscripts on auction tonight?" she asked and handed a Christie's catalog to Vincenzo.

"Yes, please. Thank you," he said with a soft voice, sending the woman a smile.

"You're just in time. They're just about to call the auction," she said.

"Perfect. I was running a little late because I had some business to attend to," Vincenzo replied. A bell rang and cut their conversation short before an omnipresent and distinctly British voice requested that the attendees of the auction please move to the auction room.

"Good luck! I hope you win your lot," the woman said as the crowd began to move.

"Thanks. I'm sure I will," he said and proceeded upstairs to the auction room with the rest of the crowd.

Blake was downstairs in the foyer observing the cluster of low-ranking CAC agents posing as newly arrived auction guests and waiting for the vampire buyer to arrive. Suddenly, he got the call in his in-ear headphones that the vampire had just arrived. The voice of Clarence Jacobs explained that it was the young, sleek woman with the dark A-line bob who had just walked through the front entrance. Blake quickly made her out among the crowd and signaled to one of his agents that she should present the vampire with the Christie's catalog for the night's fake auction. The catalog had been fitted with a microscopic wireless microphone just in case they needed a tap on the vampire. As the vampire took the catalog, Blake gave the go ahead to call the fake auction. It was twelve minutes until the real auction would start, which Blake figured was perfect. This would allow the real auction to fill with those auction attendees who were running late, as well as a second team of CAC agents on standby. Yet, there was no question about who would be the buyer of tonight's star lot number three: the Flamel manuscript. No one would be able to outbid Dæth or Mr. Ferre. As the auction was called, Blake left Clarence Jacobs in charge of setting up the second group of CAC agents to attend the real auction. Then Blake followed the vampire buyer to the fake auction himself. Vincenzo walked up the stairs amid the crowd, following the Christie's usher to the auction room. As he sat down on a chair in the back, he noticed Blake casually walk into the room and sit down on a seat two rows behind him. This was turning out to be one of the best nights of his life, Vincenzo thought as he unfolded the first stage of his revenge against Blake Beck. For minutes they sat there in the relative silence of an auction room filled with strangers who saw little reason to chit chat with the possible competition.

The auctioneer took the stand ten minutes late and the crowd was growing restless, although the grace and conservative form of British high society prevailed, making for little ruckus. To make sure that all went as planned and that the CAC buyer won the real auction, Blake's earpiece transmitted all that was going on at the real auction simultaneously. Almost in unison, the two auctioneers opened the auctions.

"Welcome to this evening's auction of rare books and manuscripts here at Christie's. This is a highly anticipated auction as tonight's lots include a hither-to unknown manuscript written by the famous medieval alchemist Nicolas Flamel. Lot number three." Blake heard the words in a strange stereo, the sounds of the real auction in his right ear lagging slightly behind the sounds of his surroundings. But the words were the same.

"I will open the bidding on lot number one: a mid-thirteenth century Bible that was produced in Tuscany. This four hundred-page, illustrated vellum manuscript contains a prologue with Latin interpretations of Hebrew names, and the bidding will start at 12,000 pounds" said the auctioneer from the real auction through Blake's earpiece at the same time as the first lot of the fake auction was presented in front of Blake.

"I will open the bidding on lot number one: a commonplace fifteenth century book including rules and grants concerning ecclesiastical benefices under Antipope John XXIII. The manuscript consists of twenty-three leaves in a single binding, and the bidding will start at 9,000 pounds." A man raised his paddle. Then another joined in and soon bidding was well underway. The auctioneers in both auctions called off "12,500 pounds" and "13,000 pounds," and "16,500 pounds is the lady's bid over here" until the bidding subsided and the lots were sold. Lot number two was sold in a similar procedure before the evening's star lot was opened.

"Now I will open the bidding on tonight's star lot, lot number three: the Flamel manuscript. This 68-page, leather-bound vellum manuscript dates back to the early 15th century, and it was written by Nikolas Flamel in the last years of his life. The manuscript has been in a closed private collection and the seller wishes to remain anonymous. I will start the bidding at 1.5 million pounds," the auctioneer announced. Bidding began immediately and quickly reached 2 million pounds before the vampire and the CAC buyer joined in at the fake and real auction, respectively. As bidding subsided, Vincenzo joined in. In a calm and collected voice, he immediately raised the bid from 2.1 million to 2.5 million pounds, sending an awed hush through the crowd. At the same time, Blake could hear the CAC bidder in the real auction joining in, albeit more carefully, upping the bids by the standard 50,000 pound increments. An elderly, overweight British gentleman with a distinct comb-over tried to challenge Vincenzo for the manuscript, but as the price turned the 3 million pound corner, even he gave up. It was clear that the young woman in the back was more than intent on getting the manuscript.

"Sold to the young lady in the back for 3.175 million pounds!" the auctioneer said as he banged his gavel. Around the same time, Blake heard that his CAC buyer had acquired what he thought was the real manuscript for 2.7 million pounds. The deal was done, the price could be paid and the manuscript would be collected. With the outcome of the auctions, the CAC had even made 475,000 pounds selling the fake manuscript to the vampire.

"That felt good," Blake thought to himself as he walked across the street to the trailer to inanimate. He was back, the job was well done and he could leave the CAC agents to clear out under the expert supervision of Mr. Thompson. As Blake climbed into the trailer, he found Judith alone preparing the capsule for his inanimation.

"Mr. Beck," Judith greeted him.

"Judith," he nodded.

"Your gown is still in the changing room and you can just leave your clothes in there. I'll take care of them."

"Thanks, Judith," Blake replied before stepping into the changing room as Judith finished the preparations. A few minutes later, Blake emerged wearing the same white hospital gown that he had reanimated in. "I'll just get in then?"

"Yes, Mr. Beck. Just get in and get comfortable. That

should make your next reanimation much more pleasant. Then I will reposition the chamber and you can inanimate at your own leisure." Blake stepped into the capsule and tried to relax. "Mr. Beck, sir. May I ask you something personal?"

"Sure, but I won't promise that I'll answer."

"Well, it's just . . . Is it true that you were in the position that you arrived in because you died on the loo?"

"Yes," Blake said with a grin. Then he decided that a short explanation might be prudent, but decided not to go into too many details. "It's true. It seemed like the best solution at the time. It was either that or the bathtub."

"I'm sorry, sir, but I don't quite get how the toilet is a better choice than the tub?"

"That, Judith, I'll let you figure out on your own. You seem like a bright woman. I'm sure it'll come to you."

"Alright, Mr. Beck. Now have a nice trip."

"Thanks. And take care," Blake said before he closed his eyes and prepared to inanimate. Judith shut the capsule and started lowering it to a horizontal position. As she did, Blake shifted his position until he was comfortable. Then he let go. He let go of Judith, the truck, London and the rest of the world. He let his soul dissolve and let himself be pulled back into Shades.

CHAPTER 4

- MAKE IT RAIN -

I

At dawn, Blake woke up in his new home in the Entrance and ritualistically enjoyed his breakfast. Then he took a long walk along the waterfront. It seemed to him, thinking about it as he walked, that he was finally getting to grips with the concept of being dead. At first glance, it wasn't all that different. However, looking at the other souls in Shades, he could see Virgil's point. In the end it was all an act and nothing really mattered to them anymore. In due time they would all crack should they not be so fortunate as to have lived a life that would merit their departure into one of the afterlives. Blake dismissed this string of thoughts as his mind wandered off into the realm of right and wrong, and he decided that the question of right and wrong was probably not for him to argue.

When Blake returned home, he sat down in his upstairs lounge with a glass of whisky and took a well-earned look and listen through the collection of vinyl LPs provided for him by Virgil. Sending him a friendly thought, Blake sat there listening to the music, until – much to Blake's surprise – the doorbell rang. He got up and headed downstairs, wondering to himself, "Who the hell might this be?" As Blake reached the door, he looked through the peephole out of sheer habit, and he saw Marie standing on the landing in a long white dress that perfectly complemented her long black hair and the blue autumn sky. He froze like a stray deer caught in the headlights of an oncoming truck. Marie rang the doorbell again, freeing Blake from his stupor and the stream of "what, who, why, when, and how?" running through his head. With the choir of repeating questions echoing in his mind, Blake opened the door, still trying to figure out the right words with which to greet the love of his life whom he hadn't seen in years. It seemed Marie was in a similar predicament, albeit she at least had had a chance to prepare herself for the meeting.

"Hi, Blake. It's been a long time," Marie said, her smile slightly labored. Blake wished that he could find a reply both profound and cool in nature. He wanted to say something that would somehow sweep her off her feet and into his arms, but nothing of the sort came to mind.

"Marie. It sure is," he replied, feeling awkward that neither of them had commented immediately on the fact that they had both died since they last saw each other. "Nice to see you. Come on in."

"Thank you," she said, still tied to her French accent.

"I have to say, I didn't expect to have you calling around – and I'm sorry you're dead, but it's *really* nice to see you!" he said and really meant it. It was nice to see her. It made him feel less alone, and despite all that had happened between them, the dream of them together hadn't died with him.

"It's nice to see you too, Blake." She tried her best to sound convincing, and fortunately for Marie, their mutual unspoken dream that this could indeed be a happy reunion made it credible. Blake led the way upstairs to the lounge and Marie followed behind him in silence. The record player had just finished the last song, and as they entered the room, the pickup raised itself from the vinyl groove and moved into its rest, breaking the silence between them with a mechanical click.

"Have a seat," Blake said as he walked over to his chair. Marie sat down in the armchair opposite Blake's, her eyes restlessly wandering around the room. "You want a drink, honey?" Blake asked.

"No, thank you," she replied. As Blake sat down, he reached for his glass and took a sip before relaxing into the leather armchair.

"So," he thought for a split second about what to say, "I'm sorry that I let us slip. Hell, I didn't even know you were dead, but then again, it's not like anyone knew to tell me."

"Blake. It wasn't all your fault. It was just too hard, too far and too long," she said with half a smile, allowing him to give a slight nod of agreement.

"You look great."

"Blake . . . Don't," she said, returning her gaze to the floor and trying to keep a hold of herself. "I'm not here to find you,

I'm here to let you go," she said, the words cutting deeper into Blake than any blade ever could. To Blake, it was as if their breakup in life had been but an intermission, as he knew full well that an eternity waited for them: an eternity in which he had felt sure that they would somehow find each other again. He looked at Marie and was taken aback by the veil of sadness that shrouded her.

"But . . ."

"Blake, dear. Please do not make this any harder than it already is. We did not manage to make a life together, and I have come to tell you that we will not make a death together either. I need you to know this."

"Marie . . ." He tried to be more assertive, but his words were immediately dismissed by her eyes, the shake of her head and her words.

"I need you to know that though we will both have an eternity in Shades, and – the gods forbid – we might even be forced to work together, I cannot go back. I need you to understand this." She looked into his eyes, begging and searching for a glimpse of understanding. However, she found nothing of the sort. Instead she saw confusion, anger and the kind of desperation found only in the eyes of animals that are trapped and facing a superior enemy.

"No! Now you goddamn well listen to me, Marie!" Blake yelled as he jumped up out of his chair. "You can't be serious. We let things fade because our times together were too rare and too far between, but look at us now. We are here now, together and forced to spend an eternity here. How the hell can these notions of too rare and far be relevant? We literally have an eternity to spend and I refuse to just sit down and let you pretend that you don't love me anymore. I know you do! And I never stopped loving you. You're right that in life we were both too busy and it was too painful to be parted over and over again, but now time is no longer an issue. We can make this work!"

"But Blake . . ."

"Dammit, Marie. Don't 'but Blake' this. There is only one reason why we shouldn't try to make this work now that we are both here. Hell, I have been walking around wondering when I would see you again since my death. I've been hoping that you would get to live a good long life before coming here, but I've been cursing each day of this eternity I'd have to spend without you." He paused. "Now, if you don't love me . . ."

"I don't," she said, completely disarming him and leaving him to suffer in the silence that followed. Blake stopped and slumped despondently into the chair as if he needed something to hold him together and in place. Out of pure reflex, he took up the glass and emptied it as if the whisky would help. "Blake. I don't love you anymore, and I really hope you can find someone for you here in death." Blake didn't respond. There was no need to. Marie got up from her chair, walked over to Blake and bent down to give him a light kiss on his forehead. A kiss that he returned with a slight shake of his head and crease of his brows, looking like a child kissed by a parent after a scolding. As Marie walked out the door, she looked to Blake who sat quietly, staring at the bottom of his glass. "Take care of yourself, Blake," she said, getting the last word before walking down the stairs and out of the house. In Blake's mind, her last words were clouded and distant – as if spoken from a different world. He felt dislodged from his being as he fought to hold onto the reins of his fate. He barely registered that Marie had walked down the stairs and out the front door. He sat there for hours with the low static groan of his speakers as his only companion, wishing for something to put out the pain burning inside. He silently prayed that someone or something would just make it rain. As nighttime approached, he saw the sky darken and heard the winds pick up outside. As the rolling thunder broke the silence, he let the melancholy flood him, closing his eyes and listening to the wind's dark moan. Then it began to rain.

II

"This is turning into the worst night of my death," Harlan McCoy thought to himself as he perched on the back of his dapple grey stallion galloping down the cobbled road towards Dæth's mansion. The auction had seemingly been orchestrated to perfection, and last night he had toasted with Dæth to their success and to the performance of their newest Hunter, Blake Beck. However, by now it had become clear to McCoy that there was no reason to celebrate. A few hours earlier he had gotten word from Liam O'Hara, the Director of Operations of the London CAC, that something was amiss and O'Hara had requested the presence of McCoy himself in London – something which was very rarely done. McCoy had obliged and traveled to London in the falling darkness to meet with Liam O'Hara: a feisty, redheaded Irishman who had no renown for softening blows or sugar-coating the truth.

"It's a right cock-up, sir!" O'Hara said as McCoy entered his office at the CAC London headquarters. "We received the Flamel manuscript late last evening and I immediately sent it down to the team working on deciphering the Voynich manuscript before I went home," O'Hara continued, leaving no time for formalities.

"Yes?"

"Well, when I got in this morning, I was called down to the lab where I was told that the Flamel manuscript provided no legible cipher, and that there was a distinct discrepancy between the photos taken of the manuscript by our agents in Bath and the manuscript bought at the auction." McCoy cringed his eyebrows as if to counter the slight hint of panic in O'Hara's voice. "Look at this!" O'Hara reverted his attention to his laptop, clicking the mouse pad to play a short film clip. It was a piece of footage from the surveillance camera in Christie's vault 3b showing a young, conservatively dressed woman with a dark A-line bob standing next to the Flamel manuscript. As the woman picked up the manuscript, clandestinely replacing it with another, McCoy felt a cold shiver run down his soul. "And there's more!" O'Hara fast-forwarded to show McCoy the footage of the young woman returning about an hour later and making the second switch. "They switched the manuscripts!"

"I can damn well see that, you idiot!" McCoy bellowed, his feelings getting the better of him.

"With all due respect, sir!" O'Hara retorted, emphasizing the word sir before releasing a torrent of disrespect. "Who the fuck are you calling an idiot? I'm not the one tasked with planning or overseeing the security of the Christie's vaults. I did my job, and to be honest, I think that I went rather beyond the call of duty acquiring these tapes and serving you this explanation in less than 24 hours!" Then he added another "sir" just to make sure that he disrespected McCoy respectfully. Knowing that O'Hara was right, McCoy let it slide. He didn't offer him an apology, but it was clear to both what the short silence that lingered between them meant. When his temper subsided, O'Hara broke the silence. "The girl that served us with our own fake was the buyer at the auction, but how and when they made the switch at Christie's King Street, I have no idea."

"It doesn't really matter now, does it?" McCoy asked rhetorically. "What matters is the fact that Mr. Ferre has the real Flamel manuscript and now Khaleel will be hard at work deciphering the Voynich manuscript, just as we are."

"Yes, sir," O'Hara replied. McCoy thought about the situation for a moment, realizing that there was nothing more for him to do there.

"Keep up the good work, O'Hara, and let me know as soon as the Voynich manuscript is fully deciphered."

"I will, sir!" McCoy left O'Hara's office and hurried back to the animation lab in order to inanimate and return to Shades.

McCoy rode in a furious gallop through the Empires of Industry in order to serve Dæth with the unpleasant news that the auction con had been a failure and that they themselves had been the ones conned. The white and grey coat of his horse glistened with beads of sweat as McCoy spurred it on up the long drive leading to the mansion. Summoned by the sound of the hooves beating the cobblestones, Elijah took his place at the bottom of the stairs in front of the mansion in time for McCoy's arrival. McCoy pulled back the reins, making the horse rear and shake its head wildly as it halted by the stairs. McCoy jumped off and tossed the reins to Elijah, leaving the horse panting.

"Sir," was all Elijah said, as always keeping up the formal facade. McCoy hurried up the stairs and into the hall. As he entered, Dæth walked out onto the upstairs landing and started down the stairs. He wore a pair of long, loose black pants beneath an embroidered scarlet robe finished with a black silk lapel. He held a black and white Meerschaum pipe in his right hand and his left hand trailed along the banister.

"I was lying in bed much savoring the presence of my wife when I heard the sound of hooves on cobbles and decided to venture out of bed in the hope that you, my friend, were bringing me joyous news that you could not keep 'till morning." McCoy looked up at Dæth and made an effort to compose himself to ready for the coming storm. "But, alas, reason has already dissuaded me that this could be the reason for your untimely arrival, for ill news does indeed travel faster." Dæth reached McCoy and put his arm around his neck in what appeared to be a friendly gesture. McCoy found himself at a loss of words. "Harlan, my friend. Let us step into the drawing room and discuss the matters you seem so eager to get off your chest." Together they walked the short way down the hall and entered the drawing room. Harlan removed his hat, looking around for a place to put it down before deciding to keep it in hand. "Now, pray tell," Dæth said as he poured hot water from a samovar onto a helping of green tea leaves that he had already deposited into a porcelain cup.

"Well, it's concerning the Flamel manuscript," McCoy started.

"Yes?" Dæth asked and sat down on the small lounge sofa,

placing his cup of tea on the table in front of him. As Harlan searched for the right words, Dæth lit his pipe, puffing a few clouds of smoke to make sure the tobacco had caught fire. The scene reminded Harlan of a time in his youth when he had been forced to confess his misbehavior to the schoolmaster. He decided not to beat about the bush.

"It seems the vampire buyer managed to pull a double con, sir." As McCoy spoke, Dæth took a long, composed draw of his pipe before slowly breathing the smoke into the air. However, Harlan noticed only the slight creasing around Dæth's eyes, his widened nostrils and the proverbial thunderstorm building in his eyes.

"What?" Dæth asked, raising his head as if to enable him to look down on McCoy.

"I am sorry, sir. It seems the vampire buyer somehow found access to our manuscript fake and the original manuscript in Christie's vault, and managed to switch the two prior to the auction."

"Are you telling me . . .?" Harlan could see the anger welling up inside Dæth, and he felt sure that it would come down on him like the wrath of God.

"Yes. We bought our own fake and Mr. Ferre managed to acquire the real Flamel manuscript." Dæth let him fry in the silence, breaking it only by taking another deep draw of the pipe. The crackling and fiery smolders of the tobacco were more threatening to Harlan than any hellish flame could ever be.

"That is very unfortunate," Dæth said as he blew out the smoke.

"Yes, sir," said Harlan, reverting his gaze to the floor. He knew that there was no way this would be forgotten, and at some point this mistake would come back to haunt him. He would walk through death, perhaps for centuries, wondering how and when, and knowing that Dæth's hold on him was tighter than ever before.

"Have you informed Mr. Beck?"

"No, sir. Not yet."

"Don't. For now, let us get our bearings and figure out our next move before disclosing this any further. I hope that at least the deciphering of the Voynich manuscript is on schedule?"

"It is, sir."

"Good. Then leave me to my tea and pipe and return when the deciphering is completed."

"I will, sir! And thank you for your time." Harlan turned on his heels and walked to the door. As he took the handle, he heard Dæth's voice and turned around to acknowledge his master.

"Harlan, when you return, bring me good news. You do know that I do not tolerate failure."

The Earl decided to take a leisurely evening stroll, his instincts guiding him to the medieval Arabian quarter of Aquraa. He donned his finest walking suit and – cane in hand – the Earl walked through the Baroque quarter with a confident stride. He soon found himself at the gates of the Arabian quarter, which lay enclosed within its own city walls like the Arabian medinas of old. From there, it was no coincidence that he made his way past the home of Bahij Khaleel, halting by the establishment across the narrow street and taking a seat at a vacant table. The Earl felt certain that he would not have to wait for long before Bahij would pass by, as he knew that Bahij had been summoned to the castle. Sure enough, Bahij soon came walking out of the gateway that led to the courtyard of his mansion across the street. While it was unlikely that Bahij would fail to notice him, the Earl took it upon himself to be sure he was noticed. Still seated, he removed his feathered hat and gave Bahij half a bow, clearly not bothering to stand up.

"Lord Khaleel! What an unexpected pleasure to find you here. Had I known that you were, in fact, not far gone but mere yards away, I should have offered you to join me on this fine evening!" the Earl called out. As Bahij eyed the Earl and steered towards his table, a stern look crept across his face and he allowed himself the slight relief of an unspoken sigh.

"Your lordship," Bahij greeted the Earl, not required by the nature of his turban to remove it in greeting. "And what, may I ask, brings your lordship to humble yourself to visit the land and time of those who have not learned the gracious and elevated ways of your European self?" Bahij inquired.

"I sought to merry myself with the nature and features of your time, aiming to delve into the vices promoted by this particular part of the city, whilst hoping that I may also become ever more knowledgeable on that which puzzles me. I, myself, do not believe that I have come from a time of perfection, as you seem to have inferred, but rather from an imperfect pearl in need of yet more cultivation," the Earl replied with a sly smile.

"While I do indeed believe you to be so full of your own merit that you would be able to fill a dozen more souls before any of them would reach a tolerable amount of self-regard, I do gladly grant you the fact that your origin was greatly in need of cultivation," Bahij retorted.

"As do I, my dear bête noire! On that we shan't disagree. Instead let us each pause in our endeavors and take a short while to debate the fate of our mutual interest, the dear Mistress Ammon," the Earl said, looking Bahij in the eye and seeing hatred, desperation and a sliver of fear creeping into Bahij's mind. It was like looking into the eyes of a rival lion whose pride was being threatened on its own territory, and the Earl knew then that Bahij had finally realized that they were equals.

"What of her?" Bahij asked, staying both his hand and temper.

"I assume that you, the great pride of our race and master of our Lord's intelligence, are already aware that the delightful Mistress Ammon and I have enjoyed each other's company on several occasions since the dance," the Earl started, his tone of voice revealing that he enjoyed twisting the blade. "I should be greatly disappointed should I have misread your affection for Mistress Ammon and should you not have found it prudent to keep an eye on the preservation of our lady's virtues – something you seem eager to preserve. Now, whilst I rest assured in this, I am also certain that you have no witness to the fact that I should have behaved as anything but a gentleman," the Earl said.

"You would not be surprised, and I gather not even offended, when I tell you that I think you no more capable of being a gentleman than I think a monkey able to govern. You may be able to play the part, but that is a far cry away from actually being one," Bahij replied, trying his best to keep a formal tone and distance between them.

"Indeed, but then again, is it not all a play that we carry out? Each playing our part in the great play that is our life and death? While I may, in fact, not be a gentleman, you are, in fact, not one yourself by the merits and virtues you find it requires. I can see in your eyes that every part of your being seeks to burst out in the most ungentlemanly ways and wishes to rid yourself of my role in our great, intertwined narrative. While I acknowledge the nature of my being, you, on the other hand, deny your nature and seek to use reason to subdue it. Our nature is the same; we each strive to be something we

151

are not. The difference between us lies not in our nature, but in our motives. We are both actors who have merely chosen different roles to play." He looked at Bahij and saw the tiny thread of doubt that the Earl so enjoyed weaving. "Now while any ungentlemanly behavior on my part would have been carried on outside the realm of prying eyes, there is no reason to debate my merits as a gentleman."

"No, but the motives you so cleverly pointed out do indeed merit much debate. Fortunately, while I may not trust your motives nor your ways, I find myself confident that Mistress Ammon is indeed capable of seeing through your act herself."

"On that account, dear friend, I think you should be greatly disappointed," the Earl said with a grin. A slight tremor in Bahij's hand and the tightening of his jaw revealed to the Earl that he was on the verge of pushing Bahij beyond the realm of his so highly valued self control. He knew that with one more sentence, perhaps just the right word, he could make Bahij snap. Yet he refrained from doing so. The Earl now knew that it could be done and that he possessed the means to make it happen. That was enough. Now it was a matter of accessing the right time and place – the right scene, so to speak – and he knew that this was not it. "Now while I know this disappointment is born from a great affection for Mistress Ammon, I have come here today to do that which you think I would not. I wish to declare my intentions, as a gentleman, so that we may both court Mistress Ammon in the open and leave our fate in the matter to her judgment – something which we both seem to believe is immaculate," the Earl said, knowing that there would be nothing Bahij could do but take up the challenge.

"If that is indeed your intention, we shall certainly be competing over our lady's favor. Now I shall bid you farewell." With a slight bow, Bahij turned on his heels and headed down the narrow streets, leaving the Earl behind to savor his own personal victory.

IV

Astrid sat on her secondhand sofa, which she referred to as vintage, and looked out over her room at the May 4th dormitory in Aarhus. The dormitory had been built as a monument to the Danish resistance, and Astrid had gotten her room because her Danish grandfather had fought in the resistance against the German occupation during World War II. Her coffee table was covered in photos of Notke's altar, most of which she had taken herself on her visits to the cathedral. She picked up a close-up of the predella painting depicting the Gregor's Mass. As she did, the TV commercial break that was running as an ideal background distraction ended, and Paradise Hotel came on. Astrid thought it was a stupid show that only added to the dumbing down of the nation and the world in general. Yet, despite taking a rational dislike to the program, she had decided that she was impervious to its influence and she was just watching it with half an eye in order to know what she was up against. "Know your enemy," she thought as she struggled to keep her focus on the medieval artwork rather than on the adventures of scantily clad teens with a formidable ability to seem even more stupid than an average doorknob. She looked at the photo she had taken of the Gregor's Mass painting that had particularly caught her attention when she began writing her thesis. The painting showed Jesus Christ appearing upon the altar during a mass conducted by Pope Gregory I to silence those who doubted the doctrine of transubstantiation – the changing of bread and wine into the body and blood of Christ. In the background of the painting, a doorway revealed a terrace and garden with the sky gilded rather than painted blue. In the empty garden sat a lone peacock, which Astrid knew was used in medieval artwork to represent the resurrection and eternal life. Although a small detail, Astrid couldn't help feeling that this was somehow significant, she just couldn't figure out how. Sadly, as no immediate conclusion presented itself, the medieval art lost its grip on Astrid's attention and her focus regressed towards the television.

Bahij was raging as he reached the castle after his run-in with the Earl. He simply could not bring himself to believe that Teresa would show such poor judgment of character that she could fall for a man like the Earl, let alone favor him over Bahij. To him, the Earl seemed an untrained whelp that had been neither broken-in nor house-trained and thus ran around at its own leisure pissing on everything with scant regard for the world around him. Except, of course, that while a young dog could be excused, the Earl could not. As Bahij walked down the corridor and into the grand hall where he had danced with Teresa just a few nights earlier, he felt his right hand tighten as if grasping the hilt of his sword. Oh, how he would enjoy putting the Earl down like the cur he was, but sadly, Bahij knew that it could not be done. Such an act could only be sanctioned by *Him*, and unrequited love and ungentlemanly behavior was, unfortunately, not enough to merit such sanction. Bahij walked across the hall that now lay silent, just a pale shadow of what it had been on the night of the feast. There were no guests and no decorations, and there was no abundance of food and drink. There was no music and no Teresa. Instead, the majestic room was dominated by the massive long table with the chair belonging to *Him* at the head. The décor was comprised of only a few select marble statues and tapestries, leaving the stained glass windows room to tell their stories of the origin of the undead. As Bahij started down the corridors towards the private chambers belonging to *Him*, he ran into Teresa who immediately confirmed his suspicions by keeping a much more formal distance than before. Feeling that it would be too awkward for the two of them to walk past each other without a word of greeting, Teresa stopped.

"Master Khaleel," she said, holding out the skirts of her embroidered black silk dress as she curtsied. She kept her gaze on the floor, leaving it for him to decide whether or not he would stop – hoping that he would decide against it. Bahij found that his manners made the decision for him. He stopped and engaged in a conversation from which they both knew that nothing good would come.

"Mistress Ammon," Bahij replied as he gave a deep bow, disappointed that she had addressed him as "Master Khaleel." However, as she had taken a formal tone, he felt compelled to do the same, which added to the growing tension between them.

"So nice to see you," she said with a smile that paled in comparison to the smiles Bahij had received from her just days before.

"Just as is it to lay eyes on you, and for my humble soul to fill with the song of your voice, my lady." Immediately, Bahij knew that he had overdone it. That which a week before would have seemed endearing and courteous now seemed false and clingy. An unforgiving change, which had taken Bahij – like so many before him – completely by surprise.

"Are you here to see our lord and master?"

"Yes, that is indeed my errand . . ." Before Bahij could finish his sentence, Teresa interrupted him, hoping to avoid the unavoidable.

"I shall announce your arrival and leave you to yours, and then I'll be on with that which is mine to do this day." She gave a bow.

"Teresa, I am sorry to keep you from your business, and I feel even worse on account of the subject of which I need to speak to you. I pray that you have but a moment." She felt cold and uneasy, but there was nothing for her to do but look to the floor as she replied.

"Of course."

"In truth, I have taken a great liking to you and I was confident that these feelings were mutual. That is until very recently you have grown cold and distant. It is as if we have once again become strangers even though I know we are not, and I fear that there is but one cause for this. Now I pray that you will gainsay this and set both my mind and heart at ease."

"And what cause might that be?" Teresa asked, her eyes still avoiding his.

"I speak, of course, of the Earl who was so full of himself as to declare to me his intentions to court you, and who was also so indiscreet as to insinuate that the battle for both your love and virtue had already been fought and lost by me." It hurt him to say it. He hated the Earl, and Bahij already felt betrayed before she answered, despite the fact that she had made him no promises. She paused and swallowed before slowly raising her eyes to look at him.

"Bahij," she said, half imploring him to stop and half pausing to prepare them both for what followed. "I am sorry if I have led you astray and I will not deny that – for a time, at least – I harbored feelings for you myself, but . . ."

"But?"

"But, since last we saw each other, I have been much enlightened. Not to any deficiencies on your behalf, but to the virtue and inner beauty of another man onto whom I have found myself compelled to cast my love." As Teresa said it out loud, she even surprised herself.

"The Earl?" Bahij said with disdain.

"Yes. There is no point in denying this. It will soon become public knowledge, and you and I have no obligations towards each other. Besides, I would much rather that you hear this from me than from idle gossip." This was the last straw for Bahij, and in a rare lapse of self-control, he let go of himself.

"Unfortunately, rather than from you, I heard this from the mouth of the uncultivated swine you claim to love, and it was a piece of news he savored much to deliver. I merely refused to believe it out of respect for you, your judgment and your virtue – all things which I seem to have held in too high regard!" Bahij shouted as his feelings got the better of him, resulting in a hard slap across his cheek.

"You will not speak to me in this way ever again! Not if you wish to harbor any hope for us to part as friends or for you to be welcomed into this house as you have always been." As she yelled at him, she felt angry tears welling into her eyes. "It is neither my judgment nor my character that is flawed here, but rather your ability to rule your own jealous misconceptions. I know John much better than you do, and you seem content to grant him far less credit and purpose than you would grant the pigs that find joy and fulfillment in rolling in their own filth. And you make this judgment without even taking the effort to acquaint yourself with him. I have chosen to give him my heart because I know that he is a much better man than you would ever dream or know him to be because your unbecoming jealousy clouds your vision and poisons your mind. I am not the one at fault here. You are! And you will come to see this!" Having said what she needed to say, she edged past Bahij who tried to grab her wrist as she moved by.

"Teresa . . ."

"You will see this, and when you do, you will apologize. Then we can talk again!" She wrested herself from his grasp and hurried down the hall, never looking back and leaving Bahij to quietly curse his own behavior. How on earth could he let this happen? After all he had lived and died through, all it took was a woman to make him lose control. While he imagined the disappointment Teresa felt at his words, it was nothing compared to the disappointment he felt himself. And the fact that the Earl was proven right was unbearable. But what made it even worse was the fact that he had not lost the fight because his opponent was superior, but because Bahij had failed himself. His own pride and a moment's weakness had been his ruin. With his inner voice swearing at his misfortune, he headed down the corridors to seek *Him* in his private chambers.

Bahij knocked on the heavy oaken door.

"Come in," Mr. Ferre said, his voice seeming to come from everywhere. Bahij entered and walked through the antechamber into the study. *He* sat ready to greet Bahij from behind his desk on which drawings and reproductions of the Voynich and Flamel manuscripts had been laid out. As Bahij entered, *He* rose from his seat to extend his greetings. "Bahij, my friend."

"Sire," Bahij replied, feeling his master's eyes boring through him as he bowed down.

"Pray tell me what troubles you on this fine day when you have been invited into the heart of my house to enjoy the spoils of your own victory." Bahij wanted to tell *Him* that it was nothing to be troubled with, yet Bahij knew that Mr. Ferre would not have inquired if *He* did not harbor a genuine interest in knowing. Not out of concern for Bahij, but because *He* – more than anyone – knew that knowledge was power.

"While I do not believe that it is worth your concern, Sire, what ails me pertains to Mistress Ammon and the fondness I have for her," Bahij started.

"Yes."

"As you well know, I have sought to court her for some time, but now it seems that she has cast her love on the Earl. Now while this in itself tears at my heart, I unfortunately did not handle the news of this as well as I had wished."

"So the lovely Teresa has fallen for the Earl, rather than you," *He* noted.

"That is the essence of it. Yes."

"I must say that she is more naive than I had credited her," *He* said, reverting his gaze to the manuscripts.

"Whether she is naive or merely a poor judge of character, I will leave for time to judge," Bahij said, clearly doing no such thing.

"As a consolation, I will say this," *He* started. "Should you still harbor a fondness for her and wish for her to be yours, you will come to stand even stronger when she realizes the mistake she has made. When she returns battered and beaten, you will be given the chance to be her graceful savior, which will atone all else. To a woman, the only man who stands in higher favor than her lover is the man who saves her from herself." *He* looked up at Bahij, and when Bahij didn't reply, *He* moved the conversation along. "Come join me and enjoy the spoils of your victory. Come witness the unveiling of the manuscript you have so long sought to decipher." Bahij walked to the table, trying to rid his mind of Teresa. "Once again you have done your job impeccably, my dear Bahij, leading me to reach a point where I am afraid that when you disappoint me one day, that fact in itself, rather than the reason, shall serve as the biggest disappointment to me," *He* said, offering Bahij a rare glimpse of a smile.

"Thank you, Sire, but, as always, I shall do my utmost to

keep that from becoming a real concern."

"This I know. Which is why you are the one I trust in these matters." With only the gaze of his eyes, *He* guided Bahij's attention to the papers set out in front of them. "Now first of all, the Flamel manuscript has proven that which we previously only theorized; the Voynich manuscript does indeed hold the secrets to the summoning ritual that will allow me to bring back those lost to the will of that whelp and his predecessors."

"I am glad to hear that my studies have not proven fruitless."

"Quite the contrary," *He* said, turning over the pages of the manuscript. "However, one concern has arisen so far." Bahij let his eyes follow his master's finger trailing across the pages. "The Sol Niger alchemists who created the Voynich manuscript were led by their master Bernt Notke, a revered sculptor and artist working out of Lübeck in northern Germany around the year 1500." Bahij nodded. "Now it seems that Notke, at least to some extent, began to doubt the prudence of the Sol Niger's creation some time during its fashioning. This led him to omit invaluable information from the Voynich manuscript, such as the names of the saints to be called upon during the ritual." Mr. Ferre looked at Bahij to make sure that he had no questions, and as *He* expected, Bahij had none.

"Yes."

"Notke hid the information in some of his own works, one

of them being the magnificent altar he was commissioned to build for the diocese of Aarhus in the state of Denmark. Judging from the documents that have been reviewed so far, he positioned the three saints mentioned in the Voynich manuscript in central positions on the altar."

"I will look into this immediately," Bahij said.

"Please do, but send Vincenzo in case Mr. Beck turns down my offer and decides to show up. I know Vincenzo much desires his revenge and will do his work thoroughly."

"Your offer, Sire?" Bahij asked.

"Yes." *He* looked Bahij in the eyes. "While you leave Vincenzo to seek out the altar and its secrets, I want you to seek out Mr. Beck and bring him to me. I have a proposition for him."

After Marie left his house, Blake had fallen asleep in his chair, his soul mimicking the ways of his life. He had drunk the entire bottle of whisky, and while it didn't make him drunk, it still seemed to aid Blake in his escape from reality. He woke late the following day with Marie's words still filling his mind and cutting at his heart. He wandered the house in an aimless stupor for a couple of hours before returning to his leather armchair, for which he had already developed a strong affinity.

Driving a green Land Rover, Bahij Khaleel pulled up behind Blake's silver Aston Martin just outside the house. The dashboard clock showed that it was 3:00 in the afternoon, which meant that the others should already be there surrounding the house just in case Mr. Beck did not come along voluntarily. Bahij gave them a few more minutes, and then he got out of the car, walked up to the door and rang the bell.

For the second day in a row, Blake was surprised by the ring of the doorbell, although this time it didn't excite him in any way. He made his way downstairs with the tempo of a man who doesn't really care. Blake peered through the peephole and looked straight into the stern and powerful presence of Bahij Khaleel. Bahij was wearing a perfectly fitted grey suit and black shirt, and he carried an ebony sword cane as his weapon to ensure that he did not look too out of place in this part of Shades. While Blake didn't recognize the man and opened the door without much precaution, he did think to check that his katana was indeed within reach and found it resting in the umbrella stand by the door. As Blake opened the door, Bahij found that Blake didn't look like the mountain of a man he had come to expect, rather he found him to look somehow broken.

"Good day?" Blake said.

"Good afternoon, Mr. Beck. Allow me to present myself. I am Bahij Khaleel, a close associate of Mr. Ferre." As Bahij spoke, he presented himself with a deep bow. Blake remembered McCoy mentioning the infamous Bahij Khaleel at Dæth's mansion during the banquet that followed Blake's initiation as a Hunter. While Bahij bowed down, Blake preemptively reached out for his katana, drawing it from its sheath and striking out against Bahij in one fluent movement. Bahij had expected that this might be a natural reaction, and with a quick flick of his wrist, he raised the cane to block Blake's blow while still halfway through his bow. The two swords met and Blake's katana cut through the ebony cane until the blade hid within stopped it. Rather than rising from his bow, Bahij jumped forward in a somersault, getting to his feet and maneuvering behind Blake at the same time. Bahij moved with an unnatural speed and agility, the grace of his movements surpassing anything Blake had ever seen. By the time Blake had readied his sword and turned to face his enemy, Bahij had already unsheathed his sword and moved to strike. Although Bahij did not seem to put in much effort, the force of the blow shook Blake's balance and almost ripped his katana from his hands as he parried the attack. Blake sought to regain his footing and gain some distance from Bahij by sidestepping towards the downstairs living room. "Mr. Beck, there is really no need," Bahij said, seemingly lowering his guard for the shortest of moments. As if to parry his adversary's words, Blake moved to strike again, going for the kill with all he had. It was now or never. Like a bolt of lightning, the blade of Bahij's sword shot between them, effectively halting Blake's attack. At the same time, Bahij put his boot to Blake's abdomen, sending him flying back through the open living room door and crashing down on the glass coffee table, shattering it into a million pieces. As Blake moved to get up, he realized that it hurt. The pain wasn't like the physical pain of life; it was more like a very vivid recollection of a pain that had once existed. Bahij stood in the doorway looking as though he might as well have been carved out of stone - unmovable and indestructible. "As I was saying, Mr. Beck, there is really no need for this now. A time may come when we may continue this, but for now, Mr. Ferre has requested your presence."

"Oh, *Him*," Blake said as he got to his feet. He looked around assessing the situation, his eyes catching sight of several figures hiding in the shadows outside his windows.

"I would prefer for you to join me of your own free will rather than having to force you to come."

"You want me to come with you? Alone?" Blake asked.

"Yes."

"Why on earth should I?"

"You should come because Mr. Ferre has requested you to do so. Now while I deeply appreciate your apprehension, I will guarantee and swear upon what is left of my soul that no harm will come to you on this day should you not yourself seek to harm others. You may view this as an offer of parley." Bahij gave Blake time to think. Outside the windows, Blake could see the shapes moving in closer – there were at least ten of them now.

"It doesn't look like you're giving me much of a choice."

"Well, truth be told, there is always a choice. Some choices merely carry dire consequences," Bahij replied. Blake lowered his katana and rested its tip on the floor, making a small dent in the hardwood.

"So, where do we go from here?" Blake asked.

"To my car."

"And then?"

"Then we will go to see Mr. Ferre."

VII

Blake and Bahij drove for about an hour until they were well out of town and deep into the hilly woodlands that rose up outside the city. Blake eventually found himself driving down something that, on a good day, could best be described as a dirt trail, and the trail soon came to an end. Bahij stopped the Land Rover and turned towards Blake.

"This is where you get off," he said.

"And?" Blake asked.

"You follow that path up the hill. Mr. Ferre will be waiting for you up there." Blake didn't see fit to argue. So he got out of the car and started up the hillside, his trench coat waving a courteous goodbye to Bahij in the autumn breeze. He walked through the woods with its withering leaves of yellow and red, and headed ever further up the hillside. It took about an hour of Blake continuously struggling to figure out what was his path and what was the wilderness around him. As he conquered yet another peak, he looked down the path on the other side and saw a man standing at the foot of a tall cliff face where the path ended. From there, a cobblestone walkway ran through a beautiful stone portal carved in the cliff face and into the depths beneath the hills. Blake walked slowly down the path towards the man who greeted him as he approached. Wearing a pair of black leather pants and boots with a simple white linen shirt, the man seemed to be unarmed.

"Mr. Beck, welcome," *He* said as Blake came within earshot.

169

"Mr. Ferre?" Blake asked.

"Yes, indeed. And I must thank you for heeding my call and granting me the pleasure of your company on this fateful day," *He* said, extending his hand as Blake reached *Him*. Blake took Mr. Ferre's hand and shook it. It felt cold and distant despite the fact that it was right there in Blake's own hand. Blake couldn't bring himself to reply "you're welcome" and instead he said nothing. "Now I assume that your mind is plagued by the question of why I summoned you here and that this is the reason for the absentmindedness that seems to have impeded your manners," *He* said. Turning his back to Blake, Mr. Ferre started down the cobblestone walkway, making it clear to Blake that he was seen as no manner of threat at all. The fact that this annoyed Blake, paired with a lack of restraint and ability to care after Marie's visit, led Blake to speak.

"No, I just don't think you're welcome, so I didn't pretend just to be polite," he said, immediately realizing that this was perhaps the wrong thing to say to *Him*, the oldest and most powerful being in Shades. Even from the back of his neck, Blake could see Mr. Ferre's eyes flaming at the insolence. But there was no immediate retort – no utter destruction, disintegration or the like – and Blake began drawing breath once again.

"For now, Mr. Beck, I will let that pass as the mistake of one who does not know better. But know this: I shall never again suffer you to speak to me in that manner, no matter what becomes of you after this day." Blake decided that it was probably best to not reply, and he followed *Him* into the darkness. Mr. Ferre slowed his walk, allowing Blake – for just this once – to walk beside him. As darkness began to envelop them, *He* held out his hand and, without a word, conjured up a small flaming orb in his palm. The orb burned like a torch and illuminated the ancient tunnel around them.

"What is this place?" Blake heard himself say as the light fought back the encroaching darkness.

"That, Mr. Beck, I shall keep to myself just a little while longer. Instead let me begin with the other question that fills your mind: that of 'why?'" Blake looked at Mr. Ferre, feeling no need to question this. "I have brought you here to enlighten you to the true nature of your undertaking, and to extend my hand with an offer of redemption," *He* said. "I know that you, Mr. Beck, have sworn the oath of the Hunters and, as such, are the sworn enemy of me and my children. However, before I will treat you as such, I wish to be certain that you took the oath because of your convictions, not because you lacked the enlightenment of the better choice."

"I'm sure that I know what I'm doing," Blake replied.

"Even so," *He* said with a smile that Blake couldn't judge to be anything but overbearing. They walked down the narrow limestone corridor, and as they went further underground, strange etchings, signs and ciphers began to appear on the walls around them. "Let me ask you this. You have vowed to serve Dæth as a Hunter for eternity. Have you done this to save yourself from an otherwise unavoidable fate, or have you done so because your convictions command you to?"

"I'm a Hunter to rid the world of your children, as you call them, not to save myself. If I were to have saved myself, I should have started long ago – foremost by refraining from doing what I've done."

"Interesting answer, Mr. Beck. Now please humor me, and pray tell me why you would seek to rid the world of my offspring?"

"Isn't it obvious? Have you seen what your 'children' do? They prey on the souls of others, devouring indiscriminately the innocent and the guilty."

"So you seek to protect the innocent from harm, sacrificing yourself as you do so. You claim such nobility?" Blake thought about it for a moment.

"Yes."

"I beg to differ that my children and I feed randomly or indiscriminately. As you know, had I permitted, we could have decimated the number of souls in life to a much greater extent, and it very rarely happens that the truly innocent are fed upon. It is something that I, in fact, do not condone, save if it has a higher purpose."

"Even if that is the case, what's the point? You still admit to eating the souls of others."

"Indeed. But those souls have been doomed to spend an eternity here in Shades."

"So?"

"I will show you." They walked for a few more minutes until the light from the orb in Mr. Ferre's hand reached the

172

end of the corridor and revealed a room up ahead. "Well, Mr. Beck. Have you had time to wonder what happens to the souls that are condemned to stay in Shades?"

"Yes. They try to go on as if nothing has happened, but eventually they stop pretending and begin pondering their life instead."

"For eternity," *He* added.

"Yes, for eternity." As they walked out of the corridor and into the great darkness at the end of it, *He* raised his hand. As if wresting reality, *He* pulled the flaming orb ever larger and brighter. Bending to his will, the orb floated into the air above them, growing in size and luminosity. By the time the blazing orb had reached the size of a huge bonfire, the light finally reached the walls on the side. Blake looked around and found that the gargantuan hall ran much further into the hill and it lay as silent as the grave. As Blake's eyes got used to the lighting, he noticed countless alcoves cut into the walls from the floor to the ceiling hundreds of feet above them. In each alcove there was a statue of a human figure sitting or lying down – they reminded him of the dead of Pompeii.

"What is this place?" Blake asked, his voice echoing as it traveled into the darkness.

"This, Mr. Beck, is what you are so gallantly protecting. It is the reason you have sacrificed your own soul." Mr. Ferre walked slowly towards the wall urging Blake to follow. Then *He* knelt down, trailing his hand along the edge of one of the alcoves where a young woman was sitting. She sat cradling herself, holding her legs with her knees pulled towards her chest. She looked profoundly sad as she stared into the room without noticing the light that – for the first time in millennia – kept the darkness at bay. Looking at the woman and catching her sad eyes, Blake realized that these were not statues.

"This is . . ."

"Yes. This is where the souls of the dead eventually reside. At least, the souls of those not pious and pure enough to move on from Shades." As *He* spoke, Blake couldn't pry his eyes away from the woman. There was a profound pain and regret in her eyes unlike any he had ever seen or even managed to imagine. Blake felt the pain and regret tear at his own heart, flooding him with guilt. Eventually, he couldn't bear to look at the woman anymore and he averted his eyes to the floor in shame. "Now Mr. Beck, when you look into the eyes of this woman, can you, with true conviction, tell me that what we do is evil and that what you do is good?" As Mr. Ferre's words rang out, Blake could feel the doubt filling his soul.

"I'm not sure I follow," seemed the best defense available to Blake on such short notice.

"While I know that the stories you have been told were told by the very people who wish to portray themselves as righteous, I simply wish to show you this and ask you the question: as you stand here before those whom you seek to protect and see the pain in their eyes, do you truly believe those tales? When you serve Dæth, you seek to uphold the regime that forces these unwanted souls into an eternity of purification in the blazing flames of their own conscience. You seek to uphold eternal punishment for a lifetime of impurity. Is that truly what you believe in?"

"I . . ."

"I know. It is hard to realize that you are not the one on the cross, but rather the soldier hammering in the nails. Now that I have offered you a much needed perspective on your own enterprises, let me continue to enlighten you to ours." Blake felt sick. "While you seek to defend this regime, we have chosen to fight, rebel and disobey the tyranny. Yes, we feed upon the souls of others in order to continue the fight, but as we do, we offer peace to each and every one of the souls we consume. For each soul we eat, another soul finds peace. The pain on this woman's face is your doing, not mine." As Mr. Ferre spoke, Blake heard the words of Harlan McCoy repeat in his mind:

"Destruction offers them a peace which we do not see fit to grant them."

"As I kneel before this woman now, I know that I am her only hope of salvation as she has been cast away by all others and deemed unworthy," Mr. Ferre said, looking into her eyes. "Should I deny her peace, Mr. Beck?" *He* asked. As expected, Blake made no reply. *He* closed his eyes and leaned forward towards the woman. As *He* did, the back of his shirt began to darken in patches and the scars on his back began to smolder, threatening to break through the garment and set it ablaze. As *He* sank his teeth into the woman, his jaw seemed to dislocate and widen like that of a huge snake swallowing its prey

175

completely. Blake thought he heard a distant scream of pain as the woman dissipated and disappeared through Mr. Ferre's mouth, like a ghost sucked through a length of pipe. Blake did nothing, and he felt something die inside. He felt profoundly unsure and he felt betrayed. As Mr. Ferre rose to his feet, a tiny bit of charred cloth fell from his shirt, partially revealing the scars on his back. "Now Mr. Beck, I pray that you will consider what I have shown you in the light I bore, and that this will allow you to find your true calling. Ask yourself if your place in eternity is to punish or to relieve. Then know that I have extended my hand and invited you into my family with the promise of atonement for the sins you have perpetrated against my children out of ignorance. It is a gift that you are not likely to be offered again." Blake said nothing. He just stood staring at the empty alcove. "Now I will leave you to choose your own fate, Mr. Beck," said Mr. Ferre, turning and walking off into the darkness of the corridor towards the light of day, leaving Blake in silence and in doubt.

VIII

Elijah Butler couldn't make it to his usual place of greeting at the bottom of the stairs outside the mansion before Blake headed up the stairs – unexpected and unannounced. Trying to remedy the situation, Elijah intercepted Blake at the door.

"Mr. Beck," he said, trying fruitlessly to halt Blake's advance. Rather than stopping, Blake hurried past the butler and into the hall. "Mr. Beck, I really think . . ." Elijah said as he closed the door behind Blake.

"Where is he?" Blake snarled.

"I take it you mean the master?"

"Yes, where is Dæth?"

"I believe that my master is in the lounge, but I'm sorry, the master does not wish to be disturbed."

"Well, I don't give a fuck, Butler!" Blake yelled as he edged past Elijah and headed down the hall. The fact that Blake was so utterly neglecting the rules and forms of good conduct nearly cracked Elijah's facade.

"Blake . . . I . . . Mr. Beck . . . You really can't just . . ." Elijah tried. Blake stopped for a second and turned to Elijah, who was trying to keep up with Blake without resorting to running.

"Elijah, this has nothing to do with you. Stay out of it!" Blake said before continuing down towards the lounge.

"But sir . . . I . . . This is wholly unacceptable behavior! I must ask you to stop," Elijah said, clearly hearing the hollowness of his own words. Several more equally vain attempts were made to stop Blake before he reached the lounge doors and pushed them open in anger. As the doors swung open, one of them smashed into a table behind the door, knocking over a priceless porcelain vase crafted by the souls of an ancient Chinese dynasty. Dæth sat on the sofa in the middle of the lounge, bent over a large, leather-bound tome containing endless rows of figures and entries pertaining to his business accounts. As Blake burst into the room and the vase shattered on the floor, Dæth looked up from the book. "I'm sorry, sir," Elijah said, clearly at his wits' end.

"It will be quite alright, Elijah," Dæth said, removing a pair of spectacles and placing them on the table. Then he slammed the book closed and turned his attention to Blake. "Mr. Beck?" was all Dæth said, much to Blake's surprise. He had expected an unrivaled tirade, which would have made it much easier for him to return the favor with a broadside of curses and accusations. Instead there was a only a calm and collected inquiry that summed up the fact that Blake was there uninvited, that Blake shouldn't be there, and that Blake had better have a damn good excuse. This somewhat disarmed Blake, although it didn't discourage him.

"What the hell are you playing at?" Blake yelled as he advanced towards Dæth.

"Excuse me?" Dæth replied.

"This isn't what I signed up for! And you goddamn well know it." Blake reached the sitting area and Dæth rose from his seat.

"SIT DOWN, Mr. Beck!" Dæth bellowed. Blake felt like he had run into a brick wall. He stopped, collapsing into the chair, and when he regained his bearings, Blake was no longer in control. "Now you will keep your seat and speak only when spoken to. And I promise you that you will never again get away with speaking to me in that tone." Blake lowered his eyes. "I take it that you have been talking to Mr. Ferre, as I can see no other cause for such behavior as you have just exhibited."

"Yes, and I'm sad to say that he had many interesting things to tell me. Things I should have already known and not have learned from *Him*."

"Mr. Beck! There is nothing he could have told you that you should not have been able to figure out by yourself, considering that you have half a mind and are not scared of the truth. I take it that he took you to the catacombs?"

"Yes," Blake replied.

"Then let me ask you, what did you think happened here? You have chosen to serve the ruler of Shades, the caretaker of all departed souls. I am sure it is not news to you that only some of the souls move on from here, which leaves most to linger in Shades." Blake nodded in silence, but found enough strength and courage to look Dæth in the eyes as he did. "Now what did you think would become of these billions of souls that have died through the ages? They have been judged to linger here, sentenced to contemplate their wrongdoings forever. This is their sentence, meted out by the powers that be, and our job is to make sure that each one gets what he

179

deserves. You know this! And Mr. Ferre has simply shown you the natural execution of these judgments."

"But I didn't think . . ."

"NO! That is exactly the problem. You didn't think. Instead you come barging in here out of place and out of order. Now your job is to hunt those who seek to undermine the order of the worlds. Mr. Ferre and his 'children' seek to subvert and corrupt that which we are here to protect, and for that reason – and that alone – you will hunt down him and his abominable offspring."

"But Mr. Ferre is right that he brings peace, and McCoy even said it himself when he talked about the Grey: *'Destruction offers them a peace which we do not see fit to grant them.'*"

"But, nothing! They devour both souls who would go on from here and souls who deserve the punishment they are given." Of the two of them, Dæth was the only one who heard the light footsteps approaching the closed lounge doors. It was perfect, he thought. "Let me remind you that you have sworn to serve me and my purpose. Now, you will either serve and be thankful, or you will join those sad figures in the catacombs. I will see to that," Dæth said just before the lounge doors swung open. Blake turned his head to see who it was, grateful for the interruption. "Now, Mr. Beck. Allow me to introduce my wife, whom I believe you have already met," Dæth said with a satisfied smile. "This is Marie." Blake couldn't believe it at first, but as he caught Marie's eyes and saw the tears welling behind them, he knew it to be true.

"Mr. Beck," she said in a low voice, frail as glass and on the verge of breaking as she curtsied, slightly lifting the skirt of her white Victorian walking dress. Blake found himself unable to react.

"Where are your manners, Mr. Beck? I am sure that you are aware that it is only polite to get up and greet a lady as she enters the room."

"Of course," Blake stuttered in a low voice, rising from the chair a beaten man. Then he walked over to Marie. "Marie. Congratulations," he said as he gave her a kiss on each cheek.

"Blake. Don't," she whispered, fighting to keep from crying.

"I hope you will be very happy," Blake lied as he stepped back to his chair. He burned with anger and hurt, but at the same time, he felt the poor relief of knowing that nothing would ever be able to hurt him more than this. Then he sat down and looked away.

"I can see this is a bad time," Marie said, trying to pull herself together. "I will leave the two of you to your business and await you on the terrace, my dear." She still had the French accent that Blake had found so irresistible in life, which cut at his heart, even now.

"Thank you, my darling. I shall be but a moment. Mr. Beck and I were just finishing. Is that not right, Mr. Beck?"

"Yes," Blake muttered.

"Mr. Beck," Marie said as she curtsied before turning to walk away.

"Marie," Blake replied, still looking away. As Marie walked out of the room, they sat without speaking, listening to the sound of her heels rhythmically tapping the hardwood floor. When she closed the doors, Dæth broke the silence.

"Now, as I was saying, Mr. Beck. You will do the job you were chosen for without lament. Otherwise, I will not hesitate to take back the gifts bestowed upon you and send you away to face an eternity of remorse for the imperfect and impure life we both know you have led. And should you – against your better judgment – for but a second contemplate betraying me and joining Mr. Ferre, you should know this. The retribution which you would deserve would instead be visited tenfold upon her, and I would make sure that you would know it and never find peace." He let his words linger for Blake to digest. "Are we clear about this, Mr. Beck?"

"Yes."

"Good. Now you will have to excuse me, for I have to attend to my wife." Blake got up without a word and walked out of the room, angry and hurt. Halfway down the hall he found Harlan McCoy waiting for him.

"Blake?" Harlan asked, probing the wounds and trying to figure out if Blake was in a condition to talk.

"What!?"

"I have to say, this was not your smartest move so far," Harlan said, following Blake down the hallway.

"What the fuck would you have me do? Have you ever met Mr. Ferre? And how come you didn't at least warn me about

Marie? Is this amusing to you, as well? Because it damn well seemed to be to him."

"No. It's not, but you have to remember who we work for. I would gladly have told you about Marie if I could, but it would have meant my neck if I did. He didn't become death by trusting others, and he always makes sure that he is holding the reins. He has something on all of us. That's just they way it is – he's a business man."

"He's an asshole."

"Well, I understand you aren't fond of him right now, but he is your strongest ally and the only thing that stands between atonement and punishment, but nothing comes free. You know that."

"Yes, but I had hoped for a little respect."

"Respect you can and have to earn, and perhaps you may even come to merit his friendship over the years, but you need to know that it is not his job to be nice. It is to be death." McCoy cleared his throat. "Now I am sorry that I was not at liberty to warn you about Marie, but it would have made no difference, it would just have given you more time to grieve."

"And perhaps would have allowed me to not be run over in there."

"Perhaps, but my bid would be that he would simply have taken a different approach." There was a silence as they walked down to the hall, passing Elijah on their way out. "So, you were approached by Mr. Ferre, and I gather that you saw the catacombs."

"I did. And I didn't like it."

"I know, but you have to accept that this is our job. Those souls in there have earned their punishment in some way, and it is not our – nor Mr. Ferre's – place to offer atonement to them."

"But he is right that he offers peace to those souls, and he is right that the vampires feed less often on the living than they could if they wanted to."

"Blake, listen to me!" Harlan said. "You cannot let him get to you. His words are just as twisted as the words of anyone else, and he seeks only to corrupt you and further his own cause. For instance, no – you're right – they could feed much more on the living souls than they do. But it is not out of morality or good nature. It is simply because no farmer will eat his crops before the seeds for next year's crops have been gathered. Each fresh soul they eat in life is a whole family line that will never come to be, and like the farmer that might pick from the young sprouts occasionally, he will never reap his harvest prematurely. There is nothing good there, trust me! Mr. Ferre and his children consume the souls of others so that their own souls will not deteriorate – and that is all. Don't let him have you believe otherwise." Blake nodded, wanting to believe Harlan's words. "Now Blake, I'm sorry to bear even more ill news, and I will refrain from placing blame and responsibility because I understand what you have gone through these last few days. Since last we spoke, we have found that the vampire buyer at the Christie's auction that you handled managed to switch the two manuscripts prior to the auction, leading us to buy our own fake and allowing the vampire to buy the real Flamel manuscript," McCoy said. However petty it might be, Blake couldn't help but rejoice in the fact that Mr. Ferre had gotten the better of Dæth this time around.

"So they also have all the information then?" Blake asked.

"Yes, and we would imagine that they, like us, are well underway with the deciphering of the Voynich manuscript. We have managed to read parts of the manuscript and have found that it does indeed contain the instructions to the ritual of summoning a chosen soul between the worlds. The alchemists saw this as the source of eternal life. However, it seems that the leading Sol Niger alchemist, Bernt Notke, hid key information about the ritual in some of his other works to make sure that gaining full access to the ritual required more than just reading the Voynich manuscript." Harlan paused for a second as he took his tobacco pouch from his belt and started rolling up a cigarette. "While we have not yet fully deciphered the manuscript, we have found that the ritual calls upon the power of three figures currently believed to be Christian saints. Exactly which figures has been intentionally omitted from the Voynich manuscript, but we have found indications that Notke hid the information in the altar he fashioned in the late 15th century for the cathedral in the Danish city of Aarhus."

"So I'm going to find that altar and name the figures for you?"

"While we decipher the rest of the manuscript, yes. Seeing

as we must expect Mr. Ferre to be planning a similar move, we've found it prudent to send one of the Hunters. So I'm asking you, if you're up to it."

"Sure," Blake replied.

"Then you will travel there tomorrow evening, and I have been told that there is a concert in the cathedral. This should give you a good reason to enter the cathedral at night, and once the concert is over, I'm sure you will find a way to stay behind." Blake replied with a nod as Harlan opened the heavy wooden front doors. As McCoy stepped out into the windy autumn night, he tipped his hat and left Blake to his own private tortures.

CHAPTER 5

- VICARIOUS -

I

Astrid had agreed to meet her friends at Sofie's Parents, a small tea salon in Frederiksgade. It was the perfect venue for new mothers in need of a baby-friendly café and a cup of coffee. Seeing as one of her friends had recently fostered a new generation, they had agreed to meet there rather than in the café they had frequented for the last five years. It was an agreement Astrid had been rather reluctant to enter into. She hated the fact that things had to change just because other people incubated offspring. However, her subconscious self tried to tell her that she was being a hypocrite, that she would have encouraged the exact same change if she had become a new mother, and that she was just jealous deep down inside. Consciously, however, Astrid's mind wandered to a wholly different place as she sat down in the faux antique Rococo chair amidst babies, coffee and cake. She thought about the strange fact that so many places in Aarhus were named after someone's immediate family. There was Sofie's Parents, but also Pappa Eskild, a bar and music scene featuring upcoming bands. There was also the bodega Kurt's Mom, and the small drinking establishment Line's Grandma. It was as if the whole town was owned and run by some kind of secret underground menopausal mafia. She imagined them meeting in a dark, rundown warehouse on the docks – wrinkled old ladies, each older than the other – sitting at a long table with Pappa Eskild at the head of the table. She giggled to herself, but she was abruptly torn from her daydream by a young child at the table behind her who began screaming because there was a shortage of chocolate milk.

"I'm just so glad that we could all make it!" said Tina who sat opposite Astrid, breastfeeding her young daughter.

"Yep," Astrid said before taking a sip from her granny-style teacup.

"So, Astrid. Any luck?" Louise asked with a smirk, having recently ceased being single herself.

"Sorry?" Astrid said, still wondering which sinister ploys the menopause mafia was plotting in order to take over the town – maybe even the world – through a series of villainous bodega and café franchises.

"Have you gotten any lately? I mean . . . it would be about time, wouldn't it?" Astrid quickly and only semi-voluntarily swallowed her tea and looked around apologetically to see if anyone else had heard her indiscreet friend bellowing out information about her sex life or lack thereof, as fate would have it.

"Uuuhmm . . . I . . ." Astrid said, rather concerned by the fact that she had gone so long that her status as single would now merit first priority at their biweekly reunion.

"Not that I should be one to judge because I know what it is like to be single, but my boyfriend and I . . ." As Louise started her monologue, Astrid gave a mental sigh of relief, glad that she was off the hook. While Tina was preoccupied with her offspring and Louise was busy talking, Astrid let her mind wander again. She thought about how nice it would be to have a boyfriend, if not for anything else than to get her friends off her back. She decided that she would do something about it, perhaps not today but no later than Saturday night, and with that problem solved, she moved on to the matter of her master's thesis. She was heading down to the cathedral later because she had promised the church servant that she would help out at that evening's classical organ concert by showing people to their seats, helping out the organist, doing odd jobs and locking up after the concert. She figured if she headed down there directly from the café, she would be able to get in a few hours of undisturbed research time by the altar. By the time Astrid had decided on her plans, Louise had just about run out of air, thus allowing the others to enter the hitherto somewhat one-sided conversation. Although Astrid didn't really manage to or feel like influencing the course of the conversation, she sat there for an hour and a half drinking her tea, laughing, becoming embarrassed, and getting angry at and making up with Louise before it was time for her to head down to the cathedral. She made no big production of saying goodbye to her friends because she knew she would meet with them again soon, so she let a "Bye, guys! I'll see you later!" suffice. As she walked out of the café, she accompanied her

189

goodbye with a short wave. Then she headed down the street, intent on enjoying the five-minute stroll to the cathedral. She walked through the streets of Aarhus, doing her best to not be bothered by the host of people who were walking far too slow and hindering Astrid's usual pace. To her great annoyance, Astrid got stuck behind a slow-moving group of teenage girls who were walking side-by-side in order to uphold the naïve illusion that their friendship was, in fact, not hierarchical. However, not even this managed to ruin her mood. Once she reached Small Square, she decided to make a quick stop at the kiosk to quench her thirst and grab a sausage roll. Inside the kiosk, she took her place in the long line of people waiting to make their purchase from the rather inefficient young man behind the counter. While this annoyed Astrid to some degree, she secretly enjoyed the fact that once she had picked up her iced tea from the cooler, she had time to have a quick look through the tabloids while standing in line. Apparently, an elderly gentleman in Zealand had been shot by his own son, and a fisherman had fallen overboard and was presumed drowned. Officially, she despised the tabloids and their sordid stories and complete lack of respect for privacy, but for some reason, she had a hard time ignoring them like she had promised herself she would. Instead, she justified flipping through them and giving them a quick read by the fact that she never ever bought any of them, but merely read them while queuing, waiting in the doctor's lobby, or perhaps when someone had left a copy behind on the train. After all, she didn't encourage the tabloid agencies by increasing their sales.

"Are you buying that?" the young man asked Astrid from behind the counter, quite harshly bringing her back to reality from the dramatic family tragedy on Zealand.

"Sorry? No, I don't think so," she said and closed the paper before placing it back in the stand. The young man sighed, indicating both that he didn't care and that he hated his job, and then he lifted an eyebrow to inquire what she was having if it wasn't the paper. "I'll just take this," Astrid said, placing the peach-flavored iced tea on the counter. "And three sausage rolls," she added a few seconds later, trying to convey that this was a spur-of-the-moment decision rather than the plan of a young woman who had no better alternative than to snack her way through dinner at her local kiosk.

"Ketchup?" he asked, still not caring.

"Yes, please," Astrid replied as she ran her credit card through the terminal. Having gotten her rolls and iced tea, Astrid headed out of the kiosk and walked up Large Square towards the cathedral, making sure not to choke on her food from the inevitable giggling. As she strolled across the square, the bells chimed and the tower clock told her that it was now 6 p.m., leaving two and a half hours until the start of the concert. This was about the same time that Blake opened his eyes.

Blake was quickly getting used to the more delicate aspects of reanimation, and he checked that he had full control over his body as the inanimation capsule rose to its semi-upright position. As Judith opened the door, Blake twisted his head from side to side, trying to loosen up his neck.

"Welcome back, Mr. Beck," she said with a smile.

"Thanks, Judith. I hope you've been well."

"Yes, thank you. And you? Did you enjoy being dead?" As soon as the words were out of her mouth, she realized that Blake might not think being dead was all that funny. Fortunately for her, Blake's sense of irony and humor hadn't died with him, and despite the fact that Blake was in a rotten mood, he managed to not take it out on Judith.

"As much as the next man, I guess. What was it your British boys said? Always look on the bright side of death," he said as he got out of the capsule.

"Something like that, sir," Judith said with a discrete sigh of relief.

"Is everything on track?" Blake asked.

"Yes, sir. It's just past six o'clock and we're parked on Bishop's Square next the cathedral. This should give you a good two hours and change to get ready and check out the scene."

"Perfect," Blake said, taking a look around, dressed only in his hospital gown. "Where's our Mr. Thompson then?" he asked, hoping that the answer would be along the lines of "far away."

"He's in London, sir. It's a medical condition," Judith said, refraining from going into further detail. "I let the rest of the crew go out for dinner since we finished the reanimation setup in good time."

"Ah, you just wanted me all to yourself," Blake jested as he headed to the small changing room, trying his best to lighten up both the situation and his own mood.

"Indeed, sir," Judith replied with a smile in her voice.

"Have you got my ticket for the concert?" Blake called from the stall.

"No, sir. It's a free concert, but I've put 50 kroner in your wallet in case you want some cash for the collection tin."

"So you did. Thanks," Blake said with the slightly strained voice of a grown man sitting down and bending over to tie his shoes. Blake stepped out from the changing room wearing a perfectly fitted, dark grey pinstriped suit and black leather shoes.

"Looking good, sir."

"Thanks, Judith. I think I'll go and have a look around. By the way, where's my sword?"

"I've taken the liberty of hiding it inside the cathedral, sir. It's taped underneath the bench just to your immediate right when you enter the cathedral – hilt towards the aisle. I thought this was the easiest way to make sure you had it with you."

"Perfect," Blake said before exiting the trailer of the truck that had made the trip from London to Aarhus while Blake had been in Shades having a lousy time. He gave Judith a wink as he closed the trailer door and headed across the square to the cathedral. He walked up to the heavy wooden double doors and pulled one of them half open just as a young woman walked up to him. She quickly swallowed her last mouthful of food before she addressed him.

"Undskyld mig, men kirken er altså lukket lige nu, for vi er ved at gøre klar til koncerten i aften," Astrid said.

"Sorry!?" Blake replied with a bewildered look on his face.

"Altså kirken er lukket lige nu, så du bliver desværre nødt til at komme tilbage senere," she continued, mistaking Blake for one of the many Anglophile Danes who would often use the word "sorry" as their chosen word of apology.

"I'm sorry, I don't understand, miss," Blake said.

"Oh . . . I . . . I'm sorry! I didn't . . . I thought you were Danish. I just said that the church is closed to the public right now as we're getting ready for tonight's concert," Astrid said, feeling suddenly shy.

"Oh, so you work here?" Blake asked, still holding the door slightly open, allowing the sounds of the organ playing to escape.

"No. Well, sort of. I'm just a volunteer and I'm helping out at the concert tonight."

"Well, I'm Blake," he started, letting the door close. "I arrived early, hoping to see the cathedral and grab a bite to eat." He extended his hand to her, betting himself that this polite young woman would not turn him away once they were properly introduced. He hoped she might even be of some assistance to his endeavor.

"I'm Astrid," she replied, her mind wandering into a possible future where she would not have to wait until

Saturday to begin her hunt for a man: a future in which Louise would become envious of her new, rather hot, older and sophisticated American boyfriend who seemed to have an affinity for the works of Johann Sebastian Bach which were featured in the evening's concert. Blake could see his ploy working and moved in for the kill.

"I know that you're probably busy, but here goes. I'm from out of town and only here for a few days," Blake said. A bubble burst in Astrid's mind. "Only a few days," she thought and decided that she had better make the most of it. "I was wondering, in exchange for me accompanying you inside the cathedral while you finish what you're doing, would you want to have dinner with me? I imagine that you'd know where to go for a nice dinner," Blake added. Astrid's heart jumped and she immediately discarded any notion of making an in-depth investigation into Bernt Notke's portrayal of the Gregor's Mass, deciding that the peacock and gilded sky would still be there in the morning.

"Well actually, I'm starving," she lied, feeling the weight of three sausage rolls and half a liter of iced tea in her stomach, "and I wasn't really doing anything important. I was just going to check that everything is in order, which I'm sure it is, and then I was going to do some research for my master's thesis, but that can wait."

"So?" Blake waited for Astrid to continue, still following his gut instinct that she might be of assistance.

"Well, why don't we eat first and then there's no rush and we will make it back to the church in good time. And I mean,

195

if you want to see the church after the concert, you can stay behind for half an hour while I tidy things up."

"Sure, you lead the way then," Blake said, satisfied that he had found his way in. Astrid led Blake to a charming brasserie located by the nearby stream that runs through Aarhus. The stream offered appealing scenery for a dozen or so of the city's most posh cafés, making for a lively setting and a convivial atmosphere, not to mention $8.00 cups of cappuccino. Blake opened the door for Astrid and followed her into the stylish, French brasserie where they were greeted by the maître d' who sat them at a small table by the window. The maître d', whom Blake believed to actually be French, took his leave to get them their menus. "This is really nice," Blake said, feeling his mood lift from rotten to beyond ripe.

"I think so, too," Astrid replied, feeling great that she was on a date. "At least, sort of a date," she thought to herself as they took turns staring out of the window for their own reasons. Blake was still working his way up to being in a mood for chitchat, and Astrid simply didn't know what to say. They sat there for a minute or two until the maître d' returned with the menus and handed one to each of them.

"I will bring you a basket of bread and some water. Meanwhile, I hope that you will find something to your taste on the menu, and I would just mention that our à la carte dishes are made to starter size. So, for a full meal I would recommend at least two courses or perhaps tonight's four course menu," he said with a French accent that, unfortunately, reminded Blake of Marie.

"Thank you," Blake said. The maître d' walked off with a courteous smile. Blake and Astrid sat there for a few minutes studying the menus, barely noticing when their bread and water arrived.

"What are you having?" Astrid asked, and before Blake could reply, she continued, "I think I'll have sashimi tuna to start and then the fried foie gras." She smiled at him.

"I'm not really that hungry," Blake started, mindful of the fact that the Hunters ought to refrain from eating in life because their reanimated bodies cannot digest food and thus require cleaning following any consumption. Yet he felt it rather hard to explain that he wasn't eating anything – after all, he did invite this young woman to dinner. "I think I will have the . . . autumn salad," he finally said after deciding that a salad would probably be easier to remove than fois gras or steak. Astrid began feeling bad that she had already told him that she wanted two courses. She thought it would look strange if she took it back, but she also thought it would look unladylike if she ate more than Blake. "Thank God he doesn't know about the sausage rolls," she thought to herself before realizing that she had still been swallowing when she addressed him by the church. She could have kicked herself, but didn't get the chance as the maître d' arrived to inquire about the mountains of food she was about to order.

"So, did you find anything on our menu that you would like?" he inquired with a smile.

"Yes, thank you," Blake said. He allowed Astrid to order first, like a true modern gentleman.

197

"I'd like the sashimi tuna and the fois gras, please," Astrid said.

"Very well, madam. And for you, sir?"

"Well, I think I'll stick to the autumn salad."

"And what would you like to drink?"

"Hmmm," Blake replied, looking to Astrid. "Would you like a glass of wine, perhaps?" he asked.

"Yes, please," Astrid replied.

"A glass of white wine for the lady – whichever you recommend," Blake said after a quick scan down the wine list, eyeing Astrid to see if she had any objections. "And I'll just stick with the water."

"Very well, sir," the maître d´ replied before heading off into the kitchen.

"Thank you," Astrid said. She was enjoying the experience of dining out with a gentleman – the Danish men that she was acquainted with were rarely so courteous.

"You're welcome," he replied and decided to strike up a conversation. "So, Astrid. You said you were doing research for your thesis at the cathedral. What are you writing about?"

"Well, I'm finishing my master's degree in history, and I'm doing my thesis on medieval art with a particular focus on the works of the Lübeckian sculptor Bernt Notke," she replied, expecting a sigh of boredom and a complete lack of understanding from Blake, as this was the response she usually got.

"So you were going to see the altar, I gather?" Blake said as he buttered a piece of perfectly crisp baguette and watched Astrid's jaw almost hit the table.

"You know Bernt Notke?" she asked.

"Well, not personally, but I know a little about him and his work, presumably infinitely less than you do." Astrid felt invigorated. She was on a date, or at least sort of a date, with a real gentleman who also just revealed that he understood and cared about her work. They sat there and ate and talked for about an hour before walking back to the cathedral at a leisurely pace. Astrid did most of the talking, giving Blake an in-depth lesson on European medieval art and the life of Bernt Notke. She started feeling slightly uncomfortable as she wondered if it would be better if she wasn't such an endless stream of words. It reminded her of several first dates in the past, each of which had resulted in a preemptive break-up before they had even gotten together. The message had been delivered with sentences much akin to "I like you a lot, but as a friend" or "It's so nice – I feel like I can talk to you about anything," with the "anything" being one of her friends whom the young man had wanted to hook up with. Little did Astrid know that this evening would come to no such end.

II

Marie was wearing a tight-fitting, black Victorian-style riding habit, a white shirt, black leather boots and a matching black ladies' top hat as she pulled her white mare, Amandine, from the mansion stables. Since moving to the mansion as Dæth's wife, she had taken to dressing in the appropriate Victorian style of the household rather than the style of her own time. It seemed to somehow mend some of the cracks that undeniably existed in the marriage – a marriage that she felt certain was mostly for show and practicality. However, she still hoped that this would change over time. Unfortunately, the arrival of Blake Beck so soon after their wedding had rocked its already shaky foundation, or at least Marie's outlook on it. Yet, it was clear to her that Dæth would not tolerate disloyalty, least of all from those closest to him, and no one was closer to him than Marie. While he still trusted and involved McCoy more in matters of business, it was Marie who shared his bed and his time, after all. Outside the stables, the skies darkened, threatening to envelop the lands in darkness and wash everything away, but the clouds held. Marie got on the horse and she slowly trotted off, riding sidesaddle in her long riding habit. She usually rode down the cobbled road until she was well away from the mansion, but on this day she rode straight across the lawn towards the reddened skies and the setting sun. She coaxed Amandine into a gallop, sending patches of well-groomed grass flying as the horse sped across the lawns and through the row of trees that outlined the mansion grounds where the groomed lawns gave way to the fields and wilderness. For a short while, she nearly forgot about her troubles, focusing on staying in the saddle. A few minutes later, the sun had crept beneath the horizon and Marie had reached the woods that had become her favorite place of escape. She allowed the mare to relax and once again move into a gentle trot. The small path into the woods left her just enough room to ride without having to duck and dodge the branches of the trees, and as the shadowy realm of the woodlands embraced her, her dark thoughts returned.

She still felt horrible after the visit to Blake's, and she shuddered at the thought of walking in on him at the mansion. She knew she had hurt him like never before, and she wished in the deepest parts of her heart that she hadn't been forced to. Secretly, she hoped that it had not destroyed the last hope for them, despite the fact that this was exactly what she had sought to do. She knew in her mind that she had to let Blake go, but in her heart she couldn't. As the autumn winds shook the withering leaves, causing them to fall lightly around her, she felt cold tears running down her cheeks as the wind caressed her skin. She prayed that time would heal the wounds, but knew very well that it wouldn't – not in Shades. Eternity merely meant time to regret and repent. For a good half hour, she rode on with her own dark thoughts and Amandine as her only companions until she reached the small lake where she usually stopped to let Amandine rest and to allow herself to find peace. But on this day there was no peace to be found. She jumped off the horse and led it by the reins for the last few paces down to the water. She patted the horse and stroked its sides, as if to relax the horse now that she could not relax herself. "Don't wander off now," she said, and the horse seemed to give a nod before lowering its head to drink from the lake. Marie began walking around the lake and stopped underneath a weeping willow. Its dreary branches nearly reached the water, enclosing her in a cave of yellowing leaves. She sat down and rested her back against the trunk. The lake was quiet and only slight ripples disturbed her reflection staring back at her from the murky waters. It was as if a stranger was peering back at her, she thought, and she could not for the life or death of her recognize the figure in the lake. This was not the Marie she used to be or know, weeping beneath the willow, wearing this ridiculous costume. In a frenzied movement, she tore off the top hat and chucked it away into the undergrowth before letting her hair down and shaking her head wildly. Then she looked into the lake once again, but still it was as if something was missing. The winds subsided and the ripples died out, leaving the water dead calm and the image of her as clear as in any mirror. In a moment of clarity, she suddenly realized what was missing. Unfortunately, it wasn't her heart, her love for Blake or anything like that. What she was missing was her own delusion. She realized that in death she saw herself more clearly than she ever did in life, and it was not the image in the lake that was faulty, rather it was the image in her mind. She saw how she was the one to blame for her own misery and that she had been the one telling herself lies in life. She had convinced herself that what mattered most in life was, in fact, that which mattered the least. She was the one who had chosen to be too far away, too busy and too important to care, and in the end, she was the one who had willingly, even gladly, accepted Dæth's proposal as if it was some sort of final promotion. In the dark waters, she saw a pitiful whore who had stayed true to others rather than to herself. She saw what she had become – a creature of her own creation that she despised and pitied at the same time. She looked at her own reflection, feeling as small and helpless as ever, and she drew her legs up to her chest and rested her chin on her knees. In her imagination, she dreamt of Blake walking up to her, sitting down beside her and putting his arms around her while telling her that everything would be alright. Of course he didn't and it wouldn't. Redemption was for the living; repentance is for the dead.

Blake and Astrid left the brasserie and walked along the posh café waterfront, finding themselves in the company of those café patrons who had chosen to defy the autumn winds by sitting outside, aided in their defiant ways by fleece blankets and outdoor gas heaters.

"I'm really looking forward to the concert," Astrid said.

"Yeah," Blake replied, absentmindedly wondering whether or not he would be alone in the church tonight or if one of Mr. Ferre's children would make an appearance, as well. If so, he hoped that it wouldn't be Bahij Khaleel. Not yet.

"It's a brilliant Dutch organist who is playing tonight. I think it is Bach's Fantasia or something," Astrid continued as they walked up the stairs to Clement's Bridge, named – like the cathedral – after the city's patron saint, St. Clement.

"I'm very much looking forward to it. Should I save you a seat?" Blake asked out of customary courtesy.

"That would be lovely," Astrid replied, knowing full well that there would be hundreds of vacant seats. These concerts rarely drew in more than a hundred people to a cathedral able to hold ten times that, however, she thought it was nice of him to ask. As they reached the cathedral, Blake opened the heavy door and held it open for Astrid to enter before walking in behind her. "I'll go check if there's anything I need to do before the concert. You just head on in and I'll come sit with you in a couple of minutes," Astrid said with a smile. While

Astrid went to talk to an elderly lady who was one of the other organizers, Blake entered the cathedral. He started down the walkway of the nave, and as he walked by the first row of benches, he knelt down, pretending that his shoelace had come untied and checking to see if his sword was in place. It was. He continued down the nave, eyeing Notke's altar on the far end of the church dominating the choir. When he passed the pulpit, he found that most of the other concertgoers had seated themselves on the benches looking back towards the pulpit and the entrance rather than towards the altar. Blake turned around and gazed upwards to the balcony that held the majestic 18th century organ, the pipes of which seemed to reach for the sky far beyond the Gothic arches of the ceiling. He saw Astrid close the doors of the cathedral below the balcony, which caused most of the resounding chatter to die out as the other guests directed their attention to the balcony. As Blake sat down on an unoccupied bench where he expected to be joined by Astrid just moments later, he saw the stocky, well-dressed organist walk in to take his place at the keys of the huge instrument. He was so dwarfed by the organ that he looked like Thumbelina about to attempt to play a grand piano. The man started to play, and despite being dead and freed from any natural physical reactions, Blake still felt a chill run down his spine as his soul shivered. He briefly closed his eyes and listened to the pipes sing of a profound sadness that, at the same time, offered the promise of hope – an eternal promise from a different time. The pipes spoke to him and reminded him why Mr. Ferre had not swayed him. It was because of this hope floating on top of the sadness and despair. The hope of good in the hearts of man relieved him from being a jailer to the damned. Instead he became a protector of that which was worth protecting. As the last tones rang out, Blake imagined that the pipes would no longer sing to his enemies of hope, but only of despair.

IV

The grand library of Aquraa looked more like a city palace than a library. It was built in the style of medieval Arabia with a size and majesty that have not been rivaled since the great library of Alexandria. Inside, the walls were lined with heavy wooden shelves filled with copies of all the works from life that had been deemed worthy, as well as all the great works that had been written and composed in death by the greatest scholars of all time. No place – in life or death – held more or purer knowledge than the library of Aquraa. For this reason, it was only natural that Bahij had his private study there, with all worthwhile knowledge at hand. On this evening, he sat poised over his copies of the Voynich and Flamel manuscripts, surrounded by a wall of ancient tomes that rose from his desktop. He was nearly done deciphering the Voynich manuscript, and it was just as he had thought. The ritual within was indeed the source of everlasting life, offering the ability to travel between the worlds and thus granting the ability to return to life from death. Bahij dipped his quill in the inkwell and finished his notes, which by this time compiled several hundred handwritten pages, many of them written over the course of the last few days. He was done. He knew now that there were only two things missing to complete the ritual, as Notke had hidden crucial information to keep the ritual safe. Vincenzo was already retrieving the names of the three saints required for the ritual from Notke's altar, but the second piece of the puzzle proved much trickier.

In the manuscript, Notke told of a verse to be uttered during the course of the ritual: a verse which Bahij had found that Notke had included in his masterwork painting *Totentanz* – Dance of the Dead – in the Marienkirche in Notke's hometown of Lübeck. Bahij had found that the verse needed for the ritual was the verse of the minstrel. The one playing the tune of death's dance on his pipes would also be the one able to stop the dance – freeing the dancers from death's grip. It made perfect sense. However, there were two snags. First off, the painting inside the Marienkirche had been destroyed during the allied bombings during World War II, making it impossible for Bahij to get a firsthand look. Secondly, neither the only existing partial copy in St. Nicholas' Church in Tallinn nor any written records told of the minstrel having his own verse in Notke's *Totentanz*. Bahij heard resolute footsteps outside just before the door opened. Bahij rose from his seat to look over the stacks of tomes to see who had come to disturb him against his express wishes.

"My Lord," he said, bowing down when he saw *Him* standing in the doorway.

"Bahij," *He* said as *He* entered, closing the thick hardwood door behind him. "I have come to inquire as to the progress you are making, not wishing to needlessly tear you from your endeavor to serve me."

"I am most joyous to say that I have finished the translation of the manuscript."

"Indeed?"

"Yes. I am certain that I have mapped the course of the ritual, save two parts omitted by Notke in the manuscript. One being the saint names, which Vincenzo should be acquiring as we speak, and the second being an unknown verse in Notke's *Totentanz*." Bahij let his words hang in the air between them and awaited his master's reply.

"Well, I am certain that now that the existence of this verse is known to you, you will be able to attain it for me."

"Yes, my Lord," Bahij said, showing no uncertainty though he was praying that he had not made a promise which he could not keep. "It is the verse of the minstrel who is playing the tune to which death dances, and as such, he is the one able to stop the dance." As *He* walked over to take a look at the manuscripts and notes on Bahij's desk himself, Bahij stepped back to give *Him* room. *He* peered through Bahij's notes, turning the pages of the manuscripts to follow the note references, and Bahij said nothing. He stood there for minutes that felt like hours, like a schoolboy showing his work to the teacher, and he said nothing despite having one question burning in his mind. When Bahij saw that *He* was just about finished and seemed to be satisfied, Bahij finally got up his courage. "My Lord, would you allow me to ask a delicate question?"

"Yes," Mr. Ferre replied as *He* finished reading the last of Bahij's notes.

"I ask that you would let me know who will be the first to be summoned back from the Grey." The question lingered for a moment before *He* answered.

"It will be my wife," *He* said in a tone both grave and very matter-of-fact as he rose from the books and looked at Bahij. Bahij had heard it told that *He* had once loved, but few – if any – knew if the tales were true, or who she might be or how she had come to be sent into the Grey.

"Your wife, my Lord?" Bahij said with a tremble in his voice.

"Yes, Bahij. My wife. Do not tell me that you have not heard the stories."

"I have, but I must say I had never believed them to be much more than just that." *He* didn't reply, but his gaze revealed a longing for the past paired with a deep hatred and desire for vengeance. "I . . ."

"You are allowed to ask, my friend," *He* said, turning his back to Bahij as *He* walked to a chair by the wall and took a seat.

"I will keep it to myself," Bahij said, unnecessarily underlining his own trustworthiness.

"Yes, you will." As *He* sat down, Bahij took a seat in his desk chair and looked at *Him* with marvel. He felt that he had been offered a short glimpse of the humanity of the gods and that he had just been awarded the greatest gift of all, namely that of trust.

"Who was she?" Bahij asked, still in slight disbelief.

"Her name was Hel and she was death," *He* said, his eyes going cold again. "A great while before your time, she was death to the ancient Norse and ruled a large part of Shades – a task placed on her shoulders by force rather than will. But while she carried out the bidding of the powers that be, she felt no love for them and a part of her always yearned to break free." *He* let a long silence fill the room while *He* recalled their time together so long ago. "While we first met as enemies, we also found in each other a resounding understanding and a great dislike for those who tried to rule us, and that was what brought us together in the end." *He* looked at Bahij, who lowered his gaze to the floor. Though Bahij acted as if he averted his eyes to offer *Him* the solitude to speak freely, in truth he did it because he could not hold his gaze with his master's as if they were equals. "Over time, her powers faded as other deaths encroached on her realm, and she eventually turned to me for love, aid and freedom. It was a cataclysmic treason that could not be ignored. For more than a century, the battles raged and there was no rest to be found until the fateful day came when our defenses fell and they finally had their will. I found myself unable to stop them and she was exiled into the Grey, while I remained behind, swearing my vengeance." *He* fastened his gaze on Bahij. "And now, after the better part of a thousand years, it seems that the time is nigh. And it is largely your efforts that have made it possible, which is the sole reason why I tell you this." Bahij looked into his master's eyes and saw the fires raging, and he saw the wings threatening to burst from his master's back into an inferno of flames. "When she returns, our line will have a new queen. Dæth will have his downfall. And I will have my revenge!"

For most of the concert, Vincenzo listened to the ominous wail of the organ pipes from the winding staircase of the cathedral tower. He sat on the century-old wooden steps and felt the weight of time, knowing that these steps had been there even before he was born. As Bach took him back in time, Vincenzo recalled his first years as a vampire – a time when it had been much easier to roam and feed, as news and fear traveled a lot slower in those days and the Hunters had a much harder time catching up. He recalled how people had tried to shield themselves with superstitious beliefs, such as that he could not enter a house unless invited, that garlic kept him at bay, that the sight of a cross would repel him, or even better, the belief that he could not enter hallowed ground. As the bass pipes rejoined the music with great gravity after a spell of lightness, Vincenzo was taken back to a time when he had been feeding in a small village in the Netherlands. "It would have been around the year 1600," he thought to himself. The whole village had been in an uproar after only two nights of feeding, and everyone in the village seemed to have their own idea of what or who was behind the monstrous murders. Some claimed it to be the devil, and others thought that it was the punishment of God. Some said it was the gimp who lived on the outskirts of town and somehow managed to keep herself fat and fed despite being of no good use to anyone, and yet others thought it to be the work of a wild beast come to haunt the village. As Vincenzo continued to feed regularly, the general consensus in town moved towards the idea that the gimp was a witch and that the deaths were God's punishment for the sin of the villagers suffering her in their midst. The night they burned her at the stake, Vincenzo stood at the edge of the village green and watched as the smell of burnt flesh spread and the convulsions of the gimp subsided as the flames consumed her. Like a cat toying with its prey, Vincenzo refrained from feeding in the village for a good week, allowing the villagers enough time to agree that they had done the right thing. On the night he first fed again, he took a young girl of only twelve years, and he left her on the village green where the grass was still scorched from the fire that had burned there just a week before. When the girl was found the next morning, the village panicked and the doctor from the nearest city was brought in to aid the village priest in unraveling what had happened. The good doctor, being a learned man, had heard tales from the eastern parts of the continent of risen dead who fed upon the blood and souls of others. At a village meeting, he conveyed his message that this Vampir was what was terrorizing the village. He told the villagers that the best weapon against this abomination would be prayer, but that it was also believed that the scent of garlic would keep the creature at bay, and that the sight of our Lord's cross and hallowed ground would surely repel – if not even destroy – the beast. This led to villagers carving crosses on the doors to their houses, filling their pockets with cloves of garlic and digging up graveyard dirt to spread around their houses to keep Vincenzo out. That same night, Vincenzo decided to have a banquet before moving on, knowing that the Hunters would eventually arrive as news of the village's fate spread. Come nightfall, he rode to the small convent that lay outside the village. He arrived after evening prayer, just in time to hear the abbess ensure the nuns that they were perfectly safe from the workings of the devil as long as they remained inside the convent where they would be protected by the hand and mercy of the Lord. As he recalled the look in the eyes of the first nun he consumed that night, he still marveled at the panic and disbelief that he had seen in her blue, teary eyes when she found that her God had abandoned her. He felt hungry now. As the last tones of the pipes rang out and resounded between the cathedral walls, he closed his eyes and gathered his thoughts. Soon he would feed again. There was a standing ovation, and after about fifteen minutes of waiting, the last of the concertgoers had left – save for Blake and Astrid, who had promised to lock up the church after a quick tour. Slowly and silently, Vincenzo snuck around the walkways, stairways and aisles of the cathedral like a predator on the prowl, waiting for just the right time. He kept a close watch on them, listening to everything they said. Vincenzo knew that Blake would be prepared and that he would need to find a way to catch him off guard.

"Blake?" Astrid said, picking up a used, folded-up program. She chucked it into the trash bag she was carrying around as she tidied up the church. Blake followed close to give her a helping hand. Before Blake could answer, she turned on her toes and kissed him. Her kiss started out passionate and was intended to convince Blake to abandon his interest in medieval arts in order to explore a much healthier interest in anatomy. However, it failed. Not so much because Blake failed to kiss her back, although his kiss was more courteous than passionate, but it was because halfway through the kiss, Astrid felt the cold of Blake's dead lips and immediately broke off. "Your lips . . . You must be freezing," she said.

"Oh, it's nothing. I guess it's just chilly in here with the thick, cold, stone walls and all," Blake replied, trying to weasel out of it.

"You poor thing," Astrid started, but before she could move on, Blake diffused the situation by stepping out into the aisle and turning his attention to the altar at the far end of the choir.

"Would you show me the altar?"

"Sure," she said hesitantly before joining Blake to walk up the aisle, taking his arm. As they reached the altar, Astrid looked at Blake as if to ask him if he wanted her to go through the details of the altar.

"Please explain," he said with a smile, and she did. She told him about the wings of the altar that are shifted in accordance to the liturgical calendar. She told him about the many paintings that filled the predella and the closed wings, and she even pulled out a ladder from behind the altar in order to shift the wings so that Blake could see for himself. She told him about the woodcut figures of the twelve apostles and three saints – Saint Clement, Saint Anna and John the Baptist – that dominated the center of the altar when fully opened. After a good half hour's lecture, Blake thought he had a pretty good grasp of the imagery of Notke's altar.

"So why these three?" he asked, pointing to the three central saints displayed in woodcut.

"Well, Saint Clement, holding his anchor, is the patron saint of the city. I believe it is a symbol of hope and can be seen as some kind of anchor of the soul," she said, trying to recall one of the many biblical references of her thesis. "I think it has something to do with Hebrews six, verse nineteen, which I think goes something like: 'Which hope we have as an anchor of the soul, steadfast and sure, and which enters beyond the veil.' Or something like that." She smiled.

"And the other two?" Blake asked.

"Well, at the time Notke made this altar – which was before the reformation, mind you – Saint Anna had become the closest thing to a direct line to God because the Virgin Mary and Jesus Christ himself had become too distant to pray to directly. So, by sending your prayers to Saint Anna, you would ask her to send it on to her daughter, the Virgin Mary, who would in turn ask Jesus, who would send the prayer on to God in the end. As you can see, the scene even shows Saint Anna depicted with her daughter, the Virgin Mary, and her newborn son, Jesus Christ."

"So she's kind of a God hotline," Blake stated. Astrid snickered with her head now filled with images of God – long white beard and all – sitting behind a desk taking down prayers sent to him from various celestial phone lines.

"You might say that. And John the Baptist, well, he was the one who baptized Jesus Christ in the New Testament." Astrid's phone made a faint humming sound as it vibrated in her pocket. Blake stood looking at the altar as she found her cell phone and read the text message, inaudibly cussing and rolling her eyes, making sure that Blake didn't notice her.

"So we have the anchor of the soul, a connection to God, and finally, the sacrament of baptism to cleanse the soul and offer admission?" Blake recapped, convinced that he had the right saint names for McCoy.

"Yes, something like that," Astrid said absentmindedly, quickly texting her mom back. "Blake, I'm sorry, but I have to go. There is one more thing about the altar that I would like to show you, but it will have to keep until tomorrow. I'm sorry!"

"What's happened?" Blake asked, turning his attention to Astrid.

"Oh, it's nothing to do with you. It's my mom." Blake could see by the tears forming in her eyes that there was not much chance of keeping Astrid in the church any longer that night. However, he had already gotten what he came for and he would be back tomorrow to make sure that he had gotten all the details right. "Come on. I just have to lock up before we go," she said, urging Blake on.

"So, tomorrow then?" he said as they walked down the aisle.

"Yes. Let's meet here at . . . say eight tomorrow evening. We'll have the whole church to ourselves and I can bring my notes. I'm really sorry!"

"It's OK," Blake said. They walked out of the cathedral and parted ways on the square outside. Blake turned left around the corner to the CAC truck to inanimate, and Astrid turned right and headed off across town to see her mom. Vincenzo, who had heard it all, had slipped out of the cathedral just before Blake and Astrid and he watched as the two went their separate ways in the evening light. Vincenzo had the information Bahij wanted, and he savored the fact that it was now finally time for him to undertake his revenge on Blake Beck.

Astrid walked through the quiet streets of Aarhus towards the northern part of the city to see her mother. She walked to clear her head before having to face her mom and talk her out of yet another hysterical – and probably drunken – fit concerning her midlife crisis. It was the same midlife crisis that Astrid had, on one occasion, referred to as her mother's near-the-end-of-life crisis, taking her mother's age into account. The comment had done nothing to calm her mother down. Astrid walked through the shifting lights of the street lamps until she reached the park-like cemetery that filled the gap between the city center and the part of northern Aarhus where her mother lived. Although she had been forced to admit that she didn't really like walking through cemeteries alone after dark, she had long ago decided not to let the tricks of her mind rule her life, and so she walked up the cobblestone stairway to the cemetery. As the light of the street lamps dissipated and the cool autumn darkness enveloped her, her pace unwittingly hastened. She could see the stars much clearer now that the lights of the city were kept at bay, and she told herself that it was actually a nice night and that the cemetery was more like a park than a place where the dead were buried. Astrid didn't manage to convince herself, and though she stopped for a moment in an attempt to enjoy the starry evening, she quickly resumed her walk. As she walked down the mingled pathways, she thought she heard footsteps on a path behind her and felt a chill run down her spine. For the briefest of moments, her mind suggested that it might be a werewolf following her, until she convinced herself that the idea was absolutely ludicrous and besides it wasn't even a full moon. She looked over her shoulder and found nothing, which was perhaps the worst of all. Walking ever quicker, she turned up a crossing path toward the lights that surrounded the small chapel and crematorium about halfway across the cemetery. She heard them again. The footsteps were now even closer than before, and she nearly screamed out as her mind fought to get the better of her, but didn't. Looking back as she walked on, she saw a young woman walking up one of the paths that ran parallel with the one she had been walking on. Astrid slowed her walk and relaxed, both amazed and annoyed at the power of her own imagination. It was just a young student, probably with a similarly vivid imagination, hurrying home across the cemetery. Astrid gave a small sigh of relief and turned right up the nearby path on which the young woman approached, abandoning the needless safety of the lights in order to take the easiest way to her mother's flat. Once again she turned her attention to the starry sky, but now she could actually enjoy it after her obligatory scare and realization that she had nothing to fear but fear itself. It seemed that the other young woman had not yet come to the same realization and she still kept up her rapid pace. Astrid walked on one side of the path and slowed down to allow the woman to walk past her, attempting to avoid the uncomfortable situation of walking too close to someone for too long. Astrid was about to greet the woman with a courteous "good evening," but the words never came out of her mouth. She heard the piercing of her leather jacket just as she felt a sudden, sharp pain in her upper back, and despite the urge, she found it impossible to scream. The woman grabbed her by the chest and a strong push of the knife intensified the pain. Tears welled in Astrid's eyes as she tried to fight her way out of the assailant's grasp, but to no avail. The woman was too strong. Flailing her arms, Astrid felt her legs being swept away, and as she crashed down on her back, she felt the knife forcing its way even further into her flesh and her lungs filling with blood. She closed her eyes to the pain, and when she opened them again a moment later, the young woman was sitting on top of her, holding her down. Astrid looked at the woman through the haze of tears and panic began to take her. The young woman with the distinctive, dark A-line bob smiled.

"I . . . Why me?" Astrid tried to ask with her last breath of air, but the words were made almost inaudible by the blood and mucus that filled her lungs and throat. There was no reply from the woman, and Astrid closed her eyes as her life slipped from her, tears running down her cheeks. She could hear the silence of the night and the sound of her own blood dripping from her wound, drumming on the ground beneath her.

As Astrid slipped into death, Vincenzo bent over and felt the warmth of her body. He smelled death. Moving his head in within an inch of hers, he tasted the last salty tears that ran from her eyes. He felt her last breath against his cheek, and as he ran his hand up her blouse, he felt her heart stop. Then he kissed her goodbye.

VI

Vincenzo returned from life for a short time and found himself in his room at Aquraa castle, lying still in the canopy bed. He lay there just long enough to get his bearings before getting up and walking past the open window to the writing desk in the corner of the bedroom. He sat down and dipped the quill in the inkwell on the table. Then he wrote a short note to Bahij, explaining that he intended to go back for Blake Beck. He jotted down the names of the three saints – Saint Clement, Saint Anna and John the Baptist – briefly detailing their symbolism as explained by Astrid, despite knowing full well that Bahij was well versed in these matters. Then he folded up the paper, put it in an envelope and affixed it with his own wax seal. It took him only a few minutes to find Teresa Ammon to ask her to deliver the letter to Bahij. Then Vincenzo reanimated, already planning his revenge.

The following evening, Blake walked the two-dozen yards from the CAC truck to the entrance of the cathedral, waiting for Astrid to arrive. Though he had already given McCoy the names of the three saints, Blake was still waiting for the final parts of the Voynich manuscript to be translated, and he figured that he might as well hear the girl out. Besides, he found himself enjoying her company. He waited by the door for a few minutes, watching people scuttle across the square in pursuit of their lives until he eyed Astrid walking towards him wearing a big smile and a long, black coat that suited her slightly Goth appearance.

"Good evening," Blake said just before she reached him. Astrid didn't reply. Instead, she walked up to him, stretched on her toes and gave him a kiss on the cheek.

"Hi!" she said. "Thanks for coming. I've been looking forward to it all day and I'd started to fear that you wouldn't come." She held his eyes while she took the keys from her pocket and then stepped over to unlock the doors.

"Of course I did. I promised, didn't I?" he said and moved to pull the heavy door open for Astrid.

"You did." They walked inside, and Astrid turned to lock the door as Blake walked into the antechamber and over to the small desk that was the domain of the volunteer guides during opening hours. That morning's copy of Denmark's leading tabloid lay folded on the chair behind the desk offering the day's story of fear: a young woman had died and was presumed murdered in a cemetery in northern Aarhus. The story ran under the headline: "Grave Robber?" Blake looked at the paper, which sported a full-page photo of the young woman lying in a pool of blood on a path that ran between the graves. It was a poor photo, and Blake thought it was probably taken with the cell phone of whoever found the body and decided to make a buck peddling the photo to the tabloids. He heard Astrid lock the door. A black bar had been placed over the dead woman's eyes, but Blake still found her to be strangely familiar – there was something about the black clothes and her dark, A-line bob haircut. As Astrid walked up beside him and flipped through the postcards in the stand on the desk, he had a realization. It was the girl from London – the vampire. "How the hell did she end up in Aarhus, and why and how was she killed?" he wondered. If the CAC had caught up with her, he surely would have been informed – or heads would roll. Hundreds of scenarios ran through his mind, each one having its own weaknesses and holes. The only thing he was certain of was that something was amiss.

"Did you have dinner yet?" he asked Astrid, who took his arm and leaned towards him.

"Nope, not yet," she smiled.

"Well, when we're done here, maybe we should grab a bite. I think I'd like to try that autumn salad you had yesterday," Blake said, testing a hunch.

"Yes, it was really delicious! We should do that," Her voice was flirty and hinted that something else would take priority. Blake turned his head and looked at her just in time to see the light catch on the blade she pulled from her pocket. Blake realized then what had happened to Astrid, and he parried the stab of the knife and kneed Astrid's reanimated body in the gut, sending her flying backwards.

"You fucking bitch!" Blake yelled as his knee connected. The vampire landed on her feet and her coat fell open, revealing a medieval longsword hidden in the folds within. The vampire drew the sword and started laughing.

"Who are you calling a bitch, Beck? The little tart who died sobbing on the cold ground last night, rattling as the blood filled her lungs? Or the whore you brought with you last time?" Blake looked at Astrid in disbelief as the familiar timbre of her voice delivered words that clearly belonged to another.

"Vincenzo?" Blake asked, eyeing the door to his right that appeared to be the only way out of the antechamber, save past the vampire.

"Yes, and this time I know your girlfriend won't save you because she's busy holding her legs up, pleasing your master." Blake burned inside, but rather than follow his inclination to launch himself at Vincenzo in an uneven struggle, reason prevailed and Blake decided to bide his time, striking verbally as he moved towards the door.

"Well, it seems you're all the woman I need tonight," Blake said, edging backwards. "It's just as well, as I recall, you fight like a girl anyway!" Blake saw how the muscles in Astrid's body tightened, revealing that Vincenzo was about to attack. Blake made a run for the door and ripped it open, and as

Vincenzo shot towards him, he started up the old, winding staircase of the tower.

"Beck, you goddamn coward. Stay and fight! There's nothing up there but your own demise." Blake hurried up the stairs, hearing that Vincenzo was not far behind. He felt a gentle draft through the old windows when he reached a room halfway up the tower, high above the city. The room was bare, save for an old clock mechanism in the middle of the room, a number of old cast iron clock hands nailed on display up on the thick stone walls and a series of power cables running up the wall to a fuse box. Blake ran to the far wall and grabbed one of the clock hands. Then he pulled until the rusty nails that held it gave way. It looked like a sword with its crescent ornamentation on the outer hand serving as the cross guard. However, the weight was dead off and the edge of the cast iron hand was about as sharp as a brick, but Blake knew it would have to make do. Vincenzo had made his way up the stairs, and he launched himself at Blake with his sword pulled back to strike. Blake dodged the first blow and managed to parry Vincenzo's sword as he tried to cut Blake down with a second strike. "Oh, I've been waiting a long time for this, Beck," Vincenzo said as Blake retained a good distance from him by stepping back around the old clock mechanism that was standing on the floor.

"You mean hiding for a long time. What's it been? Ten years?"

"If you hadn't fought like a fucking cur, we would have finished this ten years ago and it wouldn't have had to wait.

You would have been long gone – just another meal to me."
Then Vincenzo let his sword speak as he struck out again, and
Blake moved on his heels along the wall, dodging, ducking
and parrying as best he could, watching for Vincenzo to make
a mistake.

"Vincenzo, you're the mongrel cur hiding in the shadows
and preying like a parasite on those who deserve better. You're
the coward who doesn't dare face your own judgment."
Vincenzo pulled his sword back, and as he did, the bells above
them tolled eight o'clock, making it pointless for Vincenzo to
retort as the sound of the bells filled the room. He swung his
sword, pouring all his anger into one devastating blow. Rather
than parry, Blake let himself fall to the ground, Vincenzo's
sword missing his head by an inch and instead connecting
with the power cables that ran into the fuse box on the wall
next to him. The circuit shorted, the bells stopped ringing and
the tower lights died out. As the current ran through
Vincenzo's sword, Astrid's body flinched and cramped up.
Blake dropped his makeshift weapon and made a run for the
stairs. Vincenzo's senses flickered in and out of reminiscence
as the electricity jolted his new body and the blue flash of
sparks illuminated the small room. Blake was well on his way
down the stairs when Vincenzo regained his composure and
resumed the chase.

"You know we are the same, you and I!" Vincenzo yelled.
"Both undead and each in our own way fighting to avoid the
judgment the gods would have passed on us. We have just
chosen to serve different masters." Vincenzo could hear that

he was closing in on Blake, having the advantage of the smaller body in the narrow staircase.

"Except you serve your own desires and harm those who do not deserve to be harmed!" Blake called back as he reached the bottom of the stairs and entered the antechamber. He ran for the nave with Vincenzo close behind.

"It is your desire and hope, rather than your intellect, that has convinced you to believe in angels in the hearts of men." Vincenzo swung at Blake who just managed to outrun Vincenzo and his sword. Then Blake pretended to trip, diving forward. As he landed in the aisle, he slid the last few feet until he stopped and turned, now lying next to the first bench on the right-hand side of the aisle. Vincenzo moved to take advantage of Blake's situation and he jumped into a frenzied stab, raising his sword high above his head. Blake reached out and pulled his katana from underneath the bench. Drawing the sword and striking in one fluent movement, Blake cut through half of Astrid's arm as Vincenzo descended upon him, effectively stopping the attack and causing Vincenzo to tumble forward past Blake. They both rose to their feet at the same time, but holding his katana, Blake knew that the odds had been evened out. "Beck, you fucking fool. Why won't you see that the universe is not a place of good or evil? It is a vicarious existence where you devour or are consumed. This is the way it is. It's the way it has always been! Have you seen them? Feeding on each other's misfortune and tragedies, striving not to better themselves, but rather floating through life seeking contentment in the fact that others are worse off than themselves. I feed on them, like they feed on each other." As Vincenzo raised his blade, so did Blake.

"Have you just come here to talk, or is it that being a woman has done this to you, you piece of shit?" Blake retorted.

"You . . . I'll have you writhe as I consume your damned soul!" Vincenzo yelled, running towards Blake and striking out at his neck. Blake barely managed to stop the force of the blow, causing him to shift his balance. As he did, Vincenzo kicked Blake square in the chest, sending him scuttling backwards. Blake fought to regain his composure and Vincenzo struck again, sending sparks flying as Blake parried his blade at the last moment before Vincenzo would have cut him down. Blake lingered, appearing unsteady on his feet and taken aback by the force of the blow while he imperceptibly shifted his weight to prepare for a final strike. As Vincenzo took advantage of Blake's seemingly vulnerable position and dived in to strike, Blake pulled his katana up, putting all possible force in the attack. Just before Vincenzo's sword reached Blake, his katana connected with Astrid's abdomen, cutting her body in two and halting Vincenzo's advance as he came tumbling down over a nearby row of benches, roaring and cursing Blake. "You goddamn bastard, Beck! This isn't over yet!" Vincenzo yelled, his words echoing in Astrid's voice between the thick walls of the cathedral.

"You're damn right it isn't!"

"I'll see you in hell!" Vincenzo bellowed, his voice distorting and twisting as his soul was forced to leave Astrid's mangled body.

CHAPTER 6

- PLAY DEAD -

I

Astrid opened her eyes feeling disoriented and hurt by the great injustice that had befallen her. "Thank God I survived," she thought, deciding that she'd better head for the hospital that was just beyond the cemetery. Afraid to hurt herself further, she got off the ground slowly and tried to get her bearings. Much to her surprise, her back didn't hurt. "Goddammit!" she exclaimed to the darkness, cursing the bitch who she assumed had robbed her and almost killed her. Then Astrid started walking towards the hospital, eyeing the distant lights of the surrounding town. As she walked, it slowly dawned on her that something was off – in fact, outright wrong. Someone had removed each and every tombstone, turning the cemetery into a rather fashionable park. Her feeling of disorientation quickly turned into denial, and Astrid looked all the way around, examining the city skyline. "Where's the harbor?!" she burst out, looking for the harbor that stretched out below the cemetery. The harbor was about the size of the rest of the city, so it was usually pretty hard to miss. "Where the hell am I?!" she cried out to the darkness as she stumbled slowly onwards with no conscious aim. Her heart jumped when she saw a figure moving in the dark – a robe-clad figure that was walking straight towards her. Part of her wanted to greet the figure and run to it for help. But instead she screamed. She screamed until the clear, high pitch of her voice died out and she began to cry. Astrid sat down on the pathway and hugged her knees, ignoring the figure that was coming towards her. She had a profound feeling that somehow it did not matter at all.

"Come on, miss. Get up," the robed figure said in a friendly female voice. Astrid looked up with the disgruntled look of a young girl whose pain wasn't being acknowledged.

"What?" Astrid sniffled. "Who are you? And where the hell are we?"

"Well, if you let me, I'll show you. But you'll have to get up," the woman said. Astrid grunted and wiped her eyes with the sleeve of her coat, offering out her right arm so the woman could help her off the cold ground. The woman pulled her to her feet. "My name is Victoria. Pleased to meet you." She pulled back the hood of her dark robe, revealing pearly white skin and delicately aged features framed by a mane of flowing, curly red hair, albeit slightly greying.

"Likewise," Astrid said, clearly not pleased at all. Then they began walking slowly down the path. "I'm Astrid, by the way, and I think I might need a doctor." Then she began to cry. "I was assaulted, and for a moment I thought I was going to die." Victoria put an arm around Astrid to comfort her. "It was some crazy bitch who just came up the path and suddenly attacked me. I think she stabbed me in the back. And I might have banged my head because my mind keeps playing tricks on me." Astrid looked at Victoria. "Would you help me get to the emergency room? The hospital is just beyond the cemetery."

"My dear, I don't think you need a doctor," Victoria said, trying to soften the blow to come.

"But . . . I . . ." Astrid continued, becoming more agitated, "Didn't you hear me?! I was assaulted. I almost died!!!" Victoria hushed her like a mother comforting her daughter.

"I'm sorry, Astrid, but you didn't almost die. You died."

"What!? That can't be right. I'm not supposed to . . . I still have to . . ." But no matter what words of denial came across her lips, there was no convincing herself. She knew it was true as soon as Victoria said it. She stopped talking and began crying again, seeking refuge in the folds of Victoria's robe. Astrid cried and Victoria let her. Victoria knew that, given time, Astrid would stop crying and start to ask questions instead, and Victoria was in no hurry as she had an eternity to spend. But it didn't take that long. After a few minutes, Astrid lifted her head from the folds of Victoria's robe and looked at her. "Who are you?" Astrid asked in a low voice.

"I am one of the angels of death and I have been sent here to welcome you into Shades." Astrid sniffled. Then she straightened her back and frowned, giving Victoria the classic inquisitorial look.

"Like an afterlife?" Astrid had a hard time believing that she was seriously asking that question. She had never really believed in eternal life. When asked, she usually replied that her rational mindset had a hard time allowing for the belief in gods, metaphysics and eternal life, but that she hoped they existed. She was not so much a believer as a hoper, but she always added the disclaimer that she was prepared to offer her unreserved apology for her lack of faith if she ever stood before God or any other celestial being for judgment. Although, she had always planned on offering up the argument that metaphysics was unreasonable and thus not believable to anyone who lived by reason rather than emotion. To Astrid, any existing metaphysics would have to be considered either an error of judgment on the celestial part, or a pretty sick joke, seeing as mankind had been endowed with the power of reason. "I'm sorry I didn't have faith, but I hope you won't hold that against me. Because I have to say, it's rather hard for a creature of reason to believe in a – I'm sorry to say – rather unreasonable setup. There is nothing in the school of reason or natural sciences that would allow for this to be credible, let alone reasonable." Astrid thought more about it. "How the hell was I to know?!" she asked.

"You weren't. That's the whole point. It's called *faith* not *knowledge*." Victoria smiled.

"But ..."

"And while it all may have seemed to be unreasonable and illogical in life, remember life is just one point of view, and no matter where you stand, you will never be able to see the full picture because you're in it. And trust me," she paused to underline her point, "it does make sense in the whole."

"Hmm." Astrid abandoned the topic, still not wholly

convinced, although the woman – merely by existing – had a strong case.

"So where am I?"

"You are in Shades, the place where all souls go when their lives end. Here you will spend a good deal of time waiting for your paperwork to go through and for the powers that be to decide your further destiny on the grounds of your existence up to this point."

"Like a sort of heavenly bureaucracy?" Astrid's puzzled expression was met with a friendly laugh.

"You might say that."

"So, I just wait here and play dead or what?"

"If you want to. Or you can come with me to the halfway house where I have booked you a room until you can get yourself settled. Most other souls sort of live on while they wait – doing what they know."

"I just live on?"

"Of course not. You're dead, so none of this matters in the same way as it did before, but you make passing the time more pleasant until the judgment is over."

"Then what?" They started walking down the pathway towards the city lights.

"Well, after some time – usually a couple of decades these days because life has gotten so crowded – all the formalities have been sorted and you will receive your judgment, which will be one of two things: either they offer to send you on to an afterlife or you're stranded here.

"Like, forever?!"

"Yes." Victoria's smile faded.

"What happens then? I just get eternal life?"

"Should that be your judgment, I will let you see for yourself as time goes by. I really couldn't – and shouldn't – start to describe what eternity is like."

"So where are we going?" Astrid asked, feeling that she should probably let the subject of eternity rest for now.

"I have booked you into a nearby halfway house with some of the other new arrivals in this part of the Entrance, which is the part of Shades we are in now." Astrid didn't really answer, but hummed her acknowledgement and followed Victoria, all the while trying to grasp the concept of being dead and the fact that there was an afterlife, after all. A thought dawned on her, materializing out of the fact that Victoria said that some souls were sentenced to stay in Shades for eternity. Her mind creaked as a plan began to form. She suddenly knew what she would be doing while waiting for her judgment.

"Victoria?"

"Yes?"

"So, some of the souls here in Shades . . ."

"Yes?"

"Some of them are really old?"

"Yes."

"Even medieval?"

"Some date all the way back to the dawn of man. Why?"

"Oh. There is just someone I would like to meet!"

Teresa walked down the corridors that led to the servant's quarters of the castle, tending to her usual household business. She hadn't spoken a word with the Earl for days, let alone felt his affectionate touch. The last time she saw him was the night of her row with Bahij when spite had led her to the Earl's bed as much as love. Now, in the Earl's absence, she occupied herself by paying attention to her duties that she had borderline neglected on more than one occasion over the last couple of weeks when she had strayed with the Earl. Yet a fire burning in her stomach and a knot in her throat grew relentlessly, as Teresa was a jealous creature who could be as fierce and hateful as she could be gentle and loving. Her mind told her that she was not about to let the Earl wander off to other pastures, let alone make a fool of her, while her heart – clouded by infatuation and love – constantly tried to convince her that he surely had good reason for his absence. As she passed by a window, she saw him standing in the corner of the courtyard talking to a fledgling vampire who had been dead only a decade. Teresa stopped and watched her beloved through the stained glass. The Earl had reined in his usual flamboyant behavior, talking and gesturing low as if – for once – he was trying to not draw attention to himself. Clearly angered by the young vampire's reply, the Earl slapped him across the cheek with his glove before handing him a small scroll case and sending him away. Teresa stood and watched the two part, feeling the anger well up inside. As the young vampire headed for the stables, Teresa left her duties behind and hurried down the corridor intent on catching the young man before he headed out with what were undoubtedly gentle and poetic words of love from the Earl to her rival. Why else the secrecy and discretion of a messenger?

She reached the stables as the young man was saddling up his steed and getting ready to ride out. He didn't notice Teresa until she was standing right behind him.

"Boy!" She felt her anger shift towards the young man, as he was, in her eyes, as guilty of the imminent betrayal as the Earl himself. Startled, he turned around, leaving the saddle and bridle resting loosely on the back of the beast.

"Mistress Ammon." He bowed.

"What is your business, errand boy, in the stables and house that belong to *Him*?"

"I . . ." The young man paused, but Teresa did not leave him time to find the words he was looking for. Instead, she slapped him hard across the cheek where a slight discoloration already told of the meeting with the Earl's glove just minutes before.

"Spare me your lies, boy!" She stepped forward to rip the scroll case from his belt strap, but the boy took a step back and out of her reach.

"Mistress Ammon, I assure you . . ." he tried.

"Give me the case! I know what you are hiding, and if you do not comply, I shall see that your punishment will equal that of the Earl's!" Teresa yelled, letting her anger spill over. Her eyes lit up and her face distorted as she bared her fangs. Deep down, she knew that it was an empty threat as there was no punishment to be served for breaking hearts, save that which could be meted out by the scorned lover. But if her suspicions proved true, she knew that she would do everything in her power to ruin the Earl and all who aided him. And empty or not, the threat worked.

"I . . ." The young man started to loosen the scroll case to give it to Teresa. "Mistress Ammon, I am but a messenger for the Earl who was asked to deliver a case, the contents of which I know nothing of." Hissing at the boy like a snake warding off its enemies, Teresa reached out and ripped the scroll case from his belt as he fiddled with the strap. As she pulled the lid off the case and took out the paper within, she eyed the boy, who stood silently by his horse, saying less than nothing. Then she reverted her eyes to the paper and read the Earl's script, her hands trembling. She felt dirty and betrayed, angry and full of hatred. All her love turned to loathing and she despaired at the thought that she had been so reckless. So naive. So easy. She read the final words through a veil of tears, finding not words of love, but words of betrayal. She had been the one who had made it possible, she thought to herself, realizing that she was perhaps as guilty as the Earl. Just as he had betrayed her trust, she had betrayed Bahij.

"Leave!" she yelled, and the young man scurried past her as quickly as he could. She slumped down with her back against the wall, sitting down quietly in the straw that had been strewn on the floor of the stalls. As the horse anxiously trotted around in anticipation of a ride, Teresa wept. She wept in anger at the Earl's betrayal, and finally, she wept at her own folly.

III

Astrid slept late, dozing in the mystical, half-pretend sleep of the dead. She had stayed up half the night with Victoria, getting to grips with the notions and implications of being dead. Astrid had been set up in the halfway house in a room reminiscent of a small, lightly furnished room in a midrange hotel. The city bore some striking resemblances to Astrid's hometown in life, and according to Victoria, there was a large congregation of Scandinavian souls in the area. Astrid had tried to get Victoria to tell her as much about Shades as possible, but when it came to the subject of the other lands, Victoria closed up like an oyster out of water. However, Astrid had been able to coax a few vital pieces of information from her, such as the fact that the Medieval was located due north of the part of the Entrance where Astrid had arrived. By the time Astrid got out of bed, she had already made up her mind. Why content herself with the bleak pretend life in death when she had the opportunity to witness the past that she had studied for years – or at least witness the shadow thereof. She got dressed and shoveled in her breakfast before grabbing a coat from the hanger on her way out – a coat she assumed had to be hers as this was her room. In the hallway outside, she pressed the button for the elevator and stood still for as long as it took for her to realize that it had to be out of order because no elevator could take that long to climb a four-story building. "They've thought of everything," she said to herself as she headed down the stairs, annoyed and amused at the same time.

Outside the building, she headed down the street towards the town center. It took about an hour before she found what she was looking for. On the street, outside a small first-floor shop, she saw a sign saying "Noah's Costume Rental." She went in and climbed the flight of stairs that led to the store. Inside, she fought her way through a maze of costumes on hangers and in cardboard boxes, feeling as if she was being attacked by pirates, samurai, go-go girls and cartoon figures all at the same time.

"Hello?" Astrid called out.

"Oh, hello! Just come through here," a man's voice replied.

"I'm trying!" she jested, but there was no immediate response. Finally, she reached the man to whom the voice belonged. He was standing behind a sewing table, stitching up a rip in a two-man horse costume. He looked tired and weary, wearing a suit of clothes that Astrid first thought to be a costume itself. But soon she realized that this man – who was about thirty-five, she guessed – had probably died in the mid 1990s and still insisted on retaining the cool, hip clothing style of his youth. It was a style that reminded Astrid of the golden age of Wham! with only a few modifications.

"What can I do for you?" he asked with a labored smile.

"Well, I'm going to this medieval reenactment and I'm out looking for a costume," Astrid replied.

"OK. Let's see what I can do for you. What are you going to be?"

"Sorry?"

"What's your place in the reenactment? Harlot or

241

housewife?" He gave her a stern look, letting her know that he had little time to waste, although it seemed to Astrid that he probably had all the time in the world.

"I'm going to be a maid at the manor," was the first thing that popped to mind and out of her mouth.

"Well, I think I might have the right thing back here. Give me a minute or two," he said before heading deeper into the labyrinth, leaving Astrid with little choice but to oblige. About five minutes later he returned with a roughly textured, earth-colored garment, complete with underskirts, a headdress, shoes, belt and all the accessories. "Now all we have to do is see if those hips fit," he said as he laid the costume on the counter. Astrid had already removed her jacket while he was away in the back room, and she quickly slipped the dress over her head. "It seems to fit well enough," he grunted under his breath. "I guessed you are a size 38," he said as he handed her the leather boots.

"That's about right," Astrid replied as she sat down on a nearby stool, shoes in hand, to try the boots on. When the outfit was fully donned, she walked to the tall mirror on the wall to have a look. She looked like one of the women she had seen so often in the illustrations of her history books. "It's perfect. I'll take it!" As Astrid began removing the clothes, the man walked over to a small counter with an antique cash register.

"How long do you need the clothes?"

"Uhhhm . . . Through the weekend," she said, not quite

recalling which day of the week it was.

"Well, I will bill you until Monday then and take a security deposit that will be refunded when the clothes are returned in good order."

"OK," Astrid said, feeling up her pockets and wondering how she was going to pay for anything. She grabbed her jacket and gave it a pat, locating a wallet in the side pocket. Paying in cash, she put the change back in her wallet as the man folded up the clothes and put them in a plastic shopping bag. Astrid grabbed the bag and headed out of the maze of clothing, offering up a simple "thanks" which found no reply. As she headed out, she thought about whether or not she was going to need to pack food and drinks or perhaps even a tent, but then decided against it. She guessed that it was not like she could die of thirst or anything like that anymore. Instead, she headed north out of town, thumbing down a car heading in the same direction. She could hardly believe that she might get to meet Bernt Notke in person.

IV

Teresa sat in the stables for hours until her despair had matured into resolve. She brushed her clothes and straightened her hair before leaving the stables and the castle behind, hurrying to the Earl's home in the Baroque quarter. She didn't knock or announce herself, but rather flung open the street door and hurried up the stairs, leaving the door to close itself at its own leisure.

"John! You *will* see me now!" she yelled, allowing her words to precede her to whatever room he was in. As she raged to his study and found it empty, she heard a rustle from the bedroom down the hall, a place she had so enjoyed visiting on previous occasions. When she made it down the corridor, she found the Earl coming towards her wearing only a white lace shirt, leaving his privates to dangle vulgarly at her.

"My dear! Pray tell what has gotten you into this dreadful state and what I may do to relieve you of said ailment." He smiled at her. For the first time, Teresa saw his smile for what it was. It was not charming or endearing, but arrogant and playful – like the grin of a cat toying with a mouse.

"You bastard!" she yelled at him, forcefully attempting to wipe the smile off his face with the stroke of her hand. "You son of a whore! Your mother must have bedded the devil with buggery and born you out of her arse to bear such a filth as you!" She could feel the tears pressing on, but still anger overcame sadness.

"Oh joy! To hear such words from such a noble and pretty mouth." His laugh made her even more furious. "What manner of abomination has made you capable of such words?"

"YOU!" Teresa screamed, holding out the scroll case. The Earl's smile stiffened and faded like dew evaporating in the sun.

"How did you acquire that?"

"I took it off your lackey, who, mind you, is still obliged to obey me in our master's house, whether or not he has sold his soul to you and your deceitful ways. And to think that I merely sought your written words out of jealous thoughts and fear that I might find that you had another."

"To find that out, you need not look in letters, but rather in my bed." As soon as the words were out of his mouth, Teresa moved to slap his face again, but this time the Earl caught her wrist and forced her to abandon her endeavor.

"How could you manage such betrayal and yet make yourself out to be so kind? How can a mind as sharp as yours find its way to betray your family like this? And me?" The tears began to run down her cheeks.

"My dear. Are you really so naive? So slow, as to really not know why?" He looked at her with eyes that conquered what power was left in her, resigning her to be at the mercy of his words. "I act not to favor or betray, but to stay alive. You think I betray our family as I write Dæth and tell him what you have told me. You think I betray you, like you betrayed your beloved Bahij – and you ask me why? I act because I have to. I play dead! I play the part because it is what the play calls for. Where you act to ingratiate and further yourself, I act not for my own sake, but for the sake of the play. I play dead because it stops the hurting. I play dead to escape the boredom of eternity, and without the joy of that, I would prefer absence of existing as this would at least set me free of the boredom and trivialities of being. I have and never will take the spectator's seat or that of the lowly actor! I direct my own play for the better story. Always. Like I have done now by telling Dæth of Bahij's discoveries and plans, allowing the suspense and tension to build rather than to dissipate by way of an uneven game. Like I have seduced you and guided you to my bed, making myself a rival to Bahij and thus making your relationship much more interesting than the passionless and unspoken affection you previously harbored – like that of an old married couple unable to speak words of love out of fear for the response." He paused and looked at her beaten figure. "I play dead to best the trivialities and boredom of eternal death and to offer the better story – often at my own expense lest I be a hypocrite. You and all your fellows, whom you call our family, wander aimlessly from one feeding to another, postponing the inevitable and fleeing from the end rather than walking towards it knowing and smiling. You built a stage, but dare not act upon it. You claim to serve and uphold your precious principles and rules, yet in the darkness of the chamber, it takes nothing more than a simple prick to wrest your secrets from you. That's all it took to lead you astray and turn you from the narrow path of honor and unto the beaten path of betrayal. You who claim to serve so easily betray, yet you accuse me in much stronger terms than you do yourself. I make no pretense of serving others than myself, and thus can hardly be said to have betrayed anyone at all."

"You liar! You said you loved me!"

"No. I claimed to make love to you, an act that I find unlikely for you to deny to have taken place. I spoke to my lover, not my beloved. You listened to what you wanted to hear rather than to the words I spoke."

"You betrayed me and our family!"

"No, I made you no promise that what you told me would be kept private. You betrayed Bahij, who in turn betrayed *Him*. I did not betray you, but merely by my act sought to make the possible consequences of your actions actual. I merely made sure that your betrayal carried weight and got to play the part it deserved. And that is also why you will never tell, for it will hurt both you and Bahij much more than I. For while you will regret your ways all the way to the gallows, I will dangle with a smile on my face, certain that I played my part to the fullest."

"I . . ." The hatred burned inside her, but she knew the battle had been lost.

"My dear, I know you yearn for revenge, but let me tell you that you will not take it now. That would not be true to you. You will go away plotting, and only time will tell whether it heals your wounds or offers you the pleasure of a long-awaited vengeance." She looked at him with the full fury of a woman scorned, finding a mixture of amusement and slight pity in his eyes, which angered her even more. She slapped him hard across the cheek, allowing her nails to rip at his features like the claws of a cat, and he did nothing to stop it.

"This is not the end of it!" she yelled in his face before leaving with the last word. The Earl stood still, looking down the corridor until he heard the outer door slam shut. Then he raised one hand to his cheek, feeling the scarring gashes that would undoubtedly leave her mark for prosperity and feeling his crotch with the other. He felt his member, half stiff and soon ready for more. Then he returned to his bed.

CHAPTER 7

- DO YOU LOVE ME? -

I

"Butler!" Blake hailed Elijah who was on his way down the hall to the servant's quarters of Dæth's mansion. Carrying an arrangement of used china on a tray, Elijah stopped and turned and made his way towards Blake with a controlled, almost majestic, stride.

"Sir," Elijah nodded, discretely indicating that it was not due to a lack of will, but rather the presence of the tray that he did not make his customary bow. Blake produced a slightly crumpled piece of paper from his trouser pocket and placed it on the tray.

"Elijah?"

"Sir?"

"Would you be so kind as to bring this to the lady of the house?"

"Of course, Mr. Beck." Balancing the tray in his left hand, Elijah lifted a china saucer and slid the note underneath.

"And need I say that . . ."

"Not at all, sir," Elijah cut him off. Despite Elijah making every effort to maintain his professional demeanor, it was clear to Blake that Elijah found the situation uncomfortable and did not approve of Blake's affairs, nor his choice to involve Elijah in them.

"Thank you. This is very important to me. I won't forget it." Blake tried to smooth the waters.

"Quite, sir. Now would that be all you require from me tonight, or may I be of further assistance to you?"

"No, thanks. That's all."

"Then I bid you a good night, sir." The words were barely out of his mouth before Elijah turned and headed towards the kitchen, leaving Blake to ponder how Elijah managed to carry a full tray of porcelain without even the slightest rattling. The house was quiet, save for the distant, delicate sound of skillful hands caressing a grand piano. Blake closed his eyes and listened. He felt the distant, dark tune envelop him from afar, the minor keys trying to pry open the lock on the deepest parts of his soul. Slowly and quietly, he walked to the coatrack and put on his trench coat before picking up his hat. He ran his thumb across the brim of the fedora, savoring the feel of the felt as if it was a lover's skin. As he opened the door and felt the cold autumn winds invade the hall, he reverently put on his hat and walked into the darkness and away from the sorrowful ivory moans of the piano.

In his note, Blake had asked Marie to meet him about a mile away on the moot hill that overlooks the mansion grounds. He had chosen to summon her there because he felt sure that it was a place where they would be far enough away from both prying eyes and overactive ears. As he walked across the lawns, he felt the first bite of frost. He saw the bony white moon with its frozen halo beyond the thin, wild brush strokes of clouds high in the sky, promising him a cold and sober night. He followed his shadow up the hill, and he sat down on one of the heavy boulders of the moot circle placed there ages ago by souls now long gone. "Probably to the catacombs," he thought as he sat down, fastening his gaze on the distant lights of the rural village a few miles off. He sat there alone while the silvery stars crept across the sky, and he felt the cold of the night etch through him. He saw lonely torches floating through the night as villagers gathered in the church. Those souls were still so close to life that they yet harbored the hope of redemption or even salvation. He closed his eyes for a second and found himself pitying them, and as the ringing of the church bells filled the night, all Blake heard were accusations. The rustle of cloth pulled him back, and as he got up and turned around, there was Marie standing before him dressed in the shadows of Victorian lace, cast in the light of her hooded lantern.

"Blake."

"Marie." He tried to find the words that he had rehearsed over and over again in his mind, but standing in front of her, he found none.

"Why did you want to meet like this? I thought we . . ."

"Stop!" He cut her off and stepped towards her. "I need to ask you to come back. To reconsider. To come to your senses because in every fleeting glimpse of your eyes, I see you struggling to be free. Fighting to let yourself love me."

"I don't." She shielded herself.

"That's fucking crap and you know it!" He didn't mean to yell, but he did, drawing tears to her eyes. "Don't you tell me that you love him and that you don't wish that we could spend eternity together – in Hell or not. It was clear as day when you walked in on Dæth and me. I know it. You know it, and he goddamn well knows it. And he is using it to keep both of us in line." The words died out, leaving silence in their wake as her tears broke through.

"I . . ." she started, but nothing more came. As she covered her face with her hands, the lantern fell to the ground, breaking the glass and extinguishing the fire. She sat down on the rocks. Blake walked over and sat down next to her, and after a moment's contemplation, he put his arm around her.

"Marie, I'm sorry."

"Why can't you just leave me be?" She looked up at him angrily before helplessly pounding him with her fists. "Why? You know it's too late. You just keep making it hurt more!" She sobbed as he grabbed her arms and held her tight.

"Marie," Blake said, feeling her slowly relax before he loosened his grip and left her to rest against his chest. "Marie, it's not too late. It never is. It just costs more. I know that I will spend an eternity here burning in the fires of my own conscience, and while I do, I know that being with you will offer me some relief. Your love will offer me the closest thing I will know to redemption and rest, and I hope that I may in turn offer you the same. That's the reason why I've come here." She wiped her eyes as she sat up and looked at him.

"No. You have come to doom me by asking me to make the choice I cannot." He let go of her and got up. "By asking me to choose," she finished.

"Dammit, Marie! I'm not the bad guy here – he is! And you will never be free of him if you don't break free now! But even worse, you will never be free of your own fears. The same goddamn fears that kept us apart right from the start. Now is the chance to turn around and make it as right as can be!"

"You don't know what you're talking about!" she yelled at him, getting up to make a stand.

"Listen Marie. I'm sorry – I'm not here to fight. I'm not here to blame you, let alone to claim that I am without fault in this." He stepped towards her. "I just need you to know that I love you and that I always will. And that I will face the fires of Hell willingly, as long as we do it together. Hell, I might even wear a smile!"

"Blake," she implored, never finishing her sentence as Blake moved in to kiss her. He kissed away her tears before letting their lips meet. They both allowed the kiss to linger as long as possible, and then she kissed him goodbye. A heavy silence broke out, wedging between them, until Blake spoke.

"Marie, I promise you this. This will be the last time I ask." He paused again and held her gaze. "Do you love me? Do you love me like I love you?" For a moment the words filled their world. Then she smiled a bittersweet smile and tilted her head.

"I do . . . But I can't." He looked at her, eyes narrowed and head slightly shaking, slowly peeling away any dignity she had left as he let his eyes bore through her. She felt herself shrinking and she tried to shield herself with a helpless smile that – if anything – only made matters worse. "Blake, I'm sorry." She straightened her back and tried to regain her composure as Blake turned his back on her and gave her leave.

"Don't excuse yourself, Marie. You've made no promises and I can't lay any claim to you. I simply offered you love and you turned it down." He looked at the moon hanging low in the clear sky, all battered and mangled.

"Blake . . ." She reached out to him.

"Marie, don't," he said, halting her advance.

"I really am sorry," she tried.

"Marie . . . No more." He lifted his hand into half a wave, shunning her while offering her a last goodbye at the same time. Neither of them said anything more. While Blake looked towards the dark horizon and listened to the distant chapel bells ring out, Marie turned and headed downhill towards the mansion, too busy with her own grief to notice the figure heading up the hill not a hundred yards away. She looked back at Blake through a veil of tears only to see his back against the ominous backdrop of the bone-colored moon. She wiped away her tears with an embroidered handkerchief, feeling like Sisyphus watching the boulder rolling down the side of the mountain for the very first time.

Marie was well away when Blake turned around, thinking that he was alone. But rather than finding privacy, he found Harlan McCoy standing there resting one boot on a boulder.

"So, are you done?" McCoy asked before licking the rolling paper and rolling up his cigarette.

"What?"

"Is it over?"

"Yes. It is."

"Good." Blake knew it was, at least from McCoy's point of view, but nevertheless, the remark annoyed him.

"What do you want, Harlan?" Blake sneered as he put on his fedora and snapped the brim.

"I want you to stop chasing skirt and focus on what you are doing. We brought you here for a reason and I need you to have a clear head. I need my best man on this and, unfortunately, right now that's you."

"So, spill it. What do you need me for?"

"I need you to go to Kaizerheim in the Medieval. I need you to find Notke and his *Danse Macabre*, and I need you to make sure that the agents of Mr. Ferre don't get there first." Blake pulled half a pack of delicately crumbled cigarettes from his trench coat pocket and lit one. "Can you do that, Mr. Beck?"

"Sure." Blake blew out the smoke, letting it fill the night air like a lone phantom, slowly drifting away. "Might as well."

II

Bahij was sitting in a chair by Vincenzo's bed in Aquraa Castle when Blake cut down Astrid's body and sent Vincenzo back to Shades. As Vincenzo immaterialized behind the wavering curtains of the canopy bed, Bahij looked at him with a stern gaze, saying nothing until he sat up.

"Well?" Bahij said, taking Vincenzo completely by surprise, leaving him little time to gather his thoughts and quench his anger.

"I . . ."

"Has Beck been taken care of? Or, judging from the look in your eyes, am I right in assuming that you have failed again?"

"He . . ." Vincenzo wasn't able to find the words he needed because there were simply no words that would excuse him. But soon the silence forced him to admit his failure. "You are right. Beck has been neither defeated nor devoured as I had promised he would be," Vincenzo replied in a vain attempt to somewhat redeem himself by taking his defeat as a man and admitting to it. Bahij let his failure dangle there for a while.

"How is it that you keep disappointing Mr. Ferre and yet keep counting on his mercy and blessing?" Bahij asked, rising from the chair and turning his back on Vincenzo as he walked over to the window.

"It was not my intention to disappoint *Him* or you, my lord."

"I care not for your intentions, only for your actions. Now get up!"

"My lord," Vincenzo said as he got out of bed and straightened up, standing with his back against the wall.

"I have no more patience for you, Vincenzo! But our Lord is merciful in his love for all his children, so you will be offered one last chance of redemption – and one last chance for revenge."

"Thank you, my lord! I will not fail you again." Bahij turned around and walked towards Vincenzo.

"Well, only time will grant us the blessing of knowing if you will persevere. But know this – if you fail to do my bidding, you will be alone. *He* will revoke his blessing and you will be food to his children like all others," Bahij said in a low, controlled voice, letting his eyes reveal the flaming anger Vincenzo would invoke should he fail *Him* again.

III

After her visit to Noah's Costume Rental, Astrid hitched a ride that took her all the way to a small town on the outskirts of the Entrance. From there she made her way on an old, battered bicycle that she found abandoned by a streetlight. Finally, she reached the dead end of the road where the souls of the Entrance halt their advance and the borderlands take over. She even made it beyond. She left the bicycle behind on the last stretch of asphalt and walked off into the uncultivated fields of the borderlands without knowing that it ought to be impossible for her – a simple soul, blessed with neither dark nor light magic. The sky whispered to her that she did not belong there, while the blades of grass clawed at her boots in a vain attempt to halt her advance, but it made little difference. Astrid walked relentlessly onwards and soon found herself in the Medieval without even knowing it. Days passed, wilderness turning into fields and paths becoming dirt tracks before she saw any sign of life. One afternoon, while walking along a track running between stubble fields and small congregations of trees, Astrid came over a hill and saw a small, rickety cart tied to a grey mule that was busy eating oats from an old leather feedbag. An old, slovenly man sat by the side of the road chewing through some dried meat and stale bread, which were softened by a dip into a mug of ale to let the man's remaining teeth chew the food. The man eyed her, but Astrid kept her pace despite feeling the weight of his gaze on her chest. As she neared the cart, the man yelled to her.

"What's a woman like you doing out here all alone, far from the safe bosom of her husband?" The man spoke in a low-German dialect, which Astrid partially recognized from her studies. She walked over to the man before engaging in the conversation, and she prepared herself for the most realistic role-playing game she had ever played. She decided not to excuse herself, but to use her lack of a husband to her advantage.

"My husband is dead by the plague, and consequently, I have been taken into the employ of the Duke of Niederwald-Saxonberg as a chambermaid. My cousin who is a cook in his lordship's household has arranged it. Now, I'm heading for his lordship's mansion in the city, but I seem to have lost my way." She spoke with conviction despite the fact that she was sure that his lordship the Duke of Niederwald-Saxonberg had just been born wholly out of her imagination. The man looked at her and snorted before wiping a cocktail of beer and beef from his beard with the front of his mantle.

"My apologies, madam. The plague took from us all, reminding us that we are all sinners by both our own deeds and the deeds of our fathers." He looked down at the piece of dried meat softening in the dark ale, appearing to contemplate whether to offer Astrid a bite to accompany his apology. However, if that was his thought, he decided against it and instead raised the mug to his lips and drank before taking a bite of the meat, passing wind as he chewed. He looked up at Astrid.

"Can you tell me how far off I am?" she asked.

"Well . . ." A trickle of beefy ale ran from the side of his mouth as he began talking with his mouth full. "I'm headed for tomorrow's market in the city, but I'm planning to make it there by nightfall." As he didn't offer her a ride, Astrid demonstratively refrained from replying, letting the silence do all the work. It took about thirty long seconds before the man cracked with an annoyed snort, spitting out an indiscernible yellow lump before continuing. "Now if you would want a ride on the wagon, I'm sure Elfi will manage to pull the extra weight." He looked at her, squinting his eyes.

"That would be very nice, thank you," Astrid said with a smile before walking over to the mule and patting it on the back. "I hope it's alright with you, Elfi." The mule whinnied and nodded. She looked over her shoulder towards the old man, who had just about finished his lunch. "Should I remove the feedbag?" Astrid called to him. He reminded her of the mule as he nodded. She bent down to remove the feedbag from the mule's muzzle, stroking its mane as she did. "It's time to move on, Elfi," she whispered to the mule and unclasped the bag. It fell heavily to the ground and spilled its remaining contents of maggots and rotten grain all over. The mule looked at her with a thankful gaze and snorted violently, forcing the last maggots from its muzzle. Astrid nearly retched and felt tears well in her eyes. She turned around and stepped between the man and the mule, drawing breath to give him a verbal lashing, the likes of which the world had never seen. But as she saw the man walking towards the mule, she found herself completely disarmed. She saw not only the absence of guilt in the man's eyes, but also a complete lack of knowledge of any wrongdoings. He'd seen the maggots and fed the mule, but seemed wholly unaware that there was anything wrong about it. The mule nudged her away and walked over to the man for a pat, leaving Astrid petrified. It had eaten the rotten grain and made no notice of it. Neither of them knew. It was as if it didn't matter to them and they had simply forgotten how it once was. She swallowed the spit that had accumulated in her mouth to lubricate her unspoken curses. The man turned to her.

"Get in the cart, madam, while I put Elfi in front. We'd better get going if we want to make it to the city by nightfall." Astrid didn't know what to say or do other than as the man asked, so she lowered her head and got in the back of the cart, finding a vacant spot between cloth-covered crates and baskets. Soon the cart rolled on down the tracks with Astrid in the back and the old man at the reins. For a long while they said nothing, as the old man seemed to have no desire for talk and Astrid was preoccupied with overcoming the image of maggots crawling out of the mule. In her mind, the maggots still filled Elfi's muzzle, silently and slowly gnawing their way deeper and deeper into the beast that was kept from the relief of death because it was already dead. Tracks became roadways, and as night fell, the cartwheels met the cobblestones of the main road leading to the city.

"Sir, how big is the city we're headed for?" Astrid asked, finally breaking the silence that only she had found uncomfortable.

"Well, it's the seat of the Holy Emperor," he said. Astrid waited for him to continue, but he said no more. She gathered that it was because the man didn't know the numbers, and she told herself that she should have known that this man probably knew neither math nor how to read or write. She decided not to speak anymore, but instead lay down to rest as best she could. An hour passed before Astrid sat up to see what the man's recently uttered, indecipherable grunts were referring to, and she saw the majestic city of Kaizerheim. Thousands of torches and braziers illuminated the miles of city wall and created a glowing halo that rose high above the countless tents and campsites that lay strewn around the fields outside the main gate.

"This is the end, madam," the man mumbled, pulling back the reins and halting the cart.

"Thank you!" Astrid said as she got off the cart. She tried to make it around the side to give Elfi a pat goodbye, but before she reached the mule, the man shook the reins and Elfi trotted along the cobblestones, leaving Astrid behind. She started off toward the city gates, keeping to the main road. As Astrid walked the last mile to the gates, campsites lying side by side on either side of the road, she could feel the eyes of those around her, their gazes scrutinizing and penetrating her soul. They paused their routines and looked at her in silence with despairing gazes, awed by the presence of a being not long bereft of true purpose and determination – something most of these people had not witnessed for centuries. Astrid kept her pace and made sure that her eyes did not linger. She saw the empty faces turn back to their own dealings, each returning to their own memories and regrets, failing to relive the details of their past properly. Like a tailor working with his needle unthreaded, each of these souls went about their business, but to no reason or consequence. She pondered their strange behavior as she walked along the cobblestones. It felt as if she had been allowed to gaze into the past, only what she found was history breaking at the seams, decaying into patches of incoherence until each soul stood alone. It took her about ten minutes to make it to the city gates, and she eyed the soldiers keeping guard outside before making her next move. They stood straight with a proud pretense, wearing heavy armor with swords sheathed and halberds resting on the ground. But walking towards them, Astrid could see that they were broken inside and that time relentlessly gnawed at their souls. As Astrid approached, a young captain stepped out of the ranks and walked towards her, raising the visor of his helmet.

"My lady," he said with a hollow smile, giving her a courteous bow that resulted in the clacking and rattle of his chain mail against the plates of his armor.

"Sir," Astrid said with a curtsy. "I would like to ask permission to enter the city."

"Then I would ask on what business, my lady?"

"I'm on my way to enter service as a chambermaid in the household of the Duke of Niederwald-Saxonberg, but for tonight I seek merely board and lodgings and the safety of the city walls." She looked at the man with an endearing smile, trying to shield herself from further inquiries into her wholly imaginary story.

"In that case, I welcome you to our city and hope that you will find all that you seek." He signaled with one hand for the guards to allow a door in the massive gate to be opened.

"Thank you, kind sir. Then may I, in turn, ask you a question before we part ways?" she asked.

"Naturally," he replied, removing his helmet completely, letting a mane of blond, curly hair loose in the wind.

"I wish to light a candle and offer prayer and thanks to our Lord for the safe passage I have had coming here. Could you please tell me the way to the cathedral?" she asked in the most pious voice she could muster.

"As a lady, I would imagine that you will want to keep to the main roads. You head on from this gate until you reach the Emperor's Walk – the stretch of road leading from the emperor's castle on your left down to the cathedral to your right. So you should have no trouble finding your way."

"Thank you, sir," Astrid said. She walked through the gate and hurried down the cobbled street with massive brick and timber-frame buildings rising around her. By this time of night, the deserted streets, alleys and pathways that crisscrossed between the houses looked like a labyrinth of shadows to Astrid. The city was bereft of life or motion, save for the flicker of a lone torch flame and stealthy shadows of the odd man or beast hurrying on. As she walked past one of the many back alleys, a coarse, mechanical rattle ripped through the night, bouncing from wall to wall. Astrid picked up her pace, and she looked down the alley and into the darkness. A hooded figure of a man coming her way stopped and looked at her with old eyes that implored her to cease. Without letting go of Astrid's eyes, he put down the cart that he was dragging. She stopped and they stood still, looking at each other and saying nothing. Although her heart screamed at her, Astrid found herself unable to tear her eyes away from the man. He looked dirty and drunk or perhaps mad. Suddenly, the man shot his right hand out from the folds of his robe, violently shaking his rattle at Astrid. Had she, in fact, not already been dead, she probably would have died of fright. Then he began to laugh at her with his mouth open wide enough for Astrid to see into the depths of his toothless maw. Pocketing his rattle, the man turned from Astrid and returned to his work of clearing the gutters and emptying the barrels of feces that lined the back alleys of the city. Astrid hurried on towards the cathedral, but despite trying, she failed to shake the visage of the man from her mind. The image of his maddened eyes and toothless maw remained locked in her mind, threatening to consume her, like a promise of what was yet to come.

IV

Late in the evening, Bahij was interrupted in his studies by his house servant who informed him that *He* wished to see Bahij. Without delay, Bahij left his home and paced through the streets of Aquraa until he found himself walking through the castle courtyard atop the hill. It was a clear and cold night and the distant moon loomed above him. He knew it was not the same moon that he had set his eyes on in life, but merely a shadow of that moon, part of this world only to maintain the illusion of death being like life – although it was nothing of the sort. He eyed Teresa heading towards the servant's quarters with two chambermaids trailing behind her. She kept her usual stride and dignified walk, but it was clear to Bahij that something had changed. She had changed. Yet he dismissed the thought of her, at least for the time being. He made his way through the castle to Mr. Ferre's private chambers, pondering the inanimate soul statues that *He* had displayed on the walkway that led to his study. Bahij knew those souls had all been chosen by *Him* as *He* had passed through the ages – each one selected for its own distinct and compelling display of sorrow and regret, the exact nature of which would forever be kept from the observer and left to the memory of the soul itself. Bahij walked in silence through the hallways until he reached Mr. Ferre's private chambers. He knocked and waited for a reply.

"Bahij, I trust it is you, my friend. Come in." His dark voice filled the world and resounded down the hallways as Bahij opened the door and walked through the antechamber.

"Yes, my Lord," Bahij called out.

"Join me in my study. We have much to attend to." As Bahij entered the study, he found *Him* relaxing in a deep leather armchair with a glass of soul and Bahij's pile of notes on the manuscripts neatly arranged on the side table next to *Him*. Bahij bowed graciously. "Please, my friend. In private, I believe we have moved past idle courtesies. Take a seat."

"I see that you have read my notes, my Lord," Bahij said as he walked over and lowered himself into the armchair on the other side of the side table, lifting his cape slightly avoid sitting uncomfortably on it.

"Yes. It was most enlightening, but before we move into the matters of the ritual itself, I must ask whether or not you have attained the minstrel's verse from the *Danse Macabre*?" *He* sipped his soul, deliberately looking at nothing, which was located just beyond the rim of his glass.

"My Lord. I am not yet in possession of the verse, but I am confident that I will be before the dawn, lest Vincenzo fail me."

"Let us hope that he does not. I would be greatly troubled by that outcome."

"I am confident that he will do all in his power to complete his task, for I have enlightened him to the consequences of failure."

"And Beck?" *He* poured Bahij a glass of soul from the crystal decanter standing underneath the table on a small shelf.

"Well, I have made sure that Vincenzo can relay his findings to me with haste, but I would be much surprised if he did not remain behind to face Beck, who is surely on his heels." Bahij nodded his thanks, closing his eyes in reverence before taking up the glass. "While I would have gone to Notke myself, I assumed that you would prefer for me to prepare for the ritual?"

"Yes."

"My Lord," Bahij started, but was promptly interrupted.

"I wish for the ritual to be held in Hel's tomb, and I wish it to be ready at nightfall tomorrow."

"I am sorry, my Lord. This tomb . . ."

"Yes. Beneath the grave mound beyond the eastern gate, I laid her tomb centuries ago on the site of the last great battle. It is where she fell and was sent into the Grey. It is where I have commemorated and honored her undeath and love, and it is where I will have her returned to me. It is where our vengeance will arise!" His eyes sparked and Bahij could feel the anger like the heat of a blazing fire.

"I've never . . ." Bahij said.

"No. No one but I has ever set foot there, but on tomorrow's eve they will. And those who attend will witness the rekindling of a fire that will burn this world into the ashes from which a new world will grow." *He* looked at Bahij, eyes flaming and wreathed in hatred. "Our world!"

"Your word is my law, my Lord. It will be done as you wish."

"I know, my friend. That is why you are the one sitting at my right hand." *He* subdued his anger and shifted, offering Bahij a discrete hint of a smile. A delicate hand knocked on the door to the antechamber. "Enter!" *He* called out.

"Yes, my Lord," Teresa replied, her voice accompanied by the sound of her heels tapping the stone floor as she made her way into the study.

"I've let Mistress Ammon summon those nobles whom I wish to have present at the ritual, and I am confident that she is merely here to inform me that this has been done." Taking a deep breath of the stale, dusty air of the study, Bahij calmed himself despite the fact that each step Teresa took towards him tore at his heart. As she entered, her confident smile stiffened when she saw the pair of them rise from their seats to greet her.

"My Lord." She curtsied, offering *Him* the smile of a daughter before she turned to Bahij to greet him. "Master Khaleel." She lowered her gaze as she curtsied again to his bow. "I did not expect to have the pleasure of your company tonight," she said with a shudder in her voice.

"Call me Bahij, please. Rather than for us to shield ourselves with titles and family names, I still wish us to be so close as to grant each other the use of our first names, no matter what words we may have exchanged in the past." He offered her a smile to relieve her of any awkwardness, but much to his regret, she did not seem to notice as her gaze was still seeking relief in the cracks of the floor.

"Mistress Ammon, I expect that you have come to tell me that the nobility has been summoned?" *He* asked, sparing both Bahij and Teresa the silence that would otherwise have followed, pulling Teresa back from her own inner darkness.

"Yes, my Lord. I have sent your word to the lords of each of the houses, as well as to those other members of the nobility that you requested."

"Good. Then there is merely one last thing before you may leave us to prepare for the feast."

"My Lord?"

"Until the feast, you will oblige Master Khaleel in any request or desire that he might have, setting his needs above your own and those of all others, save mine."

"Master," Bahij tried to enter the conversation.

"Until the feast, Master Khaleel's word is my word to you, Mistress Ammon. And his word will be done," *He* said, leaving no room for uncertainty.

"As you wish, my Lord." As her words died out, Bahij tried to catch her eyes to ensure her of his completely honorable intentions and irreproachable character, but again her attention eluded him. "My Lord. Master Khaleel." She curtsied and then turned around and walked out of the room. As they heard the door close, *He* turned to Bahij.

"Should you still harbor the fondness for Mistress Ammon of which you have previously spoken, it seems now is the time to heed my words, my friend: the only man who stands in a higher favor to a woman than her lover is the man who saves her from herself." Bahij lowered his eyes, knowing full well that *He* was right, but uncertain of his own desires and ability to save her. "Alas, we are not here to debate the matters of a lover's quarrel, but rather the matters of the ritual," *He* said as *He* sat down and took up one of the heavy tomes from the side table.

V

It had been four days since Vincenzo had received his orders from Bahij, and Vincenzo finally reached the city of Kaizerheim with darkness falling. He had travelled across half of Shades with the knowledge that the agents of Dæth would be onto his every step, knowing that he was in great danger without a body to animate into should he need to flee into life. To draw as little attention to himself as possible, he had refrained from feeding, though his soul ached for nourishment and his mind tried to convince him that each and every soul he met along his way was a meal to be had. Wearing a simple dark robe and posing as a Franciscan monk, he glided with purpose through the camps that had been set up by traders and travelers outside the city walls. Most of the other souls ignored him, keeping to themselves, their own ailments of mind and their own private tortures. Only the odd call from an aching soul asking Vincenzo to offer God's salvation, along with the flickering flames of torches and braziers, threatened to uncover him. Vincenzo saw that the gates to the city had been closed for the night, so he made his way east along the walls until he was well away from the camps. Away from prying eyes, he stopped and looked at the damp stone face of the wall. He pulled up the sleeves of his robe and let his fingers find a minute crevice in the wall. Then Vincenzo began his climb. With a spider's ease, he scaled the wall and paused only to make sure that the parapets were clear before making the final push over the wall and onto the parapet walkway.

With the moonlight as his sole companion, Vincenzo made his way along the wall and down the nearest staircase, finding himself safely inside the city, just a stone's throw away from the cathedral. As he looked up, a black raven touched down on the roof of the cathedral, and Vincenzo noticed the Gothic spires reaching towards the dark night sky. A host of gargoyles grinned down at him – a telltale visage that revealed to Vincenzo that this was not the house of a merciful God. This was a house of God built by those who had been abandoned by God, and in a strange way, Vincenzo felt welcome. He made his way to the nearby side entrance, finding the heavy wooden door unlocked. As he pulled open the door, the hinges gave out a low moan. Inside the antechamber, the silence pressed down on him under the weight of the heavy stone vaults high above. The silence was broken by the sound of a wooden mallet masterfully directing a carving gouge through heavy wooden planks, creating bursts of sound that echoed through the cathedral.

Astrid entered the cathedral, and using her knowledge of medieval Catholicism and its rituals, she lit candles and gave thanks to several saints depicted in their own shrines lining the outer walls of the cathedral. She didn't mean anything by the prayers, nor was she seeking any degree of atonement; she was merely trying to remain inconspicuous. She quickly eyed the old craftsman who stood alone in the choir measuring and assessing the progress of the unfinished church altar. It was akin to the Aarhus altar in style, yet it far surpassed it in both execution and elaboration. Even at a distance, it was clear to Astrid that a small army of craftsmen was carrying out the work on the choir and altar, but only one man had stayed behind for the night to correct the mistakes of others and plan for the rest of the fateful eternity awaiting. As Astrid walked through the cathedral, she kept quiet and kept an eye on the man. She wanted to be sure that it was him, and if it was, she wanted to see him work without him knowing she was there. After a few minutes, the man picked up a wooden mallet and a gouge and began carving the layout of the altar's main scene. Suddenly, Astrid heard the distant grind of heavy hinges as someone opened the door in the south wing antechamber. In a matter of moments, she scaled the stairs to the pulpit and hid, safely out of sight but with a view of Notke through a small crack in the pulpit. A Franciscan monk entered the nave from the side entrance. The monk appeared to float across the floor with nothing but the barely audible sound of his robe dragging across the marble slabs to give away his presence. Her eyes followed the monk up the aisle into the choir. The monk tossed back the hood of his robe and as his voice filled the cathedral, the craftsman finally looked up.

"Notke?" the monk asked, his voice somehow familiar to Astrid. She recognized characteristics of the voice and she realized that she had, at some point, shared one of the most intimate and significant moments of her life with this monk. As her mind peeled away different parts of the voice, leaving only a sickening feeling in her stomach, she knew. Astrid knew that somehow, as impossible as it seemed to her, this man was the woman who had killed her in the graveyard just days ago. Her heart gasped, and she felt like the body she no longer had was struggling to breathe.

Notke steadied his mallet and laid down the gouge. Shaking slightly as his old knees struggled, he frowned as he rose slowly, clutching his mallet firmly in one hand.

"How come a lowly monk feels entitled to break the bishop's promise that I would not be disturbed in my work?" he snarled in an aged voice.

"My friend, I am no monk, and not even a promise from your false God would have kept me at bay."

"How dare you speak those words of our Lord . . . and even in his house! Blasphemer!" Notke raised his mallet and – though it was a feeble attempt – lunged his old body forwards. Vincenzo grabbed the old man by the wrist, revealing to the sole spectator hiding in the pulpit that this would be an uneven struggle. Holding the old man dangling by the wrist, Vincenzo moved his head in close to Notke.

"I dare speak these words because I – like you – have long since been abandoned by the gods. Like you, I have been left to fend for myself in Limbo. Left to rot. Left to pain. Left to pine for absolution. Left longing for peace. That is why I am allowed to speak such words – because your God has abandoned you to be consumed by the flames of your own conscience." He let the old man fall hard on his back among the boards and tools scattered on the floor, and Vincenzo took a step to stand over him. "But where you keep praying for mercy that will never come, attempting to atone your deeds in life by building a house already forsaken before the first stone was laid, I have chosen differently." Looking into the eyes of the old man, it was clear to Vincenzo that he was quickly quenching every last morsel of resolve, and pain and despair began spilling into the old man's gaze, narrowing his eyes.

"You are one of them?" Notke asked, his voice near the point of breaking.

"Yes, but you need not be afraid. You shouldn't be." Vincenzo's voice became friendly as he extended his hand to the old man, offering him an easy way to his feet.

"What do you want from me?" Notke took Vincenzo's hand and got up.

"I want knowledge, and in return my master offers you a last chance for the peace and absolution that you so deeply desire." Notke looked around, searching for a savior, but finding none. "My friend, you should not worry. We will not be disturbed. The bishop has made a promise, I hear." Vincenzo smiled.

"What knowledge does an old craftsman possess that could be of any interest to a child of Lucifer – let alone to Lucifer himself?"

"You know very well why I am here. Offer me the final verse of the *Danse Macabre* and I will grant you both peace and absolution." The old man started laughing. At first, it was a rough, staccato laugh that sounded more like choking. It quickly shifted to a full, rolling laugh that took his old, coarse voice by surprise, making him cough and sputter and hold his chest to keep his composure. Then Notke smiled sadly and looked Vincenzo straight in the eyes.

"You . . . You have no way to offer atonement for what I have done, and I will lose my life and soul before I ever relinquish what little knowledge I have to the depraved bastard children of the dark one. I have been doomed before, but will not find myself doomed again. The only way you can offer atonement to me is by offering me a last chance to keep my secrets from you." As Vincenzo's face morphed in anger, the old man lowered his head and relinquished his smile as he surrendered his soul to the mercy of the vampire.

"I come here offering you that which you desire most, and you dare spit in my face, citing your precious uncompromising morals and holding yourself as my better. Well, old man, where was this backbone in life when temptation so easily led you astray, dooming you to an eternity in this hole? Here those morals will offer you no satisfaction nor salvation, but rather earn you a measure of pain and suffering that you could never have imagined." Vincenzo took the old man by the neck and raised him off the ground, catching Notke's lowered gaze with his eyes. "And I promise you that I will have your secrets. In the end you will break to your own desire to rest in peace – a gift that you know very well is mine to offer!"

CHAPTER 8

- BY THE RIVERS DARK -

I

Most of the household had retired to their own quarters, save for the lady of the mansion. Marie sat in silence resting on a black ebony bench at the grand piano in the drawing room. Her long black hair was fashioned in a tight bun revealing her pale neck. She felt a lonely bead of sweat run down the back of her neck until it was absorbed by the white lace collar of her shirt. She shuddered as if to cast off her shackles of lace before carelessly unbuttoning her dress. Having unhooked her corset, she drew a deep breath and placed her hands on the piano keys. Then she started to play, softly drawing out the minor chords, letting the piano lament what she herself could not. She played long and sorrowful tunes, feeling like she could go on forever and thinking that perhaps she should. She didn't notice her husband walking up behind her, his shirt missing its jacket and his silk vest unbuttoned.

"I always enjoy this time of the night when the house sleeps and there is no longer a need for pretense." As Dæth spoke, he placed his hand on Marie's shoulder. She stopped playing.

"There is not?" she asked.

"No. I would think that, for better or worse, a husband and wife should be able to leave pretense behind in the night." Solely for his own enjoyment, he caressed her neck and traced a finger along the lace of her shirt, running it halfway down her chest. "I understand that you met with Mr. Beck again."

"Yes, and what of it? Am I not allowed to meet whom I desire?" she said as calmly as possible, looking straight ahead.

"My dear," Dæth said, bending over covering her with his body as he held her shoulders and whispered in her ear. "You may meet with whom you wish, as long as you never cross me. But I am certain that you will not, for without Mr. Beck to tempt you, you no longer have any reason to. Now you have finally earned my trust, my dear."

"You mean to tell me, that . . .?"

"Of course, my love."

"Blake is here because of me?"

"Naturally. What better way to prove your loyalty and faithfulness?" As his words sank in, tears formed in her eyes and poured silently down her cheeks. "I appreciate how you might feel offended by this gesture, perhaps even feel betrayed, but you are a bright woman. In fact, you are as bright as they come, which is one of the reasons why I chose you. Therefore, I am certain that you will be able to understand and perhaps even forgive me one day." Her shoulders shuddered at his touch. "After all, time is on our side, and from here on I shall promise you that I will treat you with the respect that you deserve." He stroked her shoulders. "I should not keep you from playing, my love. I will retire to our bed for the night and you may join me when you please."

Late at night, Blake entered Kaizerheim Cathedral, which lay silent as the grave. The heavy wooden door creaked as it closed behind him with a low groan. He walked into the nave, removing his soft, rounded hat and placing it underneath the belt that held his embroidered silk doublet in place. When he had first put on the attire befitting a medieval nobleman, he had felt like he was going to a carnival, but now he felt comfortable. As he walked up the aisle, he could see the unfinished altar in the choir and it was unmistakably the work of Notke. Blake rested his hand on the hilt of his sword. He stopped and looked around, knowing and hoping that he might run into Vincenzo. In the distance, he heard someone crying. He walked toward the choir searching for the distressed soul. He eventually found himself walking up the small wooden staircase to the pulpit halfway up the nave where he found a girl hiding. She was curled up with her legs drawn to her chest, rocking herself slowly back and forth and quietly sobbing with her face hidden in the palms of her hands.

"Miss?" Blake inquired, reaching out to calm her. Taken aback by the fact that she was suddenly no longer alone, Astrid shot away from him, cowering and screaming.

"Don't touch me!" Her voice bounded between the cathedral walls. "Get away from me!"

"I'm not here to hurt you," Blake said to calm her down,

taking a few steps down the stairs. Then the girl slowly removed her hands. "Astrid?"

"Blake?" Astrid sniffled.

"Yes. What are you . . . How did you get here?" Blake asked in disbelief. Astrid sat up, her back to the wooden wall of the pulpit.

"Well, I walked most of the way." She dried her eyes on her sleeve, trying to muster a smile.

"But you can't!"

"Well, I did, but I wish I hadn't," she said, tears filling her eyes.

"Why did you?"

"I wanted to see Bernt Notke. Victoria, the lady who welcomed me here, told me about this land and I decided to come here. It's not like I have anything else to do." She made it onto her knees and scooted towards Blake. "I'm so glad to see you!" She hugged him like she had never hugged anyone before. "I'm so glad it's you." Her voice quivered. "That it's you and not that monster." Blake put his arms around her.

"Don't worry, I'm here," he said, hoping that this would stop her most recent spell of crying. "Now calm down and tell me - what are you talking about?" As he spoke, he gently urged Astrid to sit down on the pulpit floor to allow them to talk face to face.

"I was hiding here to watch Notke work when this thing came in through the door over there," she said, pointing towards the south entrance. "I'm sure it was the girl who killed me, even though it couldn't be because it was a man."

"And?"

"Then he, or whatever it was, walked up to Notke and they quarreled."

"Did you hear what they were talking about?"

"Only some of it," she said. "I remember Notke calling him the child of Lucifer, and I remember the man wanting to know about a last verse of Notke's *Danse Macabre*."

"His name is Vincenzo – the one who killed you," Blake said. "What happened afterwards?"

"Notke laughed at this Vincenzo thing and told him that nothing he could offer would be worth his secret. Then he – Vincenzo, I mean – raged and told Notke that he would have his secret and that when he was finished with him, peace would be the only thing he needed to offer."

"Then?"

"I saw Vincenzo hold Notke, and it looked like he began to eat him, but not with his mouth. Well, I mean it was not like he bit him or anything. With his head distorted like a snake swallowing a whole goat, he seemed to inhale Notke. It looked like Notke began tearing apart and he screamed. It was like no scream I have ever heard." Astrid covered her face as she started crying again. "His scream filled the whole world, echoing between the walls. No matter how hard I pressed my palms to my ears, I could not escape it. And it didn't go away. He screamed and screamed, and even now I can still hear it."

"But they're not still here?"

"No. In the end, a few words made it through the screams. I think Notke cried, 'It's in the empty tomb – the Emperors' Tomb.'"

"The Emperors' Tomb. Are you sure?"

"Yes." She moved towards Blake for comfort and he couldn't help but put his arms around her.

"Listen, Astrid. This is very important. I have to go."

"No, you can't," she muttered.

"I have to, but I will be back to get you."

"NO! You can't leave me here alone!" she cried, holding him even tighter.

"Astrid." He tried to calm her.

"I won't stay behind. You have to take me with you." She sat up and looked him in the eyes. "I won't stay here!"

"You do know where I'm going?"

"Yes."

"And I can't promise that I can protect you."

"I'm not asking you to. I'm only asking you to take me with you."

Riding a black Frisian steed stolen from a stable in Kaizerheim, Vincenzo sped across the Kaizer Marshes following the trail leading to the Emperors' Tomb in the heart of the marshland. An empty tomb, it was built as the final resting place for emperors that would never find rest or peace in death. The horse panted heavily, unable to find relief in death after an hour-long gallop that Vincenzo had ceaselessly spurred on with the tip of his sword. As he rode on, Vincenzo looked to the reddening sky and eyed the dark silhouette of a lone raven against the backdrop of the setting sun. He could see the straight shapes and sharp contours of the tomb rising from the flat marsh horizon in the distance, which told him that there was not far to go. Looking back, he saw nothing but marshlands. It took but a few more minutes before he reached the majestic granite mausoleum that could easily have been mistaken for a Gothic cathedral long bereft of a parish and presiding over nothing but defiant blades of grass. The horse reared as Vincenzo pulled back the reins and jumped down where the trail ended. He left the horse behind and made his way across dry patches of land to the entrance. He lifted the heavy iron bar from the oaken double doors that kept the peace of the tomb. As he pushed open the doors, the light of the setting sun passed through the opening, carving a wedge into the darkness. Vincenzo looked around and found a small brazier that had been carved out of the stone wall. Using a cigarette lighter, he set the remaining oil alight and watched as the fire spread through the oiled channels in the walls to the countless braziers lining the tomb. First, one sprang alight, and then another and another until the tomb was flooded with light and the smell of burning oil filled the dusty air. As Vincenzo headed further into the tomb, the raven flew through the door and landed on his shoulder, shaking and shifting its feathers back in order. The sound of Vincenzo's steps echoed through the empty hall. Arching pillars held the Gothic ceiling aloft, and the raised foundations for heavy stone coffins remained vacant, forever waiting to receive dead emperors that would never arrive. The tomb lay as a silent hope for peace that would never come, and it was a stark contrast to the tombs built by the same emperors in life, which were meant to ensure their eternal death. But there was no hope for them, and they would find neither peace nor rest. Instead, like all other souls in Shades, these emperors would decay and end their time in the catacombs, for in death all are equal. On the far wall, Vincenzo recognized the *Danse Macabre* running the length of the wall. It eerily resembled real people dancing. Vincenzo picked up his pace and he soon stood before the people dancing in the painting. They were as tall as he was, each painted in such detail and color that it seemed they could step out of the wall at any time. Vincenzo recalled how he had spent a whole day in life pondering Notke's original in the Marienkirche on a visit to Lübeck. He had been there with his father, who was doing business with one of the wealthy Hanseatic merchants in the area. Vincenzo walked along the wall until he stood before the preacher who

286

was addressing the dancers from the pulpit. As Vincenzo read the verse of the preacher, he noticed that this work was different from the original that Notke had created in life. "See, raven?" he said, to which the raven turned its head. "The piper. In life, Notke painted this figure not as a man, but as death playing his own tune." Vincenzo looked at the raven, and it cawed and twitched before leaning its head sideways. Vincenzo walked slowly along the painting, examining each of the dancers and reading their verses, until he came to the end. "Now raven, look at the minstrel playing his pipe again here at the end. This is what Khaleel is concerned with." The raven cawed again. "Listen carefully as I read, for it will be your doom should you forget the words." The bird nodded. Vincenzo sat down on one knee and began to read, the raven sitting on his shoulder.

"'Please, death, do not forget me!
You bid all to dance and all pay heed.
As the people of the world join in your dance,
you lay claim to their attention and receive their prayers.
While you listen to their lament, each dance to my tune.
But I beg of you to give me what I am due.
For without my pipe, there is no dance,
and I shall take my credit.
As my pay, I ask only to keep playing in favor of dancing.'"

Vincenzo looked at the raven, and the bird urged him to go on with a flick of its beak.

> "'Oh minstrel, you have not been forgotten
> and I will give you what you are due.
> But hear my premonition.
> I shall let you stand by while others dance.
> To play your pipe for all those who join.
> Alas, in the end, your fingers will be worn through,
> and you will come to ask me to dance before the end.
> And I will take what is mine then.'"

Vincenzo turned to the raven. "Do you remember?" he asked. It cawed and nodded. "Then go! And inform Khaleel that I will remain behind to reclaim my honor or to face my undoing." He sent the raven away with a jerk of his shoulder, and at the sound of its fluttering wings, Vincenzo rose to his feet and turned around. Keeping his eyes on the setting sun beyond the doors, he straightened his belt and drew his sword halfway out of it sheath before easing it back, making sure that it was as ready as he was.

IV

Bahij sat in his study memorizing the words and gestures from the Voynich manuscript and preparing for the ritual he would conduct later that night when he was interrupted by a knock on the door.

"Yes?" Bahij called out, annoyed by the disturbance. His house servant opened the door.

"I am sorry, master, but mistress Ammon is here to see you and expressly bade me ask you for a moment's time."

"Mistress Ammon is here?"

"Yes, master. She is waiting for you on the south terrace."

"Tell her that I will be but a moment."

"I will do that, master," the servant said, leaving Bahij to the company of his books. As hard as Bahij tried to finish memorizing the words he was reviewing when the servant entered, he found that no words or gestures would stick. There were too many questions filling his mind to leave room for anything else. Finding no use of his efforts, he got up and walked to the mirror that hung on the wall, and he looked at himself. He poured water from a pitcher into the porcelain bowl standing on a table beneath the mirror, washing his face quickly and making sure that he looked presentable. He straightened his robe and consulted the mirror one last time before walking out to face Teresa. He found her standing on the south terrace that overlooked the Arabian quarter of the city. She heard him approach by the sound of his footsteps, but refrained from turning to face him.

"Teresa. I did not expect you to come here," Bahij said as he walked onto the terrace.

"Neither did I," she replied as much to herself as to Bahij. She trailed her hand across the sandstone railing. "But I found that I had to. I hope that you are not disappointed."

"Not at all, but I cannot help asking myself why you have come?" He walked slowly towards her as he spoke.

"Perhaps you should ask me rather than continue to ponder?" she said in a tone that made Bahij uncertain whether she meant the words as an endearment or an insult.

"Then why have you?"

"Is it not obvious to you? I have been given to you, should you choose to take me," she said, still standing with her back to him. He halted his advance. As he stood and looked at her, the shape of her body shielded his eyes from the setting sun that blazed like a mocking halo around her head. She was flooded and filled by light, but the shadow she cast towards him cut a dark, fanged silhouette across the length of sandstone floor that kept them apart. He thought all the way through the silence that followed, locked in a battle between his longing for her caress and his own ideals.

"I should not then," he finally said, forcing her to turn around.

"You should NOT?" she asked.

"No."

"I come here and degrade myself. I offer myself up to you,

and you turn me down?" she yelled.

"Yes. I shall not take you if your reason for coming here is that you have been given away. I will not once again seek your love if there is none to be found. I shall not take you, lest your reason for coming is that you choose to by your own inclination." As he spoke, he stepped into her shadow and slowly approached her, like a shepherd nearing a stray.

"But . . ."

"Mistress Ammon. You say that you degrade yourself by coming here. You present yourself as a common whore who has been cast out from one bed, used and discarded, and who now finds herself compelled to seek out another. If that is true, then I will not have you."

"You . . ." He could see that she was on the brink of crying as she took the final step toward him and slapped his face to relieve her anger and fear. "Fiend! How dare you?" With a hand on her shoulder, he halted any further outbursts.

"Teresa. Please do not say or do anything that you will come to regret, for you will have eternity to lament. I have said nothing but what would be found in your own words. I would claim you as my companion in an instant had your words offered me a different reason for your visit. But I will not take you as a whore. I would take you should you want me to." As he spoke, her tears broke through and she leaned into him, seeking relief in his embrace. But rather than put his arms around her, he kept her from his chest and took her by the shoulders, insisting on looking into her eyes. "I will not take you by pity, order, or spite, or because that bastard Earl would not have you. I would take you only if you desire me to."

"But I do," she said, her eyes pleading for mercy.

"Why have you come here?" he asked.

"I have come here to be with you, Bahij." Then she moved to kiss him, and his ideals could no longer overcome his desires. As their lips met, Bahij felt the warmth of the sun for the first time in centuries. Sadly, even in this moment, Teresa could not forget the image of the Earl, and it tore at her heart.

Accompanied by the light of the waning moon high in the night sky, a procession of two-dozen souls walked slowly through the streets of Aquraa. Some carried torches with flames flickering wildly in the autumn winds, while others played medieval bladder pipes, filling the night with a sharp, wailing tune. As they walked on, the flickering lights cast shadow upon shadow of the robe-clad figures onto the timber framed houses that lined the otherwise empty street, leaving the procession to be accompanied by an endless army of dancing shadows. From behind curtains, from darkened passageways, through withered shutters and from wooden doors that had been edged open, countless undead spirits peered out at the spectacle, feeling the sorrowful tune cut through the heart of their souls. The procession continued, each figure clad in dark silken robes, and all but three of the figures were disguised by gilded half-masks that allowed them to play their pipes as they walked. In front of the procession, Mr. Ferre walked unmasked, leading his people through the night and into the new dawn of their kind. Right behind him walked Bahij, unmasked and wearing the sermon master's robe that was embroidered with signs and sigils in silver thread as prescribed by the ritual. Then came Teresa leading two masked figures carrying a heavy chest containing the ritual artifacts. Walking about halfway down through the procession, the Earl looked out from behind his mask at the stage he had set. He wore a slight smile, holding the reed of his bladder pipe between his lips and playing with little conviction, as he knew it would make no difference now.

"How fortuitous that misconception takes such mercy upon those of little talent and slow minds, and that their deficiencies do not resign them to ruin the play as they take the stage. It saves them from having to endure the scorn of those freed from said same faults," the Earl thought to himself. "As misconception takes its mercy upon them, they need naught but their convictions to be able to play their role far more convincingly than any actor playing solely by talent. Before my eyes I see them walking with the stride and certainty of cattle going to the field, so touched by mercy that they find no rhyme nor reason in questioning their herdsman, let alone themselves, and at my eyes' report I smile. I smile at the mercy they have been shown by their own deficiencies, dreading that said same mercy ever be shown to me, knowing that it may well be as painfully short-lived as a syphilitic erection." The Earl looked ahead and saw the eastern gate with braziers of oil burning all the way along the parapets like a string of beads illuminating the night. In the light of the fires, he saw the guards standing in awe as they looked down to the procession that neared the gates. "Lest one among them possesses talents far beyond those of which I give them credit, I would wager that my eyes and mind report naught but the truth. Namely, that they can see themselves walking towards nothing but victory. Now how can I but marvel at the awe to be found in every gaze that falls upon us? Even as I search for a mere shred of tension or doubt, I find nothing but joyful anticipation of that which they believe will follow from the inevitable conclusion of this evening's play. I see eyes peering out from the darkness, and as they look at us, I swear that they see only a procession of extras filling the stage to set the final scene for the unmasked actors to play – blatantly ignorant that the director of said same play is walking onto the stage right in front of them. So sure are they, that their eyes refuse to see that the director's eyes betray him by unveiling the feeling of excitement that he harbors: the excitement of knowing that the stage is set, yet the end of the play remains unwritten. Of knowing that he has, in secret, chosen to withhold any further direction, bent on leaving the actors to choose an ending at their own accord to his amusement." As the gates opened and the procession was about to pass through the gateway, Teresa Ammon stepped aside to let the procession pass. As the lady of the house, it was her duty to close the gates behind *Him* on this momentous occasion. The Earl neared her and caught her eyes, and by the icy look that crept across her face, he found that she had realized it was the Earl who was approaching in the gilded half-mask.

"Lovely Teresa! By your unbending allegiance and unwary, credulous mind, I had deemed you merely the cow leading the herd. Yet looking into your eyes as I pass you by again, I see the change in you. As you stand waiting to close the door behind me, I see your heart broken, spilling its anguish and anger out before me and betraying a mind that has vowed never again to let down its guard, let alone be led blindly on. Only now do you give me a glimpse of a talent worth regarding, perhaps even worth respecting, as I see doubt and wonder in your eyes. You and you alone see my smile, not as that of a jester or a fool, but as that of the conductor reveling in the beauty conjured by the tip of his baton. In your eyes, I can finally mirror myself, and in this moment, I know that you share my suspense. Albeit in your mind's eye I see it take on the abominable form of fear rather than that of golden excitement." He smiled at her as he walked past, knowing that she would understand.

As the great eastern gate of the city was closed behind them, the procession walked on along the cobblestone road. The lament of the bladder pipes filled the night, and as the procession turned off the road and onto a lone path leading across the wild, uncultivated fields, the torchbearers began to sing. A low, wordless keen carried the sharp wailing of the pipes through the night. In the distance, the path ended at the foot of the grave mound where Hel's tomb lay empty and abandoned. *He* had raised her barren tomb on the very field where she had fallen in battle centuries before as an eternal testament to her undeath and fall, and as a vow of revenge. At the foot of the mound, a cobbled walkway carved its way into the grass-covered hill leading to a massive stone portal fashioned from rough slabs of granite. A huge block of granite that had been placed in the portal blocked the entrance to the tomb entirely. Chiseled into the lintel stone above the entrance, Futhark runes read "Here the fires of Hel were quenched and here they will be rekindled." As the procession reached the mound, *He* raised his hand to halt the advance and walked down the cobbled path alone until he reached the expressionless granite face. To Bahij, who stood only a few yards behind *Him*, it seemed that *He* commanded the stone to move with the mere gesture of his hand. As *He* placed his hand on the cold stone surface, the stone trembled. It cracked and crumbled as if it had been touched by time itself, and finally drifted away like fine desert sand at the mercy of the night winds. Accompanied by the cold, silvery moonlight, Mr. Ferre walked into the empty grave chamber beneath the mound, leaving the others to follow behind. The chamber was cold and still, kept in a constant chill by the surrounding earth. Coarse stone pillars lined the walls of the elongated chamber and supported the bare granite arches that kept the surrounding earth from caving in. As *He* walked through the chamber to the far end, the nobles took their place along the wall and Bahij took his stand in the middle of the chamber. The pipers silenced their pipes and joined in the low chant that spread like a blanket over the cold stone floor. Teresa signaled for the heavy wooden chest that held the ritual artifacts to be carried forth and placed in front of Bahij. Then she walked out into the chamber herself and opened the chest before taking a few steps back. As Bahij spread out his arms, the chanting subsided, leaving the chamber completely bereft of sound. Then Bahij spoke, his voice calm and clear as it filled the tomb.

"We gather here on this night to ask for summons. In earnest, beseeching the one lost to offer up the will to return. With right, we claim the power to grant passage between the worlds, and by a sacrifice of song, we bid Death honor his promise to stay his hand as long as our pipes beckon others to join his dance."

VI

Approaching the Emperor's Tomb, Blake and Astrid could see a warm, fiery glow shooting from the half open doors. The light cut into the night like a sword, trying to fend off the shadows that draped the mausoleum. Blake and Astrid were certain that they were neither alone nor in time. Blake pulled back his reins, rearing his horse and turning it around to face Astrid. The horse panted after the long ride.

"Astrid, you stay here," Blake said.

"Do you think it's in there?" she asked with a slight tremor in her voice.

"Yes. And like I said, I won't promise to protect you. So the best thing is for you to stay here. You will be safe here for now."

"But . . ."

"No! But nothing, Astrid. Stay here and let me do what I do."

"Are you going to fight it?"

"Yeah."

"But what if you can't win?"

"Listen, I've fought this one before and I can beat him."

"But what if you don't?"

"If I'm not back here by sunrise, I want you to make your way back to the Entrance. You can hole up in my house if you like – just find the woman who welcomed you to Shades and ask for Virgil. He'll know what to do. If I'm not here to take you back, I won't have much use for it myself."

"Blake," Astrid started, but Blake had already ended the conversation by pulling the reins to one side to turn his horse before spurring it forward.

When he saw Blake's silhouette drawn in the doorway against the sparse moonlight, Vincenzo stood waiting with his hand on the hilt of his sword.

"So, Beck. You finally made it," Vincenzo called.

"Yes. If for nothing else, then just to put you down," Blake said, unbuttoning his cape and letting it fall to the ground before drawing his katana.

"I'm glad that you're not without intent, for I feared for you that your aim was but to rescue the old man and keep his secrets safe. Had that been your sole aspiration, you would already have failed!" Vincenzo's tone was mocking and Blake could almost hear the laughter that filled Vincenzo's mind.

"Then let tonight be ours and let our masters worry about their own affairs!" Blake yelled and started down towards Vincenzo, rightly expecting Vincenzo to meet him halfway.

"I would love nothing more!" Vincenzo called out, as he drew his sword and set to running. A moment later, the sound of steel clashing midair filled the tomb as Blake parried Vincenzo's strike, forcing his blade to slide off along the blade of his katana. Each knew that for one of them, this would be the final battle. From here on, there would be no more. Once cut down in Shades by a blade that had been blessed by either of their masters, the best the vanquished could hope for was nothing. As Blake parried the blow, Vincenzo momentarily lost his balance. Making the most of it, Blake elbowed Vincenzo in the side as he moved past, sending Vincenzo to his knees to avoid falling flat on the floor.

"I would have thought you'd practiced, but it seems you're no better than when I last cut you down to size."

"I believe you mean when you cut down your girlfriend," Vincenzo sneered, getting up to face Blake. "That delicious whore whom I had the pleasure of watching drift into Shades at the tip of my blade." Vincenzo grinned. "This time I will not be hindered by the unfit body of a common slattern, and when I have finished with you, I promise you that I will go and find her for a second helping." He raised his sword overhead before stepping towards Blake, striking down as he did. Their blades met, sending sparks flying into the air before they dissolved into nothingness, just like anything else in Shades dislodged from its being. As their swords came to rest against each other, they found themselves face to face and Vincenzo bared his fangs, his eyes blazing at the mere prospect of sinking them into a Hunter.

"I promise that this will be the end of you!" Blake said, straining to keep the vampire at bay with his blade. As Vincenzo leaned into him, Blake moved on an impulse and bit Vincenzo's face. Vincenzo screamed and pushed Blake away with an unearthly force that sent Blake sliding across the floor. Blake felt the immaterial flesh come undone in his mouth, vaporizing into a wisp of smoke before ceasing to exist. As he looked up, he saw Vincenzo holding his face, the look of disbelief in his eyes quickly changing to hatred.

"So, you have listened to what I said, after all," he cried as he took his hand from his face, revealing a deformed visage to Blake. In place of his nose and upper lip, Vincenzo had only a dark gash from which a trickle of immaterial flowed down his lip and chin, dripping onto his chest before disappearing in discrete wisps. "You see. We're not all that different," Vincenzo said with a maddened grin, the gash twisting and writhing as he spoke. Blake could feel the power welling up inside him. It was a feeling that he immediately knew would haunt and tempt him for eternity. "Now, get up!" Vincenzo yelled, wiping his face with his sleeve. As Blake got up, Vincenzo bounded towards him and raised his sword to strike, driving the sword with hate and spite. Despite being caught off balance, Blake managed to save himself by raising his sword in one hand to parry Vincenzo's while throwing himself to one side. But as the blades met, Vincenzo's sword slid along the length of Blake's katana, cutting through the cross-guard and severing two of Blake's fingers from his left hand. Even before the sword hit the floor jangling, the fingers that had held it dissipated into thin air together with Blake's screams of pain. When Blake regained his composure a second later, Vincenzo already stood looming above him, his sword ready to strike. "Now I only have to decide whether I offer you a clean peace or not."

As Blake lay beneath the tip of Vincenzo's sword, he noticed a shadowy figure moving towards them from behind Vincenzo.

"If you want to plead for mercy, now is the time, Beck." The figure closed in, moving silently.

"I . . ." Beck started, biding his time.

"Yes?" Vincenzo smiled, the tightening muscles distorting his deformed face. Blake eyed his sword lying on the ground merely a foot away. He thought he could do it. Just as Astrid reached them, Blake moved to grab his sword. Preparing to strike, Vincenzo saw the silhouette of a woman standing right behind him reflected in Blake's eyes. He immediately turned to defend himself, seeking to strike down his newfound enemy. Armed only with a pointy rock she had picked up outside, Astrid saw Vincenzo turn and strike in one swift movement. She closed her eyes and braced herself for the end. Then she heard Vincenzo cry out, and as she opened her eyes, she saw Blake's sword passing through Vincenzo from waist to shoulder. The vampire writhed in pain as he began to dissipate and disappear into nothingness, his final words ringing out across the tomb among his cries of pain. "You still lost, Beck!"

Astrid stood paralyzed as the sound died out, her feelings overwhelming her as she desperately tried to shake the image of Vincenzo's severed body and deformed face from her mind. As Blake wrapped his arms around her, she felt her soul tremble. Then she began to cry and Blake let her, holding her in his arms. A few minutes later she emerged from his bosom and dried her eyes with the back of her hand.

"Come on. Let's get out of here," he said, and Astrid made no objections. As they walked through the doors into the moonlit night, she took Blake's hand.

"What did he mean that you lost?" she asked, and Blake began to explain.

The ritual was nearing its conclusion and the barren stone innards of Hel's tomb had been completely transformed. In accordance with the ritual, Bahij had covered the stone slabs of the floor with a labyrinth of intricate patterns and sigils drawn in lines of white chalk and black ink. Robe-clad noblemen lined the walls chanting in low, deep voices or playing lamenting tunes on the bladder pipes. The torches that were carried in the procession had all died out, but massive wax candles now burned in a huge circle around Bahij in the middle of the room, filling the chamber with a warm light. Looking Mr. Ferre straight in the eyes, Bahij signaled for *Him* to step forward. As *He* walked slowly towards Bahij, halting just beyond the circle of candles, three noblemen stepped forward, each carrying a symbol pertaining to one of the three patron saints found in Notke's altar. The nobleman to the east held in his hands the anchored cross of Saint Clement. Across from him, a nobleman held a silver scallop shell filled with water, a symbol associated with John the Baptist. Finally, the nobleman to the south held a heavy tome, a typical symbol of Saint Anna. Bahij turned to the east and held out his hands towards the anchor of Saint Clement. Then, as was required of the sermon master, Bahij called out the first of the three prayers that he had written to the saints.

"As we ask the one lost to return to us on this night, we beseech the martyr Saint Clement to raise the anchor of her soul so that she may pass freely into our world! We do so with hope of a new beginning, praying that she may return from the dark depths into which she too has been cast!" As he spoke, the nobleman to the east raised the anchored cross so high above his head that it nearly touched the low stone arches overhead.

Across the room, Teresa stood by the wall. She looked around the chamber, examining each of the noblemen that lined the wall, trying to discover which mask hid the Earl. As her eyes swept the room, she heard Bahij's voice ring out over the chanting and wailing pipes.

"By the dark waters of the river, we seek to cleanse the soul of the past and ask for it to step into our world from the wilderness. In this, we call upon the powers of Saint John the Baptist, and we ask him to herald her return from the Grey!" As Bahij spoke, the nobleman before him raised aloft the silver shell, the water inside appearing jet black in the sparse light. Teresa spied the hint of a smile across the chamber and she knew it was the Earl. She saw suspense and joy in his eyes and realized what the Earl's smile hid. A profound sense of loathing welled up inside of her as she finally realized that he had been right. She had been the one to betray Bahij's confidence. She had willfully aided the Earl in setting the stage for this play without considering the costs, let alone her own role. As much as she despised the Earl, she found that she loathed herself even more. From the corner of her eyes she could see Bahij turning towards the last of the noblemen that stood by the candle circle. "We call upon the will of Saint Anna to ask her daughter to implore the lamb to abolish any

306

sins of the one we summon. As we summon this soul, we abate the past and wipe clear the pages so that she who is summoned here may henceforth become the divine author of her own story." As he spoke, Bahij looked at Teresa over the shoulder of the nobleman holding the blank tome. When he caught her eyes, Bahij saw her doubts and pain, yet failed to recognize their true nature and origin. The three noblemen laid their symbols down on the floor amidst the chalk and ink lines and stepped back to the wall. Still searching his mind for answers to what would merit the doubt he found in Teresa's eyes, Bahij stepped out of the circle, allowing Mr. Ferre to take his place. Standing in the middle of the chamber, *He* began to speak. His voice seemed to fill the entire world, threatening to tear down all of creation if his will was not done.

"Pipers! By my power and the powers called upon this night, I bid you keep your breath and leave your reeds to the wind. You will cease your playing so that Death will halt his dance and the one we summon may break free from Death's embrace. Tonight Death will dance alone, and the fires of Hel will burn again as I demand Death to honor his agreement with the minstrels that play to his dance. I demand that she whom we summon tonight be returned to us, and in return we shall once again voice our pipes so that the dancing may carry on! I demand that she will once again be free and that she will return to us from the moonlight beyond, transforming this tomb to a place of birth. By my word, let coffin and crib become one." As his voice died out, so did the wail of the pipes, leaving the chamber bereft of sound.

307

VIII

Blake and Astrid had put several miles between them and the Emperor's Tomb, riding south towards the borderlands between the Medieval and the Entrance. There was no longer any rush. In fact, they had the better part of eternity to fill and Blake was still trying to explain things to Astrid. He decided to not hold anything back. He figured she had a right to know what had cost her her chance of life and possibly the opportunity to earn an afterlife.

"So Vincenzo was only after Notke's secret and you were meant to keep it from him?" Astrid asked.

"Yeah. But I failed, which probably means that all hell is going to break loose very soon, from what I understand."

"Because of this ritual?"

"Mmhmm. From what Dæth shared with me, my best bid is that a war is coming."

"But you said that Vincenzo needed both the verses of Notke's *Totentanz* from the tomb and the names of the three saints from the altar."

"Yeah, so? He needed them and he got them," Blake said, looking at Astrid. She took a moment to think while stroking the mane of her mare.

"I'm not sure," she said.

"You're not sure of what?"

"I'm not sure that he got it right, I mean."

"Astrid, you were there," Blake replied. "You saw him in the tomb where he had all the time in the world to send word of the verses to Bahij Khaleel, and you were there in the cathedral in Aarhus. It's pretty clear. He must have overheard you at the concert when you told me about the saints. Otherwise, how on earth would he have known to kill you to get to me?"

"But . . ."

"Astrid!"

"Blake! Shut up for one second, will you?" she said, lifting her eyebrows. "I showed you the altar and you asked me about the three central figures, so I explained about Saint Clement, Saint Anna and Saint John the Baptist."

"Yes."

"But those aren't the ones Notke was hiding! I'm sure of it," Astrid said with a self-satisfied smile, certain that she had finally found the answer that had eluded her for so long.

"What?"

"Look, it was bugging me the whole time I was writing my thesis. In the predella, Notke painted a scene depicting the mass of Saint Gregory when Jesus manifests on the altar before Pope Gregory and the congregation as divine proof of the doctrine of transubstantiation."

"The doctrine of transubstantiation?" Blake asked.

"The Catholic doctrine that the substance of bread and wine changes into the body and blood of Christ. But that doesn't matter. What matters is how Notke depicted it. In his version, a doorway in the background leads into a garden where the sky is gilded and a peacock sits alone on the garden wall."

"A peacock?"

"Yes. A symbol of resurrection and eternal life sitting under a gilded sky, which was Notke's way of showing the importance of this scene. I've never understood why it was so important, but I do now! You see, the altar in the painting of the Gregor's Mass is made to clearly resemble the altar in Aarhus itself – I mean, even the ornamentations are the same. However, this painted altar is without the wings or anything, so there are only three figures in this altar and they are definitely not Saint Clement, Saint Anna and John the Baptist."

IX

Halfway across Shades, Hel's tomb lay silent, and all those within stood with their gazes fastened on the entrance from which their queen would return. Only in Teresa's eyes could a shred of doubt be seen. As the seconds passed, the doubt began to spread among the noblemen like a contagious disease. Finally, it reached the middle of the tomb where *He* stood and awaited the return of his queen consort, his love and his revenge. Bahij looked around in despair, desperately searching for answers, when he noticed the Earl's eyes glimmering with excitement behind his gilded mask. As Bahij turned his eyes to Teresa, he finally realized what had caused her doubts and pain. Bahij's attention was torn away from Teresa by the smoldering patches forming on Mr. Ferre's back, and then Bahij saw his master's countenance shift. Every muscle in Mr. Ferre's body began to tighten as the rage welled up inside *Him*. His clothes were set ablaze, draping *Him* in a robe of fire as his flaming wings burst from the scars on his back and flooded the chamber with fire and light. All around, the noblemen shielded themselves, cowering by the outer wall of the chamber. They all heard his furious cry.

"BAHIJ!!!"

X

Dæth sat alone by the drawing room fireplace savoring the sight and sound of the crackling fire. He ran his fingers along the black lapel of his red silk dressing gown before turning to the table next to his chair to pour that night's last cup of tea. Allowing the tea to cool, he picked up his pipe and drew smoke, the tobacco smoldering with a warm red glow. Then he picked up a pen and dipped it into the inkwell on the table before turning his attention to a small piece of paper. With perfect penmanship, he wrote "King F2 to E3." He knew very well that this would press a draw, but he found eternity lying before him, and he knew that they would certainly play again.

EPILOGUE

- THE GREAT PRETENDER -

I

Blake parked his silver Aston Martin by the curb and walked up the stairs to his front door. As he opened the door, the smell of roasting duck, caramelized potatoes and other traditional Danish Christmas dishes hit his nose.

"Is that you, Blake?" he heard Astrid call, imagining that she was probably still busy in the kitchen.

"Yes!" he said, setting down a small plastic bag on the credenza beneath the hallway mirror before bending down to untie his shoes.

"Did you get it?"

"Yeah. Half a liter of double cream and a bag of potato chips, right?" As he stood up and kicked off his shoes, he saw Astrid coming towards him from the kitchen.

"Yes. You're a dear! Now go relax, and in about half an hour you will have the best Christmas dinner of your life." She gave him a quick kiss and picked up the plastic bag.

"Well, technically . . ." he muttered.

"What?"

"Nothing. Never mind."

"OK. Now go sit down, Blake," she said as she headed back to the kitchen.

"Don't worry, I will. I'll be upstairs!"

Blake walked up the stairs to his study. He picked up a bottle and a glass from the bar cabinet and placed them on the table next to his leather armchair. Then he poured himself a drink and walked over to the collection of vinyl LPs that Virgil had thoughtfully included as part of Blake's home. Blake slowly flipped through them, unable to decide until his fingers finally made the choice for him. He lifted the cover from the shelf and removed the black vinyl disk. Reverently, he blew on it to remove as much dust as possible before placing it on the turntable. Then he pressed play, causing the pin to be slowly lowered into the groove while Blake lowered himself into his chair. He picked up his glass, closed his eyes and took a drink. All his shortcomings and the image of Marie filled his mind, just like the sound of the sorrowful saxophone filled the room as the band began to play. Then, as the chorus began, the needle skipped, mockingly reminding Blake over and over again that he was the great pretender.

Help make my dream come true

Thank you for spending your time reading my book. I sincerely hope you've enjoyed it!

In the world of self-publishing, word-of-mouth is key for the success of any author. Therefore, if you've enjoyed the book, **please take a minute to rate the book on Amazon** – or even better, write a short review. It really makes a *huge* difference to me as an author.

Also a **Facebook** Like or a **Twitter** Tweet about the book goes a long way! :)

If you want to be kept up to date on future releases and my other projects, sign up on www.widowgrove.com. Your email address will never be shared and you can unsubscribe to the mailing list at any time you wish.

Acknowledgments

A heartfelt thank you to the following people:

Iben – my wife and first reader, thank you for putting up with the countless nights and weekends of writing, for your comments on the book, for your endless support and the encouragement you have given me, and for being there for better, for worse, in sickness and in health.

Jennifer Schmaltz Robbers, thank you for your comments and painstaking copyediting. This book would not be what it is, if it hadn't been for your help.

Jan Roed Thastum, thank you for your friendship and for all the advice and help you have given me during the creation of this book's cover.

My brother Martin, thank you for helping me find my way into storytelling – from the first D&D set you gave me for my 11th birthday, to believing in me when I aimed for a career as a writer and game designer.

My parents, thank you for never telling us that we couldn't.

My test readers (you know who you are), thank you for your invaluable comments, and for taking time in your busy lives to read and respond on my first write-through.

About the Author

Anders Rauff-Nielsen is an award-winning Danish game designer and fiction writer who has made an international career working with games, storytelling and world-building since 2006 – a career based on a lifelong passion for stories and games, supported by a master's degree in Philosophy and History.

His previous work as a writer includes three years of writing fiction for the international hit trading card game *Chaotic*, a how-to book on story-telling and role-playing games, and the groundbreaking augmented reality fantasy adventure *Noorhjem*. In 2015, he was invited by the Danish Cultural Agency, under the Danish Ministry of Culture, to help investigate the future of digital literature.

For more information, please visit www.widowgrove.com

Story Blurb

For Blake Beck, it proves to be no ordinary day when he finds a razor blade in the morning mail. As Director of Black Ops within the CAC, Blake hardly expected the morning mail to include a letter from his boss telling him to kill himself.

The razor blade is intended to be Blake's ticket to Shades – the realm beyond life where all souls go to await their celestial paperwork. Following his instincts to save himself, Blake soon finds himself caught in the frontlines of the age-old war between Dæth, the ruler of Shades, and Mr. Ferre, the first undead.

As the uncovering of a mystical medieval manuscript threatens to turn the tide of the war, Blake has no choice but to embark on a fateful hunt to secure the manuscript's hidden secrets, while his old nemesis Vincenzo looms in the shadows, out to claim the secrets first. Unfortunately, the resurfacing of Blake's one true love, as well as his own sense of right and wrong, threatens to put an end to his endeavors as Blake discovers that he is merely a pawn in the chess game of gods...